FOOTNOTES

The fifth book in the NOTED! series

Kathy J. Jacobson

Duly Noted —
to my dear sister and
friend Betty for whom
new chapters keep unfolding!
Love, Solveig

Kathy J. Jacobson

LITTLE CREEK PRESS®
AND BOOK DESIGN

Mineral Point, Wisconsin USA

Dedication

In loving memory of my parents,
Merle and Loretta Thompson
and my brother, Mark

Author's Note/Acknowledgements

I'd like to thank my husband, Jeff, for suggesting the title of this book. A "footnote" is a note of reference, an explanation, or a comment used to clarify and expand one's knowledge. When I finished writing Scratch Pad, I felt my readers (and I myself) needed to know what happened next, and also what transpired in the thirty year period between the beginning and ending of that book. After taking some time to do my own grieving—the characters have become very real to me—I began Footnotes. I found my years of working with people who have lost loved ones—whether by death, divorce or other circumstance, to be invaluable as I wrote this book. I also confronted some of my own losses in the process—"facing, feeling and healing"—thanks, "Jillian," for that advice. I hope this book brings those currently dealing with a loss, some of the comfort they are seeking. And as Jillian mentions more than once in this book, she can't imagine dealing with life without faith, friends or family—neither can I!

Chapter One

Jillian stood in the foyer rubbing her finger gingerly over the handwritten words on the yellow sticky note. She had been holding the note and staring at John's words—which turned out to be his final ones to her—for the last few minutes. The note had come with a bouquet of thirty roses which had been delivered at the house, a gift from John in honor of their thirtieth anniversary. The note was a carbon copy of the one John had attached to a bouquet of roses he had given Jillian on their wedding day.

Jillian, I'll love you forever. John

Ever since then, "I'll love you forever," had been the couple's nightly refrain to one another. Jillian gently returned the note to the clear plastic stake which protruded from the bevy of bright yellow blooms. She slowly bent down toward the vase and inhaled, gripping the ebony table the arrangement was on with both hands to steady herself.

Jillian's head was swimming. It was difficult to believe that only hours earlier she and John had wished each other a happy anniversary. John had recreated a breakfast he had made for her once early in their relationship, and they had excitedly recalled the special weekend they had just shared with family and friends, over the repast. They had renewed their marriage vows two days earlier, on Easter Sunday at 5:00 p.m., the same special occasion and time as their wedding, once again at Grace Lutheran Church with Pastor Jim officiating. It had been a very moving and memorable ceremony and celebration afterward.

This day, March the twenty-seventh, was their official anniversary date, so that was why John had made the special breakfast. Jillian had offered to clean up afterward, and John took her up on it, happily sauntering off to read in his favorite room in the house, the library. But he had returned to the kitchen only minutes later with a strange look on his face, just before he collapsed. Jillian had been a nurse for many years and had instinctively known that he was gone.

"Oh, John," Jillian whispered. She felt tears sting her eyes and suddenly felt the need for air.

She walked to the kitchen where she picked up her keys and purse from the counter and opened the door to the garage. She wanted to jump into her old white Land Rover, her wedding gift from John, but it was rarely driven anymore. Instead, she climbed into her small electric car. Vehicles in California in this decade, except for collector's vehicles like her Land Rover, were required to be either hybrids or electric models. She didn't mind that, as she and John had always been huge advocates of alternative energy usage and taking care of the environment. They had been the first in their neighborhood to go completely solar, which was now the standard.

She slid into the small, sleek, black vehicle and sighed as she gripped the steering wheel. She knew where she wanted to go—where she had to go. She had driven there so many times she could usually navigate the route without too much thinking, but today, in her current state of shock, she thought she should use the navigational tools available on her vehicle, which were now also standard on most cars. She pushed a button to lift the garage door, put her destination into the computer, and let the car do the rest.

Kathy J. Jacobson

Soon Jillian found herself in the driveway of their beach house in Malibu. The warm sunshine and salty sea breeze hit her face as she stepped from the car. She loved this place. It was the very house she and John had spent their first night together as husband and wife. She would never forget that night. She had never felt so special, or so loved. Five years later, John would surprise her with the house as a gift for their fifth anniversary. Jillian would never forget that night, either.

Twenty-five years earlier

John and Jillian finished another delicious meal at Leo's, their favorite Italian restaurant, and actually, their favorite restaurant, in general. Part of the reason they enjoyed Leo's so much was the fabulous food, and the other part was the feeling of being with people who felt like family. Leo's restaurant provided both, exceptionally.

Usually, John and Jillian topped off their meal with Leo's family recipe of tiramisu. But in celebration of their fifth anniversary, Leo and his daughter, Adelina, had made an Italian almond cake for them. Jillian had once told Leo about how much she had enjoyed the almond wedding cake John's relative had made for them on their honeymoon trip to Italy. Katerina had baked it, and they had shared it with many family members and friends at Pietro and Katerina's rustic stone house with the large wooden shutters, just outside of Naples. Jillian didn't believe anyone could recreate such a special cake, but Leo and Adelina's creation came very close. Leo was so thoughtful—almost as good at caring about and loving his customers as he was at cooking and baking for them.

John's chauffeur, the gentleman he used for special events around L.A. ever since the night of his first Academy Awards ceremony, sat in the limousine outside the restaurant. Gregory was a great driver—discreet, polite, friendly, and intelligent. He was also a tall and strong man, which discouraged the sometimes overzealous paparazzi.

John had packed a small overnight case for Jillian and was taking her somewhere special, he said, when they had climbed into the limousine earlier that night on the way to Leo's. Gregory waited for them while they dined, then waited longer as John and Leo argued once again about whether or not John would pay for dinner. Once that was settled, John acquiescing again, they were ready for their ride to "wherever."

As they settled into the plush leather seats, John produced a soft, black scarf and held it up to Jillian. "If you don't mind, I'd like to blindfold you," he said sweetly.

"Really?" Jillian asked. This was a new one, even for her often surprising husband.

"Really."

"I guess you have your reasons," she replied, one eyebrow arched.

"I do. I promise, Jillian, it will be worth it," he said, and kissed her before he gently tied the band of cloth around her head to cover her eyes.

"I think it's worth it already," she said, smiling after the kiss.

She snuggled against John and just relaxed as the car pulled away from the curb. Before she knew it, they were there—wherever "there" was.

Gregory opened the car door for John, then helped Jillian out of her seat on the other side, holding on to her until John could come around and take her arm. She could smell the salty air and heard gulls overhead, so she was quite sure they were once again at a beach house, as they had been on their honeymoon. She just didn't know yet that it was *the* beach house.

Gregory opened the door to the house for them, then went back to get their bags while John guided Jillian inside.

"Is there anything else I can help you with, Mr. Romano?"

Gregory asked as he set their bags just inside the door.

"Not a thing, Gregory. Thank you so much. We will see you tomorrow afternoon," John answered, facing Jillian and holding her arms.

"Yes, sir. You and Mrs. Romano have a wonderful evening."

"You, as well," John and Jillian said in unison, then laughed.

Jillian heard the door close, and John pulled her close and kissed her.

"Ready?" he asked softly.

She smiled and nodded. John gently slipped the scarf off over her head. She looked around and was stunned to see where she was. It was their honeymoon house. There on the table in the living room was a vase of yellow roses, as there had been on their wedding night. She remembered reading his loving words on the note on the floral stake that night. She also remembered John's reassuring words to her when she had started to tremble, having been so in love and so nervous at the same time.

"John!"

"I told you it would be worth it. It is, isn't it?" he asked excitedly.

She answered him with a kiss.

Later that evening, they stood in the moonlight on the deck, the gentle breeze in their faces and the moon's rays dancing on the water. John held Jillian from behind, his arms tightly wrapped around her. She loved it when he held her that way, and she tightened her grip on his arms.

"Do you like your anniversary gift?" John asked quietly in her ear.

"I *love* my anniversary gift, John."

"That's good, because it's yours."

Jillian turned around slowly to face him, a look of confusion on her face. "What's mine?"

"This place … the house. After our honeymoon, I told my friend if he ever planned to sell it, to please call me first. He called a few months ago, and now, it's yours, sweetheart. Happy anniversary, Jillian!"

Jillian was speechless. This place, which was so special to them both, was now theirs. Jillian's eyes filled with tears of happiness, and she gave him a long and tender kiss.

"I'll take that as a thank you any day," John said, smiling.

Ever since that night long ago, John, Jillian, and their extended family members had enjoyed many special moments in this house. Jillian walked slowly through the rooms to the deck and stood there, looking out over the ocean as the sun was beginning to set. It looked particularly stunning this evening, and Jillian suddenly felt like she was getting a glimpse of another world.

With her arms crossed over her chest, she watched the yellow ball of fire seemingly drop slowly, but steadily, into the ocean. She closed her eyes, and a soft breeze caressed her cheeks. Jillian took a deep breath, and as she did, she felt something—two warm, strong arms wrapped around her own. She could feel John's chin on her shoulder and his breath in her ear. She almost turned around, but then she felt something else—even stronger arms surrounding and holding them both, like they would never let go.

Jillian knew at that moment that nothing would ever be the same again, but she also sensed that everything would somehow be okay. As she drove home that evening, and for the rest of her days, she knew that for just a moment, she had felt the peace that passes all understanding and had truly been in the presence of God.

It was late when Jillian returned home. The house seemed darker than she had ever seen it, with the possible exception of when she first came to work in it thirty-one years before. John had been a different person when she arrived as his newly hired house helper. There had been a lot of darkness in the house, and in his life, at that point in time.

She double-checked all the locks on the doors and windows, feeling a vulnerability she hadn't experienced in many decades. *Maybe I'll start using the gate again,* Jillian thought to herself, referring to the iron security gate John and she had installed at the entrance to the property. It had protected them from intruders who had emerged once John's acting career made its big comeback.

Jillian's legs felt like lead as she trudged slowly up the winding staircase. It had been one of the saddest, and longest, days of her life. She came to the doorway of their—*her*—room, then paused and closed her eyes. In her mind she saw John sweeping her off her feet and carrying her over the threshold on the first night after returning from the honeymoon at the beach house. She remembered the awe of realizing a room that she had cleaned many times as John's employee, would be the room she would share with her husband.

She opened her eyes and tentatively stepped into the room, flipping on the light switch. She felt like she could barely breathe. Reminders of John were everywhere—photos, a pair of slippers, his computer charging on the desk. And his scent—it was all around her. It reminded her of the final tour of the house she had once taken, planning to leave her employment, and John, many years before. She had been so afraid to let herself love again, that she had decided to run away.

Jillian had been standing in the circle drive later that afternoon, many years ago, her bags packed and at her side. If the taxi picking her up had arrived a few minutes earlier, the past thirty-some years would have played out in a completely different way. The thought of what she had almost missed occasionally haunted her. It was difficult to fathom a life without John, and now, that was her reality.

Jillian entered the bathroom to get ready for bed. She brushed her teeth and gazed into the mirror, barely recognizing the face looking back at her. She looked pale and gaunt, with an unfamiliar sadness masking her typically cheerful countenance. Jillian rinsed the toothpaste out of her mouth and dried her face dry with a towel, wishing she could spit out and wipe away the sorrow of the day.

Jillian dreaded entering the closet but knew she would have to, sooner or later. She turned on the light and entered the huge walk-in, which was more like another room than a closet. She stood silently, looking around as if she had never before seen the compartments and rods filled with clothing, shoes, and memories.

Jillian spied the old, soft and worn navy blue shirt John had been wearing the first time she saw him in person. She would never forget that day, when John's orange-haired cat, Lucy, had run away from him. She would also never forget the stunned look on his face when he saw Jillian holding the purring feline, who had a reputation for greatly disliking the house help.

Jillian had once told John she hoped he would always keep the shirt, and he had honored her wishes. Occasionally, he would even wear it for her sake, and that would always bring a smile to Jillian's face. She smiled weakly as she gently touched it. Jillian undressed, then took the shirt down from the shelf and pulled it over her head. It was big enough to serve as a nightshirt on her. She turned off the closet light and slowly walked to the king-sized bed.

Turning down the bedcovers was one of the hardest things Jillian had ever done. Over the past thirty years, it was a rarity that she slept alone. It only happened when she or John had work out of town and could not travel together. She didn't enjoy those nights, but she had always known it wouldn't be long before she and John would be back together. That wasn't the case tonight. It would never be the case again.

She pulled the heavyweight comforter down, then a blanket and sheet and reluctantly crawled in. She stared at John's pillow, then reached for it and pulled it tight against her body, breathing in deeply. At that moment, Jillian realized that getting used to the "new normal" was going to be one of the biggest challenges of her life.

She turned out the light, and as usual, she said her prayers for her family and friends. For those who were on their way back to her, she prayed for a safe return. She also prayed for God to heal their hearts. And then she prayed for her own heart, which felt at that moment like it would never be the same again. She held John's pillow even tighter, and with tears in her eyes she whispered into the darkness, "I'll love you forever, John."

Chapter Two

Carol, Jillian's long-time friend and mentor, was the first one to arrive the next morning. Just as she had been when she was Jillian's supervisor in nursing school at the University of Wisconsin, Carol was strong and reassuring. Together, Carol and Jillian had dealt with death many times throughout the years, beginning with the first death Jillian had ever attended in her first week of practicum, that of a father/grandfather who died on Father's Day. It had been heart-wrenching, but Carol's calm-but-caring demeanor helped both the family, and Jillian, cope with the loss.

But today was different. This time, it was John—someone they both loved dearly—who had died. Jillian sensed that Carol had never had to work so hard to act strong, and she noticed Carol quickly wipe away a tear from time to time, something Jillian had never before witnessed in the myriad of years they had known each other and worked together.

Jillian almost told Carol that it was okay to cry, but she knew better than that. If, and when, Carol chose to let go, it would be Carol's choice, not Jillian's. Carol, and years of nursing, had taught Jillian that everyone grieves differently, and in their own ways, and in their own time frame. If one day Carol cared to show more emotion, she would. In the meantime, Jillian appreciated Carol's tranquil demeanor and steadiness. Jillian imagined it wouldn't be the same scenario with many of the others who would walk through the door over the next few days, and she was correct in that assumption.

The next person to arrive was their daughter, Marty. As John had often said, there were two best days of his life—the day he married Jillian and the day he became a father to Marty, who he adopted when she was twenty-six years old. The two appeared to be a match made in heaven. John had always wanted a daughter. Marty had always longed for a father who would want her and love her. Both of their dreams had been fulfilled beyond measure in one simple procedure at a courthouse in Los Angeles, sharing a "double-header" adoption day with their friends, Karen and Robert Wilson, as they adopted their foster son, Rick.

Marty, a medical professional for many years now, also had her professionally practiced way of holding things together. But in this case, like Carol, she struggled. She and Jillian held each other tightly, tears in their eyes.

They parted and looked at each other, searching one another's face. "How are you doing?" they asked one another simultaneously. They were so much alike that it was almost comical.

"You go first," Jillian said, holding and squeezing her daughter's hands.

"I don't really believe it yet, Mom. I mean, we just had such a wonderful weekend together. I didn't see any signs of a problem, did you?" she asked, almost sounding guilty for being a doctor and not recognizing a medical problem in her own father.

"I don't think it was anything any of us could detect. The coroner said it was most likely an aneurysm. That seems the most likely to me, too," Jillian added.

Marty nodded her head in agreement at that assessment. "Now, it's your turn, Mom. How are you doing?" she asked, and gave Jillian's hands a firm squeeze.

"The word that first comes to my mind—stunned," Jillian said. Inwardly, she added *heartbroken and devastated,* but she just couldn't say it out loud yet and didn't want to heap any more pain on her already hurting daughter. And knowing Marty, Marty already knew exactly what her mother was feeling, and was probably feeling the same way, too.

Marty nodded her head, a tear escaping down her cheek. "Oh, Mom," she said and hugged Jillian tightly.

"I'm so glad you're here, Marty," Jillian said.

"Me, too. Michael will be here as soon as the doctor covering for him makes it back to the village. He should be here tomorrow sometime."

"That's great. Now, why don't you go and get settled in. I put you and Michael in the guest suite," she said, gesturing toward the staircase.

Marty picked up her bag and turned to go upstairs. "Thanks, Mom. I'll be down soon," she promised, and kissed her mom on the cheek.

Carol was in the kitchen making coffee and putting pastries she had purchased at a nearby bakery onto a plate. Carol was not one to bake, but she had wanted to bring something, as was often the custom at a time such as this.

Jillian was going to join her in the kitchen, when there was another knock on the front door. She opened it and there was John's beloved nephew, Tommy. Jillian took one look at Tommy's face, and that did it for her, and for Tommy. Tommy dropped the travel bag he was carrying, and he and Jillian held each other tight and sobbed in the doorway. Anything Jillian had been holding in was now unleashed. It was sad in some ways, but it was also cleansing.

After a minute or two of this, they both pulled back. Jillian wiped her eyes on her sleeve and smiled at Tommy through her tears. She loved him like the brother she had never had, but had always wanted. "Well, that was a fine hello, wasn't it?" Jillian asked, trying to lighten the moment a bit.

"I'm sorry, Jillian, I just couldn't help it."

"Don't be sorry, Tommy. I'm not. I needed that," she said honestly.

"Good, because I did, too," he said, picking up his bag and coming inside. "It was a long plane ride. All I wanted to do was cry. The flight attendant kept asking me if I was okay. I must have looked as terrible as I felt."

"Well, you're here now, and you can cry whenever you need to," she said seriously.

He nodded, pulling a handkerchief out of his pocket. "I rarely carry one of these anymore, but I thought it might be a good idea today," he said, wiping his face. "I guess I was right."

"Leave your things here, Tommy. Carol brought pastries and has coffee brewing in the kitchen. Marty will be downstairs soon, too."

Tommy set his case near the bottom of the stairs, then followed Jillian down the hallway past the elaborate library and the elegant dining room toward the kitchen.

Carol hugged Tommy, then directed them both to the breakfast nook. Carol was back in perfect form—in charge and calmly taking care of business. Again, Jillian appreciated her longtime friend and mentor. She needed someone in the house to be on an even keel. Jillian, on the other hand, could barely think straight. She wasn't sure she could even remember how to make a cup of coffee at that moment and was so grateful for Carol. Jillian felt like she was living on a different planet. Everything felt alien to her.

Carol poured two huge, steaming cups of coffee and two glasses of orange juice and set a plate of pastries in front of them. She had small plates and napkins on the table and was doing an admirable job for someone who was not a kitchen person. It's not that Carol didn't like to cook, but all those years of working crazy hours had made it difficult for her to do much regular cooking and baking. She often ended up making a few big batches of food once a week, and she and her kids ate them all week long. Carol had often felt guilty about that, but it was the best she could do in a job like nursing, especially after she became a single parent.

Carol went to tell Marty about the goodies downstairs and Tommy's arrival, but Marty was already on her way down the stairs and met her mother's long-time friend as she reached the bottom.

"Carol, you are the best friend my mom could ever have," Marty announced and gave the blushing Carol a huge hug.

This made Carol's eyes mist, and she had to look away. "Go and join them, Marty. I'll be with you all in a few minutes. I have to make a phone call."

Marty was quite sure that what Carol really needed to do was regain her composure. They all would have a lot of practice doing that as the day wore on.

Tommy stood up when Marty came into the kitchen. He turned to her and hugged her tightly, tears in his eyes once more. It made Jillian want to cry again, too, and she realized that this was only the beginning. With each person who would be arriving, or who came to greet them at the visitation or service, or any who called over the next few days, it was going to be the same. Each time it would be another person whose life had been touched by John, and that was going to be *a lot* of people. Incredible strength would be needed to get through this, and Jillian sent up a prayer as she sat watching two of her most beloved people on earth hug one another. *Lord, help.*

They decided to have the visitation and service all on the same day, the coming Saturday. Jillian felt terrible that Pastor Jim did not get much rest that week after Easter, but of course, he said he didn't mind. The pastor had been grateful he hadn't gone away as he often did. Instead, he had opted to stay home with his wife, Janet, and relax and work on a few small projects around the house he had started, but never seemed to finish.

Pastor Jim had been wonderful to talk with that afternoon as they planned the service. He had a way of drawing out many memories and capturing everyone's best and deepest thoughts about John. Tommy and Marty both wanted, or as they said, *needed,* to share a eulogy. Tommy's son, John Anthony, had told Jillian on the phone that he planned to sing for his "Uncle John," the person who had inspired him to go into his profession in musical theater.

Jillian was so grateful for these people—the backbones of love and support in her life. She didn't know what people did who did not have family. And she certainly couldn't imagine, most of all, going through all of this without faith. As they returned to the house late that afternoon, she again felt those strong arms around her, and she smiled, even if ever so slightly, at the reassurance they provided.

Chapter Three

More family members arrived over the following two days. John Anthony was next. John Anthony's wife, Kirsten, and sons, Tommy John and Anthony, would come on Friday, as they didn't want the boys to miss too much school. Tommy John was incredibly bright, but couldn't always convey or apply his knowledge the way he desired, which made academics a real challenge for him. He was handsome and athletically talented, which was in his favor in high school, but it still didn't keep him from being teased at times or talked about behind his back, especially by some of the boys who were jealous of his looks, talent on the football field, and his popularity—especially with the girls.

Anthony was a carefree soul who never seemed to study but always managed to bring home a stellar report card. He had a voice like an angel, just like his father, and was blond and blue-eyed like his mother. Everyone adored Anthony, and even though Tommy John was sometimes jealous of his brother's abilities in the classroom, he loved his little brother fiercely, and vice-versa.

Kirsten was a physical therapist and had her own practice in a suburb of New York City, where the family resided. She and John Anthony met when he suffered a knee injury in a football game—

similar to his great-uncle John's injury—in his senior year at Northwestern. With surgical advancements, however, it could have been only season-ending, rather than career-ending. However, John Anthony's thoughts for his future were redirected during his hospitalization.

John and Jillian had visited John Anthony in the hospital just after his knee surgery. They had expected to be greeted by a sad and disappointed great-nephew who was missing the remainder of a stellar season as the starting quarterback on the team. Instead, they found him laughing and joking with a pretty, sweet physical therapist named Kirsten, who was, as he put it, forcing him walk and do exercises that were difficult. He mentioned she was tougher and harder on him than his football coaches.

"Poor John Anthony," John said as they left the hospital that day.

Recalling the friendly banter between John Anthony and the attractive physical therapist, Jillian responded, "I don't know about that. Did he look like a 'poor John Anthony' to you?"

"Well, his season is over, for certain."

"Yes, I agree. His season as quarterback is over, but I think there is another 'season' that's just starting," Jillian said, with a knowing smile.

"Kirsten?"

Jillian nodded her head. "And when I get a feeling about something like that ..."

"It's a done deal," John said. "Good for you, John Anthony," he said with a grin, and took Jillian's hand as they walked out through the hospital's automatic exit doors.

John Anthony and Kirsten began dating shortly after his hospitalization, when she was no longer his P.T. They were married right after John Anthony's graduation that spring. He never returned to football. After his surgery, he was able to fully concentrate on his studies in musical theater, and he decided that was more his passion than any sport. His coaches were disappointed. They thought they could get him another year of eligibility with a "medical hardship," but he had made up his mind.

Once John Anthony focused on music and acting, his rise to the top of the theater productions was like that of a rocket. He was the male lead in the spring musical. He did summer stock theater after the wedding, and one night he was noticed by an agent, which launched a long and prestigious career.

Now "poor John Anthony," a Tony-award winner for best actor in a musical, with several other nominations under his belt, was walking through Jillian's front door. He, like Tommy, often took Jillian's breath away when she first saw them, especially when they smiled. They both had that famous Romano jaw and grin, as did John Anthony's sons. When they smiled, it was like seeing John smiling at her. John Anthony flashed one of those smiles at Jillian, then his face turned serious.

"I don't even know what to say to you, Aunt Jillian," he said, holding her arms, his eyes growing moist and red. John Anthony had been the first person to ever call her "Aunt Jillian," and it was a title Jillian cherished. She loved this man like a son.

She looked at him lovingly. "You don't have to say anything, John Anthony. I'm just so glad you are here," she said. She suggested they join the rest of the family out on the pool deck and hooked her arm around his trunk of an arm. He was big and strong and made others around him feel safe and at ease. He was also as kind and compassionate as he was strong, which made him an even more attractive figure.

His agent had been working very hard to convince John Anthony to do more work in Hollywood, predicting he could be a huge success if he would only give it a real shot. He had done a few small parts in movies, but his first love was the stage. Also, the thought of uprooting his children and disrupting Kirsten's work was not appealing to him, either. He was very considerate in those areas. However, he told his agent that if the right opportunity presented itself, he would seriously consider it. He just didn't know what kind of role would be attractive enough, or important enough, to make him "consider it." It would have to be something exceptional, and so far, nothing had even come close.

Michael arrived in the late afternoon, much to Marty's relief and happiness. He looked absolutely beat. He was such a dedicated doctor and still did research projects from time to time when his schedule allowed it. He and Marty had been among the doctors who had tackled the Zika virus head-on, helping to virtually eliminate it from the South American continent.

They were also instrumental in developing treatments for those who had contracted the disease and helped open orphanages in remote rural villages for affected children abandoned by parents who had no means to take care of sick children. The difficult decision to go to South America, rather than Africa, many years ago had been a good one for them and for the many thousands of people whose lives were bettered by their work and others'.

Alison and her daughter, Zoe, arrived that evening. Alison's husband was unable to come, which wasn't surprising considering he was a surgeon in a large Chicago hospital. Judy Jo and John Martin, Marty and Michael's daughter and son, also in the medical field, wouldn't be there until the very last minute themselves.

The house was filling up with loved ones. Tommy and John Anthony decided earlier in the day that they were going to barbecue that evening, and readied the monstrous grill at the end of the deck for duty. Grill-ready meats and vegetables, which Jillian had ordered, had been delivered and were ready to cook.

For a while that evening, things felt like they always felt when the family was home. John had so loved simple and intimate gatherings like this, and Jillian equally relished the relaxed and loving atmosphere.

At the end of the night, the family gathered in the kitchen for their traditional frozen yogurt sundae bar finale. Then everyone headed to bed. Those who had been traveling all day were having trouble staying awake, and Jillian wasn't much better. She wasn't too upset about that, though. She felt like she might be able to get a decent night's sleep for the first time since Tuesday, or at least she prayed she would.

Once upstairs, as goodnights were said and rooms were busy with people readying for bed, Jillian overheard the tail-end of a conversation in the hallway between Zoe and Alison.

"You should tell her what's going on, Mom," Zoe said.

"Shh," Alison whispered loudly to her daughter. "Aunt Jillian has enough on her mind right now without ..."

Jillian cleared her throat loudly before coming around the corner. Zoe and Alison separated like two middle-schoolers caught gossiping.

"Goodnight, Aunt Jillian," Zoe said and hugged her before hurrying down the hall to her room.

Jillian looked at Alison. "How about a cup of tea, Alison—just you and me?"

Alison nodded, and the two women quietly descended the staircase. Jillian heated two mugs of water in the microwave, then brought them over to the breakfast nook along with a small assortment of caffeine-free teas, sugar and cream. The two sat across from one another, Jillian waiting for Alison to say what Zoe thought her mother needed to say.

Jillian thought back to the day when a teenaged Alison had whispered to her that she was looking into nursing schools. She had told Jillian about her plans even before she had told her mother, Maria, even though daughter and mother were very close. She and Jillian always seemed to have a bit of a special bond because of nursing. Alison had attended and graduated from the University of Wisconsin, just like Jillian, and later completed her education to become a nurse practitioner. She probably would have been a great doctor, but Jillian always felt there was not room for two doctors in Alison's household, unfortunately.

Alison met Dr. Cameron R. Turner when she was interning at the University of Chicago. He was a cutting-edge surgeon. He was "dashing and brilliant," as Alison described him to Jillian the first time. For some reason, Jillian had an uneasy feeling about their relationship right from the beginning. Perhaps Cameron reminded Jillian just a little bit too much of Marty's biological father, Dr. Jeffrey A. Lawrence. Even now, after Alison and Cameron's twenty years of marriage and being the parents of the beautiful and intelligent Zoe, the feeling still remained. And on this night, Jillian discovered her instincts were unfortunately correct.

When Alison's eyes started to mist, Jillian's heart started to beat harder. She hoped that whatever Alison had to tell her was not about some serious illness. She didn't really feel that it was, but her senses weren't as sharp at that moment as they usually were. Jillian didn't trust her usual uncanny abilities during this unusual time of sudden loss and grief.

"He's having an affair," Alison finally said, not even saying her husband's name. "Actually, he's had numerous affairs over the past twenty years, Aunt Jillian. But this time, he's going to have a child with this woman, and a few days ago, he filed for a divorce and moved out. I know I should be glad it's finally over, but I'm not. I always dreamed of a forever love, like you and Uncle John had. I guess I'm just a hopeless, and unrealistic, romantic," Alison said.

"You aren't hopeless or unrealistic, Alison. You just had the misfortune of giving your heart to the wrong person—this time. Remember, I did the same thing, more than once, actually. But then, finally, there was John." As Jillian said this, she again felt so blessed to have had such a love.

"Do you think I'll ever find someone who will love me like that?" Alison asked so sadly that it made Jillian's heart break.

"I will start praying for you, Alison. I think there's a really good chance of that. You're even younger than I was when I met John, and we had thirty amazing years together."

"I'd settle for thirty amazing days together. I should never have married Cameron. He was always looking at other women while we were dating, while we were engaged, and even on our honeymoon! But, I still put up with it. I was a fool."

"First of all, never put up with, or settle for, anything other than what you deserve. And as for being a fool—I'd rather be a fool with a good heart full of love than be someone who never loved, or someone like Cameron who squandered someone else's love. You have a lot of love to give. There's someone out there, Alison, who is looking for a love just like yours. I know it—I feel it," Jillian said, and at that moment, she really did feel it. She put her hand on Alison's. "How is Zoe taking all of this?"

"She's a trooper. She is a smart and intuitive girl. She's suspected, unfortunately, her father's philandering ways for quite some time now. I feel bad that Cameron is the example of a father, and a man, she has grown up with."

"But remember, she had your dad and your brother as examples, too," Jillian reminded her.

Alison nodded. "And Uncle John, too. Sometimes I feel bad that I let this situation go on so long. I tried to get Cameron to go to counseling once. He told me to 'go ahead,' if that was what I needed to do, but he wouldn't be joining me. I went, and it helped me some, but it didn't help our marriage," Alison replied with a heavy sigh.

"At least you showed your daughter that you put some effort into your relationship. You loved someone, you tried to make it work, you tried to get help, and you didn't just give up the second things got tough."

"That's true. I guess that's something, at least." Then Alison's eyes began to water and her lip trembled. "I'm not looking forward to telling my parents," Alison said, looking down.

Jillian thought about the day she had to tell her mom and dad that she was pregnant. It was the hardest day of her life. She had always been their shining star, their pride and joy. She hated the idea of disappointing them.

Of course, they weren't jumping for joy about the situation, but they told her that they loved her, first and foremost, and they would love her baby, too. Martin and Judy Johnson, who had adopted Jillian as an infant, had been the best parents Jillian could have asked for and had been wonderful grandparents to Marty.

"They will handle it, Alison. They will hurt, mostly for you and for Zoe. But they love you and Zoe and John Anthony and his family more than life itself. It will be okay," Jillian said, squeezing Alison's hand.

Tears gently cascaded down Alison's cheeks. "I'm not crying because I'm sad, Aunt Jillian. I just feel so much better than I have in months—maybe years. You are right. My parents love me. My brother loves me. You love me. Zoe loves me. It will be okay. I can feel it, too!"

The two women got up and hugged each other. It felt good to both of them, as they were both needing a reassuring touch at that moment. The two picked up their mugs and put them in the sink. They held hands as they walked upstairs to their beds, and both slept like babies that night.

Of course, before Jillian fell asleep, she prayed. She prayed for Alison, for Zoe, for Tommy and Maria, and the rest of the family. And she again thanked God for John—for his faithfulness, for filling her heart with love, and for returning her love with his own for so many years.

Chapter Four

On the plane, Maria buckled her seatbelt, then leaned her head back on the headrest. She was physically and emotionally exhausted. Last weekend, she had flown to Los Angeles for one of the happiest events she had ever attended—John and Jillian's renewal of vows and thirtieth anniversary celebration. Now, she was on her way back to California for one of the saddest situations she had dealt with in years. Not since Tommy's mother died in a car crash had she felt such searing grief. Some of it was for herself, some for her kids, but most of it was for her husband, Tommy. "Zio" (what Tommy called his uncle) had been like a father to him all his life.

She sighed, thinking about how she couldn't wait to get to Tommy and hold him in her arms. Ever since they had begun working together twenty-nine years ago, their own relationship had gone from what she had always thought was great to begin with, to what she considered to be exceptional. A lot of that, she thought, had to do with John's influence on Tommy.

Back then, John and Jillian had come to Libertyville after she had been injured in an accident. Alison and she had been out practice driving—Alison's last "night driving" segment requirement of her behind-the-wheel training—when a gentleman ran a stop sign and T-boned their vehicle. It had been a scary and life-changing event, in more ways than one.

Tommy had blamed himself. Had he been home instead of working one of a series of night meetings with an attractive new work associate, he felt the accident would never have happened. As Maria recovered from her injuries, Tommy had taken a good, hard look at his employment situation. What had once been a "family friendly" work environment, had become more about profits than people. Tommy became disillusioned with his firm and decided he no longer wanted to work for it, even though he had been with the same company since a college internship.

After a long heart-to-heart with John, and hearing how much he enjoyed working with Jillian on a movie, Tommy had decided to become the business manager for Maria's Italian deli. The two of them had been concerned it wouldn't work, but it had been the best business and personal move of their lives.

Since then, Tommy and Maria had seen each other for many hours every day, rather than five minutes at its end when they were both worn to a frazzle. They were both busy enough and independent enough, however, to give one another a healthy amount of space within each day.

Tommy was a natural, not only at keeping the books, but for promoting the business. When he was in the shop, he charmed the customers with his grin and people skills. Out in the community, he became a dedicated and integral part of the town he had lived in for so many years. Working close to the city for many years, on the north side of Chicago, he never had time to become very involved before. Working in Libertyville allowed him to be a member of various civic groups and to work closely with the Main Street Program, which became one of his passions. It didn't hurt their social lives, either. The couple had never had so many friends.

Over the years, their business not only thrived, but expanded because of their quality products, new connections, and overall love for their town. The business grew so rapidly, they ended up adding another shop in the area after two years, and eventually a third. Now, after all this time, they were preparing to sell the shops to one of their most devoted and long-time employees. They had been discussing the future and making plans for over a year, and the details and papers had just been drawn up during the past week. They had postponed a meeting on this day, but it could wait. There were more important concerns, like Jillian. *Her heart must be in shreds,* Maria thought as she closed her heavy eyes.

Hours later, Maria awakened as the tires of the plane thudded against the runway at LAX. She remembered the first time she and her family had met Jillian. Maria had loved every moment of that experience. Jillian had immediately felt like a friend and a member of the family. And John—it had been like meeting a different person. He had never looked so happy. He had been making jokes, engaging in easy conversation, and smiled more in one evening than in all the years Maria had known him put together. She smiled as she thought of that day long ago.

Tommy was waiting for her near the baggage claim. He smiled at her, but then she noticed his face contort, and his emotions appeared ready to erupt. She rushed into his arms. He held her like he was never going to let go, which was fine with her. All she could think about the last few days was what it would be like to suddenly lose Tommy, and it wasn't a very pleasant thought.

They gently parted and looked into each other's eyes. Tommy caressed her cheek with his hand and kissed her gently, yet passionately. He had been kissing this woman ever since they were both eighteen, and it never got old.

"Thank God you're here, safe and sound," Tommy said softly into her ear.

Maria was pretty sure her husband had thoughts similar to her own the past few days. Losing a loved one could be a real wake-up call. Life could be so uncertain. Everything can change in an instant.

"I'm so glad to be here with you. I love you."

"I love you, too, Maria, so much." He held her hands tightly, then the conveyor belt began to rumble and begin its rotation. They reluctantly turned their attention to finding Maria's bags, getting the car, and heading out onto the traffic-packed highway awaiting them.

Again, the evening before the funeral service, Jillian wondered again what it would feel like in tough times to not have faith or family. She was very happy that she didn't know the answer, as she was deeply blessed with both, and they were helping hold her heart together. A large gathering of her favorite people in the world sat around the flames of a huge gas fire pit table, which had been installed on the side of the pool deck toward the backyard. The deck had been extended to accommodate its construction, and an elaborate grouping of comfortable outdoor furniture surrounded the structure. The current poolside scene was a far cry from the measly lone chair and table John had poolside when Jillian arrived at this house years ago.

There was constant chatter that evening. It was different, though. There was chuckling from time to time, yet there were sniffles, too. One memory would make one laugh, another make one cry, and some, both. Laugh, cry, then laugh again. It was all good, though. Good to be able to remember. Good to be able to laugh. Good to be able to cry. Good to be together. Good to be alive. It seemed a proper warmup for the next day, the day of the memorial service for John. It would be a hard one. But it would be an important one.

Jillian looked around at all the faces of her loved ones glowing in the firelight. It reminded her for a moment of that first Christmas Eve candlelight service after she and John were married. She hadn't been able to stop marveling that John was really her husband that night. Sometimes she still couldn't stop marveling about that.

Jillian thought about the next day's service. How could just one small segment of one day be enough to honor and remember someone like John D. Romano? She felt that it could go on for a thousand days, and it still wouldn't come close to covering what John had meant to so many people, and especially to her. She sighed slightly. *We'll do our best, sweetheart.*

Chapter Five

As Jillian dressed in front of the mirror, she could barely believe that just days before, she had stood in the very same spot helping John with his tie in preparation for their renewal of vows ceremony. He had looked so handsome in his crisp, new white shirt, underneath his thirty-year-old jacket. How could things go from one of the happiest days ever, to one the saddest days ever, all in less than a week? She slowly shook her head in disbelief.

She smoothed her dress. It was one of John's favorites, black and made of some of the softest material she had ever worn, with a flattering cut due to the exceptional talent of her good friend and now famous designer, Marianna. Jillian accented her attire with a scarf John had bought for her on their last trip to Italy.

As she looked in the mirror, Jillian fingered the gold cross necklace hanging around her neck, which had once belonged to John's mother. John had thought it to be lost when his mother died, but his relative, Pietro, had surprised him with it during their visit to his home on their honeymoon trip. John's mother had gifted it to Pietro's mother, and now that she was gone, Pietro gave it back to John. John had asked Jillian to wear it that night, and she hadn't taken it off since. She said a prayer for strength as she touched it, realizing she would never need God's help as much as she would on this day.

The church was packed. The visitation and service had not been publicly announced and unfortunately, had to be by invitation. Even so, John and Jillian had so many friends they could barely fit in the sanctuary. Chairs filled the narthex for overflow.

The luncheon in the fellowship hall would be handled by a select group of members of the church, those with whom John and Jillian were closest, and who could be trusted not to leak the event to the media. The privacy issue was a major downfall of working in Hollywood.

Jillian and the family stood in the church and received a steady stream of condolences from many people who had worked with John, and later John and Jillian, in the industry. Hugs, kisses and tears were intertwined with special memories and smiles.

Finally, it was time for the service to begin, and those remaining were asked to be seated. Pastor Jim gathered Jillian and the rest of the family in the chapel for a prayer. Tears filled everyone's eyes as he thanked God for John's life and letting them all share in it, and as he reminded them of God's promises.

As they began to walk back into the sanctuary, Jillian suddenly felt dizzy and like she might fall. Tommy, luckily, was at her side, and held on to her tightly when her knees began to buckle.

"Are you okay, Jillian?" he asked in a concerned tone.

She stood still, holding on to him for dear life. "Give me a moment," she said and closed her eyes. Inside, she wanted to run away and pretend that all this wasn't really happening. She gripped Tommy's arm tightly, took several deep breaths, and with each one, she asked God for strength. She opened her eyes slowly, then nodded affirmatively to Tommy. They slowly walked to their place in

Kathy J. Jacobson

the front pew, right in front of the heavy, glass and wood pulpit, part of some recent renovations of the sanctuary.

Pastor Jim welcomed the congregation and said a prayer. They sang a congregational hymn, "Borning Cry," one of John's favorites. Then it was time to remember John.

Marty had asked if she could be first. Michael squeezed her hand before she left the pew. Marty had always been pretty, but now she was a striking, mature woman. Her long hair was darker than in her younger days, but still a shade of blonde, and her smile could still light up a room on a gloomy day. She looked at her mom and began.

"Growing up, I secretly wondered why I didn't have a father. I say secretly, because I never wanted my mom to feel bad, so I didn't say anything, although knowing my mom, she probably knew. But that didn't stop a young girl from wondering and wishing she had a dad.

"So I wondered. And I wished. But one day, a little over thirty years ago, all those years of wondering and wishing were answered beyond expectation. My mom decided to follow her dreams and moved to California to become a writer. She made her dream come true, and along the way, my dream came true as well.

"I remember the first phone calls after my mom started working for my dad. He put a serving of my favorite food she had made and shared with him in the garbage, dish and all! He only wrote notes to communicate with her. He did this, he did that, he didn't do this, he didn't do that. But when he collapsed from a brain tumor, my mom discovered something—her heart belonged to John D. Romano. In fear of what that meant, she almost ran away from him, but God intervened, I believe, because God knew that my dad was the one for her, and he was the one for me, too.

"So, I just want to say how thankful I am to my mom for following her dreams and landing at the home of John D. Romano. In all my wonderings, I never imagined a dad as wonderful as John. He was far more than I ever dreamed a father could be. I didn't have to wonder anymore why I didn't have a father growing up. I did have one, and he was out there waiting for me, just like I was waiting for him. I will always love you, Dad, and I thank God you became a part of my life. You were definitely worth the all the wondering, the wishing, and the waiting."

Marty's green eyes were rimmed with red, but she smiled through her tears as she sat back down, her son and daughter giving her hugs as she passed by them.

Tommy rose to speak. Jillian thought that today he looked old. She noticed some gray in his hair, which she was certain was not there just one week before. He walked slowly to the front, without his usual energy. Jillian knew his heart was hurting terribly. John and he had been so very close. He gripped the lectern, looking like he was hoping it would help him out somehow. Tommy took a deep breath and began.

"I just realized something. I am the luckiest person in this room. I call myself that because I had the privilege of knowing John D. Romano, or Zio as I always knew him and called him, longer than anyone else here. I knew him my entire life.

"My uncle, my Zio, was always there for me through thick and thin. When I was a small boy, Zio was my savior—literally. One time he rescued me from a muddy foundation of a house that was being built in our neighborhood. It had rained hard the night before, and it looked like a swimming pool to me, so I climbed in. It was easy getting in, but unfortunately, I couldn't get out. My feet were stuck in the muck under the water. I started crying and yelling for help. Fortunately, Zio was home from college for the summer and was coming over to our house when he heard my cries for help.

"He reached down and pulled me out with his strong hands and arms, but my shoes stayed behind. Despite having a sore knee from his football injury and surgery the fall before, he jumped in and sloshed around in the mess until he found them, as I sat sobbing on top of the concrete. We were both wet and full of mud, but he had saved me, in more ways than one. Looking back, I realize I could have been in serious danger being in that water. And I know I would have been in serious trouble with my father if I had somehow made it out of there by myself and had come home without my shoes.

"Zio took me home, helped me get cleaned up, and took the brunt of my father's ire and blame for the entire incident. Zio made it sound like it was his idea to explore the house under construction, rather than a small child's foolishness. Yes, he was my hero, my savior, my best friend, and my teacher—all wrapped up in one person.

"Zio was the one who taught me to throw a football. He was the one who taught me to laugh and to love, and to be faithful to those whom I loved. Despite not officially being a father until much later in life, Zio was the one who taught me how to be a dad, too. And in my later years, he still continued to teach me to have integrity, to use my abilities to help others, and to reconcile with and forgive others, even those no longer with us here on earth.

"He was a wonderful Zio and the best man I have ever known, and I know he was a wonderful husband to Jillian. I am forever grateful, too, like Marty, that Jillian followed her dreams. We almost lost Zio many years ago, and I'm not talking about his medical incident, but when he was filled with fear and cut himself off from life and those of us who loved him. But, as Marty said, God knew John was the one for Jillian, and Jillian, God knew you were the one for him. You brought him back to us. And not only was he back, but he was the best-ever version of himself. He was the happiest I had ever seen him. I know how much he loved you, Jillian, and your life together, and the joy you brought him. And for that, I will be forever grateful.

"Right now, however, I feel a bit like I did as that frightened little boy stuck in the muck. I am counting on God to pull me, and all of us, out of the pit this time. I know it will happen. Zio taught me that, too—to trust, and believe, that nothing is impossible. So, yes, things will get better, but we sure will miss you, Zio."

After Tommy sat down, Pastor Jim asked if anyone else had something they wished to share. Jillian hadn't planned on it, but she felt herself rising. She wasn't sure she could make the walk up to the front, but she suddenly felt bolstered and felt that double set of strong arms supporting her as she proceeded. She boldly stood at the lectern and spoke.

"I just want to say this. You heard how happy Marty and Tommy were that I came to California thirty-one years ago, but no one is happier or more grateful than I am. What a blessing it was to love John, and to be loved by him. You probably know that feeling, too, as he loved each and every one of you. We are the most fortunate people on earth to have had John D. Romano in our lives. We will never forget him. Our lives have all been changed because of him. And they will never be quite the same without him." After she said that, she started to become a bit emotional. "And one last thing. John, I'll love you forever."

Then Jillian went back to her pew and sat down, feeling once more the invisible strong arms guiding her back to her seat.

Pastor Jim got up. He read the Twenty-third Psalm, then Second Corinthians 5:17: "So if anyone is in Christ, there is a new creation: everything old has passed away; see, everything has become new!"

He continued, "I'm not sure what more there is to say about John. I'm not sure there are enough words to express them, anyway. I do know that in all my years of ministry, I never had anyone come to my office and repeat back to me my entire sermon, except John. John did that shortly after I met him, when he asked me to consider performing a marriage ceremony on Easter Sunday, because it was a day all about new creation.

"The theme verse of that sermon had been Second Corinthians 5:17. That verse was John and Jillian's wedding verse and was shared again just six days ago when they renewed their vows to one another, and it was shared here today as well. John and Jillian were, and are, living examples of that verse—both bringing out the best

Kathy J. Jacobson

in one another and being changed for good, all because of the love and grace of God in their lives. They let love into their hearts, and more love followed. Their love blossomed and bloomed for thirty exceptional years.

"But now, John is once again a new creation. We don't know exactly what all that entails, but we do know we are promised it will be wonderful and that this new and wonderful creation will be endless. So we mourn a great loss, but not without hope. We will always remember John and the many ways he blessed our lives. And we remember God's promises, for which we are truly thankful. Amen."

Pastor Jim always seemed to say what Jillian needed to hear, and this time was no exception. She thanked God once more for this wonderful and faithful servant, who had been a gift to her and John from the very beginning of their marriage, to its end.

The message was followed by music. Jillian was surprised that she was able to hold herself together as well as she did when John Anthony sang an old song. It was one John and Jillian had often remarked about when wondering about heaven—"I Can Only Imagine." Marty accompanied him on guitar. There wasn't a dry eye in the room when they were finished.

After the Lord's Prayer and a prayer of commendation, they sang one final hymn, "How Great Thou Art." Jillian remembered this being sung at both of her parents' funerals and how it made her feel strong and hopeful. It had the same effect on this day as well. Maybe it was because people always seemed to sing out its timeless and familiar words, making its message that much more poignant and believable.

The luncheon after the service was perfect. Jillian had thought she might not have an appetite, but the food, like the loving people who had prepared it, convinced her otherwise. She just couldn't say no to Lorraine and Carolyn, two of the women in charge. Few meals compared to a church luncheon in Jillian's book, and she often thought the preparation and serving of a funeral luncheon, in particular, should be considered an act of ministry. No caterer, with the possible exception of Leo's family, could come close to providing such a loving spread of savory comfort foods.

Jillian took the last bite of her meal and hugged yet another well-wisher. Even though everything was very important and special at church, Jillian couldn't help but think about how good it would be to get home to be with the closest of their friends and her loving family. Leo's sons and daughter would be providing food for the evening at the house. Jillian had called to invite them to the events of the day. They would not be there for the service, but offered to cook as their way of honoring John. Jillian wanted to pay them, but in the same fashion as their late father, they absolutely refused to accept money. Cooking was their way of expressing their love and condolences to Jillian, just like the people at church. So, as John had always done with Leo, she finally gave in and let them give to her from their hearts.

After the lunch crowd had dispersed, Jillian and the family met with Pastor Jim at the church's new columbarium. John's ashes would rest there, with the exception of a small portion which would make its way back to Illinois to be buried at John's parents' graves, right next to his brother's. Jillian thought perhaps a trip to the Midwest in the summer would be nice. She hadn't been back to her own parents' graves in a long time, and she suddenly felt a renewed interest in doing so. Jillian thought about how her parents, John's family members, and John, were now all together. It was a very comforting thought on a very hard day.

That night Jillian crawled between the "too cool" sheets and pulled John's pillow close to her body once more. She sighed after she breathed in his scent, which was already starting to fade, and closed her eyes to say her prayers. She was exhausted, but she couldn't stop thinking about the day. While she knew there was no way for everyone to cover the depth of all that John had done, or meant to them, she thought it had been an admirable attempt.

She thought about all the people who were a part of her life and how precious they were to her, especially those who had been with her that afternoon and evening at the house. They were God's best gifts to her, and she didn't know what she would do without them. She thanked God once more for bringing them all into her life and prayed for their health and happiness. Then she said out loud, as she had every night for the past thirty years, "I'll love you forever, John," and fell into a deep sleep.

Chapter Six

Jillian opened the refrigerator the next morning to get out some orange juice, milk, and berries, and was taken aback. It was completely packed from top to bottom, front to back. She had known there were leftovers from the night before, but hadn't realized the magnitude of the food gifts that had been brought over by friends and family or delivered to the house. Carol had been fielding these offerings of comfort on her behalf.

After some careful maneuvering, Jillian retrieved what she needed and made her simple meal. She was the first one up, and for a moment, she was grateful for the peace. As Jillian sat in the breakfast nook with her usual bowl of cereal and berries, her thoughts drifted to her mom. Her late mother, Judy, had been on her mind a lot lately. This time it was the food in the fridge that brought on the memories.

Judy had often made her "funeral hot dish" for family and friends who had lost a loved one or had taken it to church for a funeral luncheon. In some places, they referred to a "hot dish" as a "casserole," in other places it was a "covered dish." Where Jillian had grown up, a "hot dish" was a common title. Her mom's specialty was a chicken, rice, and broccoli combo that everyone raved about.

Jillian and her dad had enjoyed it, too, and were happy if there happened to be some left over, or if her mom made extra on purpose.

Before her mom had moved to Florida, Judy had finally broken down and shared the recipe with other women in the church, submitting it to the new church cookbook. Judy thought perhaps someone else would take over making it for funerals at the church after she was no longer around to make it, and she had been right. When her mom has passed away, and her service was back at her home church, it had been the main dish served at the luncheon in Judy's honor. The thought made Jillian smile. *Maybe I'll make that hot dish sometime soon, while Marty is still around.*

As if Jillian's thoughts had summoned her, Marty appeared in the kitchen at that very moment wrapped in a robe from the guest suite closet.

"What are you smiling about, Mom?" she asked as she hugged her mom, then slid into the bench of the breakfast nook across from Jillian.

Jillian told her, and she responded with a resounding "yes" and a huge smile of her own. Marty's smile was still as brilliant as ever. It still lit up a room, and Jillian was so glad it was lighting up the one she was in at the moment.

As she looked into Marty's eyes, however, Jillian felt again that something was "up." Jillian had noticed it the moment Marty had arrived, but then things got frantically busy, and so many people kept arriving or calling that she had no time to ask. Jillian had decided it was just her emotions playing tricks on her. But studying Marty's face this morning, she sensed it again, and rarely were her instincts wrong when it came to her daughter. Many years of being each other's "one and only" played a huge part in that.

Just as Jillian was about to say something to Marty, Tommy and Maria, Alison, John Anthony and Kirsten appeared. Michael, who had barely made it back in time for the funeral, was still sleeping, as were Tommy John and Anthony. Judy Jo and John Martin had to leave the night before. Jillian and Marty had been thrilled that they could attend at all, given their work and school commitments.

Tommy went to the refrigerator and opened the door. "Whoa!" he exclaimed, gazing at the bulging shelves.

Maria joined him and ogled the mountain of food. "I know what I'll be working on after breakfast," she said matter-of-factly. Dealing with food was her thing, and if anyone could straighten out a mess, it would be Maria.

Everyone scrounged, helping themselves to a wide variety of items from the over-packed appliance or from the almost completely covered kitchen countertops. They filled mugs with a bold morning blend coffee or tea and filled their glasses with fresh-squeezed California orange juice, finding seats in the nook or along the higher eating counter in the kitchen. The steady and easy banter of family filled the space, and Jillian felt like the house was home again.

Jillian tried to catch bits and pieces of all the conversations. She had some questions in the back of her mind based on her observations from the evening before. She wanted to know why Carson Stone, Jr. spent so much time in deep conversation with John Anthony. She noticed Ricardo talking to Alison near the end of the evening. It was nice to see Alison smile. However, they only spoke for a moment before Zoe interrupted her mother with a concern.

Jillian also wondered about a handshake between Tommy and Darius, the son of her longtime friends, Buck and Nancy. Darius and his wife and sons now ran the cattle ranch Buck and Nancy had once owned. Darius was also a candidate for mayor of their community and had a strong lead on his opponent going into the upcoming primary. Not only was Darius a great rancher, but he was a very respected community leader.

Buck and Nancy, in their late nineties, were in a small nursing facility, the one Jillian had briefly worked at many years before.

Jillian and John had seen them the day before his death, taking them some tiramisu from their anniversary celebration and showing them photos on their tablet. Jillian was not looking forward to telling them about John. Darius had offered to, but she told them she would do it.

Jillian was brought back to the moment by Marty, who bussed her dirty dishes for her. Everyone pitched in that morning, clearing and cleaning dishes and silverware. Then Tommy and Maria opened the refrigerator and made a plan as to how to proceed. They would throw out anything that was not in good shape, freeze some items that might make a good dinner for Jillian after their departure, and keep others which would make good lunches and dinners over the next day or so.

Unfortunately, John Anthony, Kirsten and the boys, and Alison and Zoe had to leave that afternoon. Tommy would take them to the airport in a few hours. Tommy and Maria planned to stay a few more days, and Marty and Michael were still up in the air on their plans.

Marty asked, "So, Mom, what else needs to be done?"

Jillian thought for a moment, then gazed at a huge wicker basket filled with cards. Marty's eyes followed hers. "Oh, boy!"

"You said it. You take half. Go through them and make two piles. I would like all the memorial gifts and cards from flowers or food gifts from family members and our closest friends in one pile, then all the others in another, and make sure to keep a list of each gift. I'll begin sorting this pile," she said, grabbing the top half of the basket's contents with two hands. "I think this is the best plan of attack."

Marty took the basket to the dining room where she would have more room to work, and Jillian moved her stack to the breakfast nook to get out of Tommy and Maria's way. She grabbed a tablet, along with some pens and note cards, and sat down. Jillian began to read, and floods of memories were unleashed.

Chapter Seven

Jillian fingered the small handwritten florist card. It had been on the floral arrangement sent by Monica Morgan. Monica had even drawn a little heart next to her name. Jillian thought about her first dealings with Monica. They had come a long way since then, actually becoming close friends. Monica had sobbed uncontrollably when Jillian told her about John's passing. The only other time Jillian witnessed Monica break down like that was when Monica's son, Brent, had been arrested after a serious drunk-driving accident.

Jillian picked up a pen and began to write on one of the notecards she had been given by the funeral director. *Dear Monica.* Jillian paused again, deep in thought. Sometimes it was hard for Jillian to fathom that the Monica Morgan she knew now was the same Monica Morgan she had met thirty years before. Monica, John's former costar on *O.R.,* and also former girlfriend, had been one unhappy woman back then. Her marriage to Ben Bastien had been in shambles, and she took it out on John during a film project, pursuing him and behaving in inappropriate and demeaning ways. Not until Jillian flew all the way to Alaska where they were filming and confronted Monica, had things begun to change. Afterward, Monica apologized to John for her behavior on the set and for the way she had hurt him in the past.

Kathy J. Jacobson

It wasn't long afterward, just when Monica had thought her life was getting back on track, that one of her twin sons, Brent, was arrested for causing bodily injury while driving intoxicated. Monica and Ben paid a large settlement to the young woman, and Brent served a jail sentence, followed by community service and probation. It was a tough stretch, but it brought about some needed changes. Since that time, Monica's life, and her family's, had taken many new turns—good ones.

Jillian remembered many years before when Monica told her about her intended plans, just after Brent got out of jail. "I have a bit of news, Jillian. We have sold this place," Monica had said, gazing at her over a cup of tea. They had been sitting at a table on the huge, circular brick patio in Monica's backyard, surrounded by beds of flowers and neatly manicured topiaries. Monica had mentioned at Marty's adoption celebration that they were thinking of putting their mansion in Bel Air up for sale, but Jillian had not been convinced she would actually go through with it.

"Where will you live?" Jillian asked, trying to sound less surprised than she was feeling.

"I cannot believe I am saying this, but I'm ... we're ... going home. We found some property just outside my hometown. We are building a house on part of the land, and now we have received permission to build an aquatic center on the other end, closer to town and just off of a major highway. I'm going to train swimmers and offer scholarships to talented kids who have potential but don't have the means to pay a coach. I got the idea from you and John, Jillian, with all you are doing with the Esperanza Center."

Jillian had thought she was surprised about the house, but this was an even more startling announcement. Jillian was pretty sure that Monica had been the one who had given an anonymous million dollar donation to the Esperanza Center, so she guessed she shouldn't have been so terribly surprised. But this was Monica's *very own* idea. Jillian forced herself to take a sip of tea so she could hide the huge smile that was trying to force its way out. She was happy for Monica, but she didn't want Monica to think she was laughing at her in any way. She was so proud of her new friend, something she also couldn't get over—that they were actually *friends*— after all that had transpired.

She had hugged Monica—something Monica still had to get used to at that time in her life. Now, Monica was often the first one to throw her arms around Jillian or John. The transformation had been incredible.

Monica and Ben made their move shortly after that conversation. Luckily, it was only two hours from the city, as Ben continued to act steadily over the next ten years until he retired to help more at the Aquatic Center. He did come back to L.A. once in a while, though, to teach an acting class at the Esperanza Center, as did Monica. She also gave inspirational talks to athletes at the center, often bringing her Olympic gold medal for them to see, touch, or even hang around an occasional neck. She inspired many young people to never give up, and one of them even ended up being trained by her in her program. The young woman eventually earned a scholarship to swim at the college level. Yes, it had been quite a remarkable journey.

As she sealed the note, Jillian wondered how Monica was doing. She had really struggled the day of the funeral. Jillian said a prayer for her friend as she put a stamp on the envelope.

Ben came into the living room of his and Monica's spacious home north of Los Angeles, where Monica stood staring out the floor-to-ceiling windows. The view of the mountains never grew old. He could tell from her posture, however, that she was not in a good place right now. Her slender, yet muscular, shoulders drooped, and her hands dangled at her sides. She turned to him when he stopped beside her and tried to smile, though her face was wet with tears.

Kathy J. Jacobson

"What can I do to help, love?" Ben asked.

"Hold me," she said quietly.

He pulled her close. He had loved this woman from the moment he met her on the set of *O.R.* Ben had known she was in a relationship with John D. Romano at the time, yet when their eyes met the first time, there was some sort of special connection. He hadn't intended to fall in love with Monica, but by the end of his several episode guest star stint, he knew he wanted to marry this woman, and he had never even given marriage a thought before meeting Monica.

Ben had tried putting her out of his mind, but he thought about her day and night while they were filming. When they finally had a scene where they had to kiss, he hadn't wanted it to end. He felt he needed to act on his feelings for her. She might tell him to go away, but he had never felt that way before about anyone, so he had felt it was worth a try.

He had waited for her to come out of her trailer one day, acting like he was there by accident. He had purposely bumped into her, literally almost knocking her down. They had laughed, and when he grabbed her to steady her, their eyes met again, and there was an even stronger feeling of connection this time. He knew she was an actress, and maybe she was just acting, but he thought he saw something special in the flicker of her eyes, and when she asked him into her trailer to look over some lines, he didn't have to be asked twice.

Ben had felt guilty during the rest of the filming, but he couldn't seem to stop his heart. He was in love with Monica Morgan, and she appeared to love him right back. Ben started shying away from John Romano whenever he could. He felt sorry for the guy, but at the same time, John always seemed so serious. Back then, John was nothing like the man he had become friends with over the past thirty years. And Monica—the way she spoke to John and about him didn't sound like a person who was in love with the man.

Then again, Monica definitely had, at that period of her life, what one might refer to as a "sharp tongue." She was like that with pretty much everyone except Ben. Over the years he had concluded it was a defense mechanism. Monica had had a mother who did nothing but push, push and push her in swimming. She had a father who thought it was all very foolish and told Monica she should become a secretary for a CEO. She was "pretty enough," he had told her.

It was no wonder that when Monica left for college, she never went back home, not even for school breaks. She always used swimming practice as her excuse, then her Olympic training. Her mother thought it was wonderful. Her father didn't care.

Over the years, the pressures of being a star college and national team swimmer, winning a gold medal at the Olympics, and later becoming a Hollywood star, all took their toll on a woman who had had no real loving base in her life—until she met Ben.

Monica buried her face into her husband's chest. If it weren't for Ben, she didn't know how she could stand it. She had never felt the loss of anyone in her life so deeply.

Monica thought back to the first time she met John. They had just read for what would become their respective roles on *O.R.* They had done two different scenes—one where John had to be bossy toward Monica, the other one in which they had to kiss. They were shocked, as millions of viewers would be when the pilot aired, when they learned these two characters were actually a couple.

Monica didn't mind kissing John. He was very handsome and appeared very athletic, except for his limp. When he revealed he had been injured playing Division I college football, she felt like he was somewhat of an equal. Few men she had dated knew what it took to be on a competitive team at that level, and it was one of the things about John she found attractive.

She and John hadn't intended to become involved, but between the romantic scenes they filmed and the network insisting they make numerous appearances together as one of America's favorite

Kathy J. Jacobson

TV couples, they actually became one. Monica realized she never truly loved John back then, but she had loved all the attention and publicity they received. Her career was in its early stages, and she was enjoying its meteoric rise. She and John were not only seen as sweethearts, but as a "power couple," before the term was even coined, on and off the screen. They even made the cover of several popular magazines. It was fun and exciting—for a while.

After a few years, it started to feel like "work" to be in a relationship with John. They really were not each other's type. John always seemed serious, and Monica was tired of being too serious about anything. He was also a decade or so older than her, and she was starting to think about having a family. John had seemed focused on his career at that point in time. Later, she discovered he would have been okay with getting married and having a child, but it was too late for that by that time she gained this information.

Ben had appeared on the set in their final season of the series, and she was instantly attracted to his sense of humor and his light-hearted, sometimes silly ways. She felt comfortable around him, like she could be herself. He made her laugh—not an easy accomplishment—and when he made a comment about loving children one day, that was it for Monica. It was easy for her to quickly dismiss John. She just wished that she had been nicer about it all. She had been quite blunt, even cruel, at the time. It would be many years before she would officially apologize to John for her poor behavior. Remarkably, he had forgiven her.

Now, Monica knew she had truly learned to love John over the years as a dear friend. He and Jillian were the best friends she and Ben had ever had and, she was certain, would ever have. The thought that he was gone seemed incomprehensible. She tightened her arms around Ben's waist and sobbed in his arms.

Chapter Eight

J illian realized she had daydreamed away almost twenty minutes. At this rate, she should be through the pile before her in several weeks—maybe months. She stood up and went to get a glass of water when her cell phone rang. Carol's name flashed across the screen. Jillian had finally convinced Carol to go home and get some rest. She was surprised to see her calling so soon.

"I thought you were going to get some rest, Carol," Jillian said into the phone.

"Jillian, it's Jerry," Carol's husband almost whispered into the phone. "Carol's sleeping for the first time in days, so I thought I'd call you," he said, a concerned tone in his voice.

"Is everything okay, Jerry?"

"I don't know. Maybe, maybe not. Carol is not herself, Jillian. She isn't eating well, she isn't sleeping, and I've come upon her several times when she's been crying—*sobbing,* Jillian. I guess that might not seem strange for most people, given the recent events, but in over thirty years of marriage, I've never seen her like this. I guess I don't know what to do, or not to do. I'm at a loss, Jillian."

Now Jillian was concerned. She had known Carol for what seemed to be forever. She had recognized days before that Carol was trying extra hard to be strong. Carol had even appeared at times to be fighting back tears, or even wiping one or two away. That was about as much emotion as Jillian had seen from Carol—ever. Even when Carol lost her first husband in a work accident, she had been a rock.

"What can I do to help, Jerry?" Jillian asked, not really sure what else to say.

"I'm not sure, Jillian. You two have been great friends for such a long time. Maybe when she's had some rest, you could talk to her. Perhaps tomorrow, or in a few days. I'm worried there's something she's not telling me. What if she's ill, Jillian?"

The thought of Carol being ill made Jillian feel ill. In her practiced way, taught to her by Carol, she tried to reassure the frightened Jerry, even though she was beginning to worry herself. Perhaps Carol's emotions had been so close to the surface because she was having troubles of her own. Jillian felt bad for not paying more attention to her friend. She hadn't even asked Carol how she was doing.

"Call me tomorrow, Jerry. Let me know when you think she may be rested enough for me to call, or even stop over. She's been so very helpful here and worked so hard. I'm hoping she is just tired from all her diligent work."

"Yes, I'm hoping that as well, Jillian," Jerry said, sounding a bit better. "Thank you for listening. I will record your number when I hang up, and I will call you soon," he said, and the call ended.

Jillian sat down on the stool at the kitchen counter, feeling dazed. *Lord, nothing can be wrong with Carol ... please.* It was half statement, half prayer. She wanted to share her concerns with John but remembered she couldn't—not now or ever again in this lifetime. *This was* going to take *some* getting used to, she thought, and sighed heavily.

If it hadn't been for all the company still around the house and a ton of cards calling to her, Jillian would have been obsessing over Carol. She returned to her seat and looked at the next card. As if her thoughts about her longtime friend brought it on, the next one she picked up was from Mark, Carol's son. She shook her head, thinking of the unhappy, troubled young man he had once been, and the happy, amazing one he had become.

When Jillian first met Mark when she was a nursing student and Carol was her supervisor, he was a highly intelligent, busy, and happy-go-lucky four-year-old. Later, when Jillian had left to be a missionary nurse in Tanzania, he was still a bright, energetic, big-for-his-age boy who excelled in football and told anyone who would listen that one day he would play for the Green Bay Packers. If that fell through, he planned to be an astronaut. But two years later, everything changed.

Jillian had never wished she had been back in the States as badly as when Carol lost her husband, Len. It was a freak accident. He was a foreman at the plant, and he died pushing two of his workers out of the path of a wayward piece of heavy equipment. It was all over in a fraction of a second. He died instantly, and the lives of Carol and her children were changed forever.

Carol's daughter, Carrie, had been Daddy's girl. Like her mother, she rarely let her emotions show. She threw herself into her schoolwork and ended up at the top of her class. When she graduated from high school two years later, she decided she had to get away from Madison and enrolled at the University of Minnesota in Minneapolis. She met her future husband there, got a high-earning job in software engineering, and never returned to her home state.

With Mark, it was a different story. There was always some sort of problem at school after his father died. Once a straight-A, well-behaved student, his grades eroded, and he earned numerous detentions. If it hadn't been for football, he might have ended up in even more serious trouble.

His dad had been one of the assistant coaches on his school team the year he died. He had drilled into Mark that he should always be respectful and loyal to his head coach, no matter what. And Mark tried as much as he was capable of doing at that point in time, but he was an angry and sad young man. One minute, your dad is a healthy, active man, cheering you on or balling you out from the sideline of your football game, and the next, you're standing at his grave.

Despite getting good test scores on college entrance exams, Mark's grades were poor, and his school records were filled with "red flags" for potential college coaches. His dreams were dashed. The next nine years were filled with problem after problem until he ran into his former junior high football coach one day, who had not only coached with his dad, but had been one of his father's friends. They had a long talk over a burger and fries.

It had been a turning point for Mark. He went home, got online and set up an appointment with an advisor at a technical college. The next fall, he began his studies to become a plumber. Jillian hadn't seen Carol so hopeful about Mark in years as when he went back to school—at least until one day in January many years ago.

Twenty-six years earlier

Carol's cell rang very early that morning. Her phone indicated it was her son, Mark, calling from Wisconsin, and she momentarily panicked. Mark rarely called her, and if he did, it wasn't usually at 4:00 a.m. her time.

"Hey, Mom," the deep voice on the other end of the phone said.

"Mark! Is everything okay?"

"Yes. No. Well, I don't know."

"Are you hurt?" Carol asked.

"No, nothing like that. I just got home," he said wearily.

Carol waited for him to continue. She didn't want to think about all the possibilities about why he just got home. Her mind flitted back to his high school and following years, with principals, and even a police officer or two, calling to tell her there was another issue with her son.

"I'm tired, Mom. This was my fifth call for busted frozen pipes this week. I'm sick of getting called out in the middle of the night, and I'm really tired of freezing my...." he hesitated, looking for words that would not offend his mom. "Mom, could I come out there for a visit?"

Carol almost dropped her phone. She thought she heard her son, whom she hadn't seen in several years, ask if he could come and stay with her.

"Of course! Anytime, Mark. We have a very nice guest room! We would *love* to have you. Come whenever you would like, and stay as long as you would like!"

Mark arrived a few days later and never left, except for two short trips back to sell his business and his house, both which sold quickly. His life, as was his mother's, was changed in many ways, the moment he set foot in California.

Carol and Jerry had been foster grandparents for an adorable, sweet girl named Angela, for almost a year when Mark made his winter escape. The almost eleven-year-old Angela was immediately drawn to Mark. He didn't know what to make of it at first. He had never been much of a "kid person." But for some reason, he liked the girl who smiled a lot and liked to play games, especially card games, one thing Mark had always enjoyed.

On one of their first meetings, they were playing a card game when Angela told Mark that her favorite subjects were math and science, and that one day she was going to be an astronaut. His head snapped back at that one, remembering his own desires to be one when he was about the same age.

That got them on the subject of careers. When he told her he was a plumber, she asked for more details, like what kinds of things does a plumber do, and did his job use math and science? He explained that it did use math and science skills and told her about some of the jobs, both big and small, he often did. He explained that the frozen pipes that had thawed too quickly and burst had been the last straw that sent him on his first vacation since he started his own business. He told her the problems were not always that serious—sometimes his work might be as simple as fixing a clogged sink, or a leaky pipe.

When Angela heard that, she gasped, then exclaimed, "Great! You can fix the leak we have under our sink at my house!"

Carol happened to be listening in from the next room, and entered the den. "Angela," Carol said, in a tone that sounded slightly disapproving of her remark. "We don't want to impose on Mark when he's out here on vaca—"

Mark surprised her by cutting her off. "I could do that," he said to Angela, "but you have to let me win a card game one of these times." The girl was a "killer" card player.

Angela giggled and went on to beat him again a moment later. "My mom says I shouldn't let boys win just to make them happy or like me."

"It sounds like you have a smart mom," Mark said.

"I do. She's pretty, too," Angela said nonchalantly, then changed to a new subject.

"Want to teach me a new game so maybe you could beat me?" Angela asked innocently.

That made Mark laugh. It felt good to laugh. It'd been too long since he'd laughed.

Even though life was definitely better than it had been in his teens and twenties, he still felt empty inside most days. He had just turned thirty-five. His life consisted predominantly of work, with an occasional outing to the bowling alley. He'd gone on a few dates over the past few years, but there had been no one he cared to ask out more than once or twice. There had never been anyone special in his life. When his mom got remarried, he felt like an even bigger loser in the love area. He was happy for her, but he was certain he would never find the kind of person with whom he could share his life.

Mark did teach Angela a new game, and he finally beat her—barely. He thought the girl very well could become an astronaut one day. She was very sharp.

When Carol took Angela home that evening, she told Lena, Angela's mom, about Mark's offer to fix the sink. She was ecstatic. She was a single mom, and plumbers were expensive. She was able to do some home maintenance projects but had heard that plumbing issues could be tricky, and that people sometimes ended up with bigger problems by trying to fix things on their own. Carol gave Lena Mark's phone number so they could set up a time for the repair job, and she called later that evening.

Mark had no tools with him, so he asked if she had any around her house. Lena said she had one toolbox and described its contents to the best of her abilities. She would be home the next day, as it was Saturday. Lena was so excited that he was going to fix the problem under her kitchen sink. It had been tedious remembering to empty the bucket under the sink every day for the past two months. She had been saving up extra money so she could eventually call in a repair person. Lena had a good position working in information technology, but it was still difficult to make house payments and raise a child on one income.

On Saturday, Mark drove Carol's car over to Angela and Lena's house and parked in the driveway. It was a modest two-bedroom ranch set on a small but well-kept lot. He jumped out of the car and headed up the sidewalk toward the door. It opened and Angela ran toward him. "Hi, Mark!" the girl shouted enthusiastically.

He wasn't used to such cheerful greetings. He was getting spoiled these past few days. Between his Mom, Jerry, and Angela, he had felt so welcomed and more cared about than he had in years. Angela hugged him, and he hugged her back—another uncommon experience.

"Come on in and meet my mom!" Angela was excited and pulled him toward the house. A figure appeared in the doorway, and when

Mark saw the woman, he came to a slight halt. Angela had said her mother was pretty. He figured every kid that age thinks their mom is pretty. Lena wasn't pretty. She was breathtakingly beautiful.

Mark suddenly wished he had dressed in nicer clothes, but he was going to be crawling under a sink, so that wouldn't have been a prudent idea.

Because Mark had stopped on the sidewalk, Angela pulled even harder on his hand, snapping him back into the moment. He followed her up to the door, still in a bit of a daze. Lena backed up so they could enter the house.

"Lena," she said, extending her hand to him.

Mark hesitated. He wasn't sure he remembered his name, but he croaked out "Mark." He cleared his throat, then said it again more confidently.

"This is so incredibly nice of you, Mark. We are getting tired of emptying the bucket every morning and evening, aren't we, Angela?" she said, pulling her daughter close to her and stroking her silky dark hair, which matched her mother's.

"No problem," was the best he could muster.

She showed him the culprit pipe under the sink. He was going to need a part. Luckily, he could pick it up at a hardware store.

"I'll be right back," he said, after he pulled up directions to the nearest store on his phone. He also made sure he had the right tools in the box. He thought he might buy a particular wrench, if they carried it.

"Can I go with you?" Angela asked.

"That's up to your mom," Mark said.

"I guess it's okay. You don't mind?" Lena asked, slightly amazed.

"She can come as long as I can teach her another card game that I might be able to win."

Angela smiled, then ran to the car and jumped in when he opened the passenger door for her. Lena watched her daughter go on her first ever hardware store run and smiled at the sight.

Mark and Angela returned shortly with the necessary part, a new wrench, and a treat for later. Why they sold candy in hardware stores, Mark never understood. But when Angela saw the bin filled with bags of candy near the checkout and mentioned it was her mom's favorite, Mark found himself picking one up, even though Angela hadn't asked him to buy it.

The plumbing job only took an hour, but if Lena had called a plumber, it could have gotten pricey. He knew what his usual charge was for a call, and his hourly rate, and he was certain it was likely double or more for both in Los Angeles.

After crawling out from under the sink, Mark ran the water in the basin to make sure everything was truly fixed. When he announced it was a success, two great cheers went up from Lena and Angela.

"I wish I could repay you somehow," Lena said sincerely.

"Maybe he could stay for dinner, Mom," Angela said. Turning to Mark she remarked,

"She's a really good cook."

"I don't want to impose," Mark said.

"You wouldn't be imposing, but we aren't having anything special tonight—just our favorite, chicken and rice."

Mark was thinking that if Lena knew the kind of meals he usually ate, all alone, she wouldn't be worried about what she was making for dinner. Anything would be an improvement over what he usually brought home or took out of the freezer to microwave. Meat on the grill was his specialty, the one thing he really cooked. His dad had taught him how to grill the summer before he died, and in the warmer weather, most of Mark's meals were prepared outside. Somehow, the simple act of cooking on a grill made Mark feel like he was still somehow connected to his dad.

"That sounds great to me. Are you sure?"

Lena nodded and smiled. Mark couldn't take his eyes off her, and he was glad when Angela broke the spell he felt like he was under.

"Good, now you can teach me a new card game," Angela said.

Kathy J. Jacobson

"Only if your mom doesn't need any help."

"No help needed yet. I'll make dinner. You two play cards. Later, you could set the table, Angela," she said.

"We both can," Mark found himself saying. Lena looked very surprised. She wasn't used to someone, especially a man, volunteering to help her with anything.

Lena began the meal preparation. Mark dialed his mother to tell her of his plans and make sure she didn't need her car back. Carol didn't need her car, so Mark and Angela played cards at the wooden table in the dining area, just off the kitchen, until it was time to set the table.

Mark left Lena and Angela's house at 10:00 p.m., after a wonderful dinner, washing the dishes, then eating the candy he had bought at the hardware store for an impromptu dessert. He and Angela taught Lena a card game, and she won. Mark could see where Angela got her abilities. They kept score on a sheet of paper. Mark wrote down their names at the top of three columns he had drawn. When he was writing Lena's name, he started spelling it L-A-Y.

Angela quickly jumped in and corrected him. "It's L-E-N... ." she said. Mark looked funny for a moment, and Lena noticed.

"Is something wrong?" she asked.

"No. It's just that my dad's name was Len, Leonard actually, but no one ever called him that, except maybe my grandma when he was a little boy and in trouble. It just surprised me. Your name is spelled so similarly to his." He couldn't really tell her, but inside, he felt like it was some kind of sign from above.

After a number of games, it was clear that Angela was getting very sleepy. Mark said he should be going. Angela hugged him goodnight and headed down toward her room to get ready for bed.

Lena saw Mark to the door, watching him as he got into the car. It had been a wonderful day. The best day she could remember in many, many years. Mark was thinking the very same thing as he waved to her, then drove away.

When Mark returned home, Carol was sitting at the kitchen table eating a small bowl of fresh fruit. Jerry was in another room reading. She could tell by Mark's face that it had been a good day.

"Mind if I join you?" Mark asked his mom.

Carol wanted to shout a hallelujah. She had waited for what had seemed a lifetime for a moment like this—to have her son want to be with her. Instead, she just smiled and nodded, afraid that if she spoke, she might cry.

"Mom, when you met Jerry, or even Dad, how did you know you had met someone special?"

Carol could hardly speak. She was unaccustomed to her son asking her a personal question, especially one that mentioned his father. Mark had been devastated by his father's unexpected death and never wanted to talk about him. She pulled herself together. This chance might never come again.

"Well, your dad—I couldn't keep my eyes off him. We were at a Super Bowl party hosted by his men's dorm floor for my women's dorm floor. We were supposed to be watching the football game, but all I could watch was him, and vice-versa. He asked me out at the end of the party, and that was that. And Jerry—it was at John and Jillian's wedding celebration at their home. I remember walking toward where he was standing and noticing him for the first time, and I stopped for a moment. My feet didn't want to move. Then, when Jillian introduced us, I could barely remember my name," Carol remarked with a chuckle.

Mark's eyes became huge at her comments, as many of the same things had happened to him earlier in the day.

"I never thought I would find love again," Carol said wistfully.

"You were lucky, Mom ... twice," Mark said, softly and sincerely.

Carol's eyes misted, and all she could do was nod. Not only was her son acknowledging the love she had shared with his father, but he was validating her relationship with Jerry. She was so very grateful at that moment, and her heart felt full.

The next day, Mark asked Carol and Jerry if they would watch Angela that evening. He had asked Lena out to dinner, and she had accepted the invitation. Then he asked Carol to take him to the nearest men's shop to get some decent clothes and then to a barber for a haircut.

Carol had been in heaven, and the story kept on getting better and better. Six months later, Mark and Lena were married, and Angela, their foster granddaughter, became their first grandchild. One year after that, a grandson, Len, short for Leonard, and named for Mark's father, joined the family. It had been a dream come true for Carol and her son.

Present Time

Jillian wrote a note to Mark realizing she had been daydreaming once more. It was good, though, to remember, even if it did take her forever to write her thank you notes.

She hadn't even noticed that Tommy and Maria had taken a break from purging the refrigerator until she glanced out the huge windows facing the backyard. She saw Alison directing her mom and dad to a table near the pool and sitting down, a serious look on her face. Jillian said a prayer for Alison, as she was quite sure she was about to tell her parents about the end of her marriage.

Jillian pulled another card from the pile but was interrupted by John Anthony, who came bounding into the room. He was so much a combination of his father, Tommy, and his Uncle John, that it sometimes took Jillian's breath away.

"Aunt Jillian," he said, giving her a much-appreciated hug. "I hate to bother you, but I have a big favor to ask."

"You are never a bother. Ask away," she said, smiling.

"Carson Stone, Jr. wants me to come back to L.A. in a few weeks to talk about a project he says will be perfect for me. I think that is doubtful, but Kirsten says I should explore it more, or I'll probably regret it later. And you know, she's usually right about things like that," he said.

Not only did John Anthony have many of John's qualities, but he and his wife had a relationship which often reminded Jillian of her own with John. That made her very happy, because she and John had surely been very blessed.

"So, I was wondering if I could stay here when I come back?"

"Of course. You don't even have to ask that. You are family. This is your home, too," she said.

"I thought you'd say that, but I just wanted to make sure," he said.

He was so considerate. Actually, she thought it would be great to have something to look forward to. She was dreading everyone's departures in the next day or so.

He gave her a big hug, then reluctantly went upstairs to pack, make sure his boys were moving, and to oversee their packing. He mentioned it was probably a good thing he was coming back soon, as he was certain there would be something left behind by accident. There always was. Jillian smiled, remembering those days like they were yesterday.

Jillian looked back out the window where she witnessed the tears and hugs of the unconditional love between parents and child, no matter what age they were. Tears of happiness and thankfulness came to her own eyes, and she said a prayer of gratitude for this wonderful, loving family she had inherited.

Chapter Nine

By the next morning, the decibel level in the house had greatly diminished as only Jillian, Marty and Michael, and Tommy and Maria remained. Despite the calmer atmosphere, the day was full of interesting developments.

Marty and Michael were teaming up in the dining room with the seemingly never-ending mountain of cards. Marty wrote and Michael put them in envelopes and put stamps and return address labels on them. He had a serious case of "doctor's penmanship," he claimed. Marty had somehow escaped that malady, even though she was a physician, too.

Every once in a while they would take a break from their work and talk in hushed tones. Every time Jillian came into the room, the conversation would come to a screeching halt. Jillian decided that if no one came forward with any information soon, she would ask Marty what was going on that evening.

Tommy and Maria had done a remarkable job organizing the refrigerator and freezer, carefully identifying and dating items. They had taken the break to talk to Alison, and now they asked Jillian to sit down with them in the breakfast nook.

"We have something we need to discuss with you, Jillian," Tommy began, sounding serious.

Jillian looked a bit alarmed, and he grasped her hand. "It's not anything bad, Jillian." Jillian relaxed and looked at him expectantly. "We are selling the shops," he announced.

Jillian looked surprised. Tommy and Maria's delis had been their life for so long now, it was difficult for her to imagine them not running them.

"We were thinking of buying Buck and Nancy's former condo from Darius, too, but now, we are not sure, with all that is going on," Tommy said, traces of sadness and disappointment crossing his face.

"You aren't doing all of this because of John ... me ... are you?" Jillian asked, a sudden feeling of guilt washing over her.

"We began discussing this two years ago and have been negotiating the sale for a year now. The paperwork is all ready to be signed for the sale of the business, but not for the condo. That was a more recent thought. We had hoped to live out here and be closer to you both. We hoped it would all be one big, fun surprise. But now with Alison's development, we'll just have to play it by ear," he said.

Maria chimed in, "This was not some last-minute decision, Jillian. We feel the need to take more time for ourselves, and for our family—including you," she said with a smile.

Jillian smiled back at this sweet woman. She never had a sister, but Maria was like one.

"I believe that's a wonderful idea," Jillian replied. In her mind she was thinking, *one never knows how much time one has left with those we love.*

"By the way, Jillian, thank you for your help with Alison," Maria said.

"I just happened to be in the right place at the right time. I caught part of a conversation between Alison and Zoe which was not intended for my ears to hear, and that started the conversation. Perhaps I was meant to hear it. I didn't do much. I just told her how hard it was when I had tough news to share with my parents, but how they loved me no matter what. I also shared how well things eventually turned out for me. And most of all, I reminded her of the daughter, parents, brother, and all the other people in her life who really do, and always will, love her dearly."

Both Tommy and Maria were growing emotional. "Well, we really appreciate it," Tommy remarked quietly.

"She will need all the love and support every one of us can give her," Jillian added. Tommy and Maria nodded their heads. Then they all held hands and prayed together for their beautiful daughter and great-niece. Alison would need all the prayers they could send up as well.

The sun was shining outside, flowers were blooming in her yard, yet it felt like a dark, gloomy day to Carol. Jerry had gotten up hours ago, but she couldn't seem to make the move out of bed. She looked at the clock. It was 10:00 a.m. When had she ever laid in bed until ten in the morning? If she had, it was so long ago she couldn't recall it.

Carol finally forced herself to get up and shower. Again, as she had each day of the past week, she began to cry the moment the water hit her face. She was unaccustomed to this loss of control and such unbridled, raw emotion. She made herself stop, feeling upset with herself as she turned off the water.

Carol dried off, then dressed slowly and deliberately, feeling like a robot. When she entered the kitchen, Jerry was sitting at the table doing the morning crossword and sipping on a cup of coffee. He looked up when she came into the room and tried to act like it was normal for her to sleep half the morning away.

"Good morning," he said.

Usually, Carol would have come up with a smart retort like it was practically afternoon, but she just didn't have it in her. She weakly returned his greeting, and poured herself a cup of coffee. Jerry had gone to the bakery and fresh muffins sat on a plate on the counter. She was grateful she didn't have to make a breakfast. Even pouring a bowl of cereal felt like too much work.

"I was thinking of popping over to the garden center today. Would you care to join me?" Jerry asked. Jerry knew Carol loved to shop for things for the garden. Even when they didn't end up buying anything, they always enjoyed looking.

"Not today," she said quietly.

"Do you mind if I go?"

"Of course not. Go ahead, dear," she said sincerely. He was trying so hard to be kind and helpful, but she just couldn't go—not this time.

Jerry got up from the table. He hugged her shoulders and kissed her cheek before he headed out. "I won't be long," he said.

She just nodded in response.

Once Jerry was outside the house and in the car, he called Jillian. He hoped she could come over—soon. Maybe she could find out what was going on with his beloved wife. He was growing more concerned with every passing minute.

It was 11:00 a.m. when Carol answered the door, still in her robe. If it hadn't been Jillian, she never would have opened it.

"I'll save you the trouble of having to make up an excuse for coming over," Carol said matter-of-factly. "Jerry called you."

Jillian eyebrows raised slightly, then she nodded her head.

"Come on in," Carol said softly, leading Jillian back to the table where her muffin sat half-eaten. She just didn't have much of an appetite lately.

They sat down and looked at one another. Jillian was not familiar with this version of Carol. Carol was the always-in-control, always-in-charge person who taught her more about nursing, and people in general, than any other single person she had ever known.

Jillian just waited silently—one of the things she learned from Carol.

"I never cried." Carol hesitated, her eyes growing moist, then continued, "When Len died I never cried. I'm not sure why exactly. It could have been for the kids. It could have been because I thought if I started, I may never stop. It could have been because I was so mad at him for dying on me. It could be that I thought if I didn't cry, it somehow wouldn't be real, and maybe he'd walk back in the door and tell me it was all one big joke."

Carol stirred the cold coffee in her cup with a spoon, then looked at Jillian.

"All these years, I've been able to avoid my feelings, until last week when John died. I think because it was so sudden like it was with Len, it brought up all the feelings I would never let myself feel before. And ..." Carol hesitated.

"And?" Jillian asked quietly after a moment.

"And now, I am afraid something will happen to Jerry. I just can't bear the thought of losing another husband," she said truthfully. "So, these past few days, instead of not being able to cry, all I seem to feel like doing is crying," she said, shaking her head a bit.

Jillian wasn't sure what to say. On one hand, she was relieved that Carol was not sick. On the other hand, she wanted to help her friend, but knew that she was struggling mightily herself these days. Finally, she put her hand on Carol's.

"That makes two of us, then," she said calmly and quietly. She was surprised that she had actually revealed that to anyone. She was almost as bad at holding in her feelings as Carol was at times—like mentor, like student. Suddenly, she realized that maybe not everything she had learned was the healthiest of behaviors.

The two stood up and held each other as tears streamed down their faces, unleashing their pent up pain.

Finally, Carol let go, then the two long-time friends looked at each other.

"Well, aren't we a pair!" Carol exclaimed.

That made them both laugh through their tears. Carol grabbed a box of tissues from a nearby counter and offered Jillian one, then pulled one out for herself. They both blew their noses at the same time, which made them laugh once more.

Slowly, they regained their composure. Carol offered Jillian some coffee and a muffin and filled her own cup with fresh, hot coffee. She started to nibble on her muffin, suddenly feeling a bit hungry. The two spent the next hour talking, crying, and sharing their thoughts and the hurt in their hearts.

"Well, you know my husband is not going to come back to the house until he sees that your car is gone," Carol said finally.

"You are right. He really is special, Carol," Jillian reminded her.

"I'm so glad you invited me to your wedding celebration, or we never would have met. I don't know how I got so lucky twice," she said.

"I do. You are a wonderful person. One of the best people I've ever known, Carol."

Carol was even worse than Jillian used to be at taking a compliment, so she just changed the subject to saying goodbye. She saw her good friend to the door, hugging Jillian once more.

"We have to do this more often," Jillian said.

"Hugging or bawling like babies?"

"Both," Jillian said with a smile. Then she was off.

Jerry walked into the kitchen almost completely hidden behind a large potted plant sporting huge, fragrant, dark blue blooms. He gently set it on the kitchen table, brushed a bit of dirt from his shirt, then turned slightly toward Carol, explaining his prized purchase.

"It's a Ceanothus 'Dark Star' California lilac. It's not really a true lilac like you used to have in Madison, but it's as close as it gets out here. You always told me how much you miss the lilacs in the spring—"

Jerry was cut off by his wife's lips against his. When the kiss ended, Carol pulled him into a tight embrace.

They parted, and Jerry spoke softly. "I thought you would love it," he said.

"It's beautiful, Jerry, but it's *you* I love," she said, then kissed him again.

He hugged her afterward, tears of happiness filling his eyes. His Carol was back. He didn't know what had gone on between his wife and Jillian, but whatever it was, it was a good thing. "Should we find a place to plant it?"

"Let me throw on some clothes. I'll be right back," Carol said, with more enthusiasm than she'd felt in a week.

They spent the next hour finding the perfect spot for the new bush and easing back to a more normal existence. Jerry knew better than to press his wife for details. If Carol wished to speak about her morning, or the past week, with him in the future, she would do it on her own timetable, and on her own terms. All he knew was she seemed to be feeling better, and that made him immensely happy.

When Jillian returned home, Marty and Michael were taking a lunch break in the breakfast nook. They were deep in conversation when Jillian entered the kitchen, the sandwiches on their plates barely touched. Their conversation stopped once again as they noticed her presence. Jillian couldn't take any more of this. Normally, she was more patient, but nothing seemed *normal* to her anymore, so she spoke.

"Maybe if you two would tell me what is going on, I could be of some help," she offered.

The two looked at each other, and Michael gave Marty a nod.

"We've been away for such a long time, Mom. It has been wonderful. Peru far exceeded our expectations, and we love so many people there. But we also love so many people here. So, a few months ago, we put the word out that we were open to making a move back to California. It began with a conversation with a colleague at Stanford. She called us a month ago with a great offer for one of us, and a decent one for the other. We were very excited. It sounded like a good arrangement—not perfect, but very good."

"But then last week happened. And I don't just mean Dad's death. The evening of the funeral, we received another call with a wonderful offer, actually *offers,* for both of us. It took us both by surprise. And we are just now feeling like we can begin to process it all. With all the emotions of this past week, it was difficult to even think, let alone make a big decision like that, especially after we thought we were going in another direction. They want to know by the end of this week," Marty said.

"It sounds a lot like the decisions you both had to make a long time ago when you went to Peru. You made a great choice then. I know you will do the right thing again. Pray about it, and I will, too. I'm sure that wherever you go, it will be okay if you two are together. You've already proven that," Jillian reminded them.

"We will, Mom. And when we finally make our decision, you will be the first one to know. We are going to do some more research on it all tomorrow, after we get those thank you notes done."

"Don't worry about the notes, Marty and Michael. You have helped me tremendously. They don't all have to be done immediately. People will understand if it takes some time."

"Well, maybe we will take a break, if you don't mind. Maybe we will take a little ride. May we borrow the car?" Marty asked, smiling and sounding like a sixteen-year-old.

Kathy J. Jacobson

Jillian smiled and handed over the key fob. "Drive carefully."

The house was so quiet without Marty and Michael. Jillian walked into the dining room thinking she might continue working on the thank you notes, but something propelled her toward the library.

The library was Jillian's favorite room in the house, as it had been for John. They spent many hours together in this room, reading quietly, discussing important ideas and concerns, gazing at the Christmas tree each December, or just snuggling together on the love seat. It was the room where the special case (which had been expanded and redesigned) resided, holding John's Golden Globe Awards, Emmys, and John's two and Jillian's one Academy Awards. The bookshelves were filled with John's incredible collection of classic books, along with the more modern tomes they had added over the past thirty years.

Jillian tentatively stepped into the room. She wasn't sure she was ready for this, but she knew she needed to go into the room sometime. John wouldn't want her to avoid their special place, she was sure of that.

Jillian stood for a moment staring at the love seat. Her eyes surveyed the small mahogany table next to it with John's reading glasses still upon it and a pen that he often used for doing the crossword puzzle in the newspaper.

She smiled as she remembered his annoyance, back when she was his employee, and she called out the solution to a clue he had unconsciously verbalized. Later, as a married couple, they often laughed together about that. As time went on, she had regularly been consulted by her husband when he did the crossword, and she had gladly given her help. They had made a pretty good team, in more ways than one.

Jillian sat down slowly on the soft seat and closed her eyes. She thought about this surprising day. Marty and Michael probably coming home to the States. She had been so surprised and excited that she forgot to ask them from whence the second job offers had come. Oh, well, she would ask when they returned home.

And then there had been the visit with Carol. It had felt good to let go with her, and she was reminded how important it is to share one's grief in some way. Then Jillian had a thought and she opened her eyes. She should bring back her first blog, the one that helped launch her debut book, *Where Broken Hearts Go*. Perhaps if she were to follow her own advice of "facing, feeling, and healing," it would be a good thing, for others and herself.

She turned to tell John about her great revelation and remembered once more that he wasn't there. She sighed and her eyes filled with tears, and this time she let them come, taking one of those tiny steps toward taking her own advice.

Jillian was getting a tad concerned when Marty and Michael had not returned in four hours time. She was just about to call her daughter when she received a text message saying they were on their way home, but traffic was heavy. Even with improved mass transportation systems, it was still unbearable at rush hour in Los Angeles.

Jillian looked in the refrigerator. Even though it was still packed, she couldn't quite think of a thing she felt like making, or eating. Her appetite had not returned since John's death, and she wondered if it ever would. She could tell that her pants were a tad loose at the waist. She knew she would have to eat better in the future. She got out her computer to see if she could find a recipe that sounded remotely good to her.

She lost track of time while surfing the Internet, and before she knew it, Marty and Michael were home bearing several bags of something that smelled wonderful. Marty plopped them down on the counter and looked at her mom. "Cheeseburgers and french fries," she said, her eyes misting a bit.

Jillian walked over to her and gave her daughter a hug. Cheeseburgers and french fries were the foods Marty had craved after being gravely ill with Dengue fever many years before when she was an intern in Senegal. John had found a restaurant in Dakar to deliver them to her door after she came home from the hospital. It had been Marty's go-to comfort food ever since.

"Perfect," Jillian said, her eyes moist as well.

They sat at the table in the breakfast nook with their tasty treats. Marty and Michael had even bought milkshakes. Jillian suddenly felt hungry and practically inhaled her meal. Just as they were just finishing up their meal, Marty and Michael made an announcement. Jillian was glad she was almost finished, or she may not have eaten another bite for her excitement.

Marty talked about how they had just driven in to the campus of UCLA, just to look around. The campus had been quieter than they expected, but they soon learned the school was on an exams break. They were checking out the medical school when a man asked if he could help them. He turned out to be one of the professors/doctors. They got a great tour, heard many wonderful things about the school, but most of all, they were so impressed with this man who took the time to speak with them and show them around, that they said they thought it was a sign from God.

On the way home they had discussed it, and they had decided they would take their second job offers at UCLA! They were moving to Los Angeles. Their job offer came with an extremely reduced rate on a condo near campus, which they had a chance to drive by, and it looked very nice. So after that, they had called to formally accept their positions, much to the school's delight.

Jillian could hardly believe it. She had thought the idea of Stanford was wonderful, but now Marty would be right in Los Angeles. It was a true gift from above.

The three of them "clinked" their waxy milkshake cups together with a cheerful toast to the future, then finished them off. The rest of the evening was filled with chatter and looking online at the campus and the inside of the condo they would be living in. It was quite nice, indeed, and would save them not only a good deal of money, but better yet, save them from commuting—a huge perk in Los Angeles.

They talked more about the positions they had been offered. Marty's time would be divided between research and teaching. Michael's time would be primarily spent on research, with some time in the hospital following up on patients involved in research studies. They both would do workshops occasionally for students considering working and living abroad in the medical field and lead special medical team trips to Peru and other countries during breaks. All these things were extremely attractive to the couple, and they felt happy and blessed.

The next day was the day before Marty and Michael returned to Peru, where they would give written notice of their departure, put their modest home on the market, and begin saying goodbye to the place they had called home for the past twenty-nine years. They were not looking forward to that part of the deal.

After they packed up, they all went on a long hike near the ocean on one of their favorite trails. Then they drove to the beach house to have a cookout, after a stop at the fresh fish and seafood market. Jillian hadn't been to the house since the evening of the day John had died. It was good to be there again, this time with family. She knew John would heartily approve, and again, as she looked out over the ocean, she felt his presence with them.

Kathy J. Jacobson

Chapter Ten

John Anthony sat in Carson Stone, Jr.'s office completely and utterly stunned. The director had told him weeks before that he had the perfect television role for him, but John Anthony never really thought any role in Hollywood could fit the description of "perfect" until now.

Carson leaned back in a soft leather chair, his feet crossed on his art deco desk. He was wearing classic brown loafers—the same type his late father had been famous for wearing. "I want to resurrect *O.R.*," Carson announced. John Anthony didn't hear much past that and had to ask the man to repeat himself.

"*O.R.*, you know, the award-winning show your great-uncle starred in back in the 1980s. I want to bring it back with you playing Dr. Nick Caruso III, the grandson of the doctor John played. If I'm able to convince her, I hope to bring Monica Morgan in on occasion as your grandmother, the former Dr. Pamela Prine."

John Anthony didn't quite know what to say. "When do you need an answer?" he asked, realizing that several conversations needed to take place if he was to seriously consider this offer.

"We are hoping to have an answer in a week. If we don't get you, I'm not sure I can get the studio on board. They will probably go with another show—another terrible situation comedy. I'm not just saying that because it's not my show."

Carson spoke again, "It's the role of a lifetime. There are still many people around who enjoyed *O.R.*, especially those who still watch network television. It's also been popular on internet media sites. Of course, medical shows will always be popular, but I think the bringing back of an old hit could really be an intelligent move. And to have an actual relative of its main star in this production would be incredible."

John Anthony nodded his head. He was too deep in thought to say too much. He shook Carson's hand and told him, "I'll be in touch soon," and walked out the door.

In the taxi ride to his Aunt Jillian's, John Anthony thought about whom to talk with first. His wife? His dad? Or should he begin by asking Jillian her thoughts? What if she didn't like the idea, or it would hurt her in some way. That would be the last thing in the world he wanted to do, after her recent crushing loss of his uncle John.

He looked up at the roof of the taxi. "Uncle John, I need your help on this one," he said quietly as the taxi drove up the circular drive to Jillian's house.

Jillian was incredibly happy to see John Anthony. It had only been ten days since Marty and Michael left for Peru, but it felt like a lifetime. It was so quiet in the house. The only consolation was that it was easier for Jillian to write her blog posts. That venture was going wonderfully. As had been the case in her first round with this subject, many readers had suffered a loss and willingly shared their hearts. Jillian realized after a few days that there was another book in the making. Perhaps in a few months she would begin gathering her favorite posts and categorizing them.

There was the other writing project possibility, too—the screenplay of her book *Noted!*. There was a lot to consider, and she had to admit, she was glad there was. It helped take her mind off the emptiness of her house and the loneliness in her heart.

John Anthony strode through the door, a small travel bag in hand. He put it down and gave Jillian a Romano smile and a wonderful bear hug.

"So, how did it go?" she asked expectantly.

"Let's sit outside, Aunt Jillian, if that is okay. I've been in a plane, in an office, and in a taxi so far today. That's enough 'in' for me," he said, sounding weary.

"Of course," she said. "I shouldn't have put you on the spot the moment you walked through the door. I'm sorry. Can I get you something to drink?"

They both decided to sip on a goblet of California Chardonnay and sat on the comfortable chairs near the pool. Jillian had a chicken salad chilling along with a fresh loaf of bread for dinner. She had brought out some falafel chips and hummus to go with their wine.

Jillian sat quietly. While John Anthony had washed up and took off his suit coat and tie, she decided she was going to stop pressuring him. If he had news to share, he would share it.

Finally, he set down his glass and let out a huge sigh. "I was offered a role today, Aunt Jillian," he said.

She smiled at him, proud of his accomplishments. "Is it a good one?"

"It's an amazing one," he said.

"That's good, isn't it?"

"Yes. Maybe. I don't know. It would be a role of a lifetime. But accepting it would mean I would either be away from my family, or they would have to move. Neither of those things sounds great to me, but this role ..."

She waited for him to continue, recognizing that he was struggling.

"Aunt Jillian, they want to bring back *O.R.* Carson Stone, Jr. would recreate it, direct and also write it. And they want me to play Dr. Nick Caruso III, the grandson of Dr. Caruso, Uncle John's role," he said quietly.

Tears came to Jillian's eyes.

"I won't do it if you don't want me to," he said, reaching out for her hand. "I don't want to cause you any more pain."

"I'm not crying because I don't want you to take the part. I think it's a fantastic idea and a perfect part. I think your uncle John would be so happy for you, and proud of you," she said. "I just wish he was here to hear this," she said.

"I do too, Aunt Jillian. But somehow, I think he knows. I feel it," he said.

"So do I," she said. She wiped her tears away with the back of her hand. "You have to talk to your family. Did you call Kirsten yet? Your dad?"

"No, not yet. I wanted to know if it was okay with you before I did any calling."

"It's more than okay with me, John Anthony, but whatever you decide in the end, will be okay, too," she said sincerely.

"Thanks, Aunt Jillian. I was hoping you would say something like that," he said and smiled.

They stood up and hugged each other. Jillian missed John's hugs, and John Anthony's strong arms felt very welcome. John Anthony excused himself to make his phone call. Jillian stood looking around the backyard and then took a little walk. The crowded flower beds were bursting with blooms of various colors, and beams of sunlight coming through spaces in the clouds were hitting them just right, making them seem aglow. It almost felt like the light was coming straight from heaven, and she began to think of it at that moment as "God's light," and smiled at the thought.

John Anthony discussed his call home over the savory salad and crusty on the outside, soft on the inside bread Jillian had enjoyed from the very first day she lived here. John had had it stocked in the guest cottage where she had first resided. The bakery it came from was family owned and still prospering after fifty years. Anyone who ever enjoyed their breads and cakes quickly understood why.

Kirsten had been very supportive, telling him, as Jillian had, that whatever he decided, she would support. She did, however, feel they should talk about it in person and maybe to some extent with the boys, too. That meant he would heading home the next morning. Jillian had hoped for a longer visit, but she understood his situation.

Jillian also realized that soon she would have Marty and Michael, possibly Tommy and Maria, and even the potential of John Anthony and his family all living close by. When she went to bed that night, she thanked God for these interesting possibilities. She was sure it was more than just a coincidence that all these wonderful opportunities were in the works, and she felt God's providing love in a new way as she closed her eyes in sleep.

Chapter Eleven

Alison stared at the wedding album in her hands. She was going through everything in the house deciding what she and Zoe would take with them after her daughter's high school graduation and they moved out. Her soon-to-be ex-husband, Cameron, had told her she could have the house, but she didn't want any reminders of the past once their divorce was final.

Instead, the house was up for sale. She wasn't quite sure where they would go when it sold, but she had a few ideas. She was going to meet her parents for lunch in a few hours. She thought they may have some good suggestions, as well.

She stared again at the album, feeling like throwing it in the trash bin. How had she been so foolish to have married someone like Cameron? She almost felt like she had been under a spell. She vowed she would never make the same mistake again. She gently closed the album, feeling like she was closing a chapter in her life. Alison decided to put it in the bottom of a box marked for Zoe. She didn't know if her daughter would want it in the future, but it would be her daughter's call if she wanted to keep it, or toss it.

It was a lovely spring day, and Tommy, Maria, and Alison sat at a table near a window at the restaurant. Alison could not believe her parents were officially retired, as they had handed over the keys and deeds to their shops the week before. She knew that their successor, Tony, would do a wonderful job maintaining the business, but it seemed like yet another era was ending. Everything in her life recently had felt like that—an end of an era.

"What are you going to do now?" Alison asked her parents.

"We were just going to ask you the same question," Tommy said. "What we do will depend on what you do, to some extent, anyway."

Alison cocked her head. "How so?"

"Well, we had thought of buying Buck and Nancy's condo in Los Angeles, but now ..." Maria's voice trailed off.

Alison suddenly realized that her parents were thinking of changing their plans because of her. "Mom and Dad, please don't change your plans for my sake. It would make this whole sad situation even sadder if I thought you were doing that. I will be alright. Zoe will be alright. I promise," she said, a sudden feeling of strength coming over her.

Tommy and Maria looked at each other not knowing how to respond.

Alison helped them out again. "Tell me more about the condo."

Tommy filled her in about the situation, then mentioned Darius would need to know soon, as there was another interested party. He also needed to get it off his plate, as it was very likely he would soon take on a major community leadership position.

"Buy it," Alison responded. "I'm sure your house would sell—" she said, stopping mid-sentence. Suddenly, she knew exactly where she wanted to move. "Mom and Dad, I think I know a buyer for your house in Libertyville."

"You do?" Maria asked in a surprised tone.

"Who would that be?" Tommy added.

"Me. I want to buy the house. I'm sure our, my house will sell quickly. Zoe's graduating, then she'll be off to school in the fall. It would be great for her to have a familiar place, filled with loving memories, to come home to on her breaks."

"I never really considered that possibility. We wouldn't have to go through a realtor, either. That would save you a lot of money, Alison," Maria said, excitement growing her in voice.

"It would be a win-win situation all around. Then, when you two want to come back and visit, you could come back to the house and stay whenever you want, for as long as you want," Alison added with a smile.

"But what about your position? It would be quite a commute for you," Tommy remarked.

"It would, but I will look for something closer. Or perhaps, I'll just open up my own office."

Maria and Tommy nodded their heads in agreement. Alison was right. There was a shortage of medical professionals, and Alison most likely could find work fairly quickly wherever she wanted it. If not, Tommy had commuted about the same distance for twenty-some years. If he could do it, Alison could do it, too. And mass transportation options had improved greatly since Tommy's days working near the city, creating another possibility.

"I have to say, I wasn't looking forward to bringing up this subject today, and now it all seems to be coming together so well," Tommy admitted. "I'll tell Darius to draw up the papers."

"And you do the same on your house, Dad. And make sure it's a fair price for you two. I don't expect any favors. You've worked too hard for that house and put in a lot of sweat and tears. I was there to see it, you know!"

"We will make certain it is a fair price," Maria said, "but remember, you are our daughter, and you are also saving us from having to list the house, have open houses, and so many other unappealing aspects of selling a home. Oh, Alison, this is such a wonderful idea, honey!"

They all held hands across the table. Alison had felt so sad that morning going through the album and other mementos of the past, and not knowing where she and Zoe would end up. Now, for a brief moment at least, she felt hopeful about the future. She would have a house that would immediately feel like home because it was home. At this point in time, home was what she desperately needed.

Their plates of food arrived, and they all said a prayer of thanks for the food and for the exciting new future plans. Then they ate heartily. It reminded Alison of the way they had devoured a meal after her mom's accident many years ago, relieved when they realized Maria was going to be alright. The same reassuring feeling that everything would be alright entered her heart once more.

Ricardo, who had shed his nickname of "Rick" over the years, twirled a pen between his fingers like a mini baton. He was deep in thought as he sat in his chair in his office in Los Angeles, inside the original Esperanza Center developed by John and Jillian and operated through the John and Jillian Johnson Romano Foundation. He was now the director of the Esperanza Center in L.A., where the organization was headquartered. As it was the parent office, Ricardo was the link between all the centers and the board of directors.

He had just been informed that the center director in Chicago was resigning due to health issues. It would be a great loss. The woman had been a caring, energetic, and talented director, and would be sorely missed. Unfortunately, she would be soon be focusing all of her time and energy dealing with a serious disease.

Ricardo felt bad for her and for the center in Chicago. The timing couldn't have been worse. They were just beginning major building renovations, had recently expanded one of their most productive programs, and had just started another new project. It would be difficult to find someone who could easily step in as a leader at such a crazy time.

Ricardo wished he could ask John Romano about it, or "Tío Juan," as he had thought of him as a boy. He wasn't really an uncle, but he had been a great friend and felt like family from the moment they met. Thinking about John made him even more upset. He was so very sad he had died. He was also sorry he couldn't call John ever again and ask for his advice.

The next person on the list was Jillian, and he reluctantly picked up his phone to call her. It wasn't that he didn't think she could help him, but he cared so much about Jillian and felt terrible for having to bother her with a work problem on top of her recent loss. Alas, he didn't know anyone better to call in this case. She would have the best suggestions, and she had to be informed about the situation sooner or later as one of the co-founders and co-chair of the board.

"Ricardo!"

"Hi, Jillian. How are you?" He hated asking that, too, but couldn't think of another way to begin the conversation.

"I'm doing okay, Rick," Jillian replied, calling him by his boyhood name, knowing he wouldn't mind. "It's been hard. Some minutes are better than others, but it helps when I hear friendly voices like yours. What's up?"

Now he really felt guilty. His "friendly voice" was going to inform her they now had a major employment opening in Chicago. There was an assistant to the director in the Chicago office, but he was new and didn't seem to be catching on as quickly as the Chicago director had hoped.

Ricardo explained the situation to Jillian in as much detail as he could, with his limited knowledge. The director had given two weeks notice. Part of that time would be spent trying to do what she could on projects and then spending a few days working with the assistant. It wasn't enough time to do a proper training. She thought perhaps they should hire an interim director in her place but did not have a candidate in mind.

"I have an idea, Ricardo. What if you were to help the assistant after the current director leaves in two weeks? You could get a feel for what is needed in Chicago and whether or not the assistant would be a worthy interim director or possibly move into the position permanently. Your assistant could hold down the fort in Los Angeles for a while. The foundation will cover your airfare, hotel, and other expenses. Stay however long you need to stay. How does that sound to you?"

"I think that is the best solution under the circumstances. Thank you so much, Jillian. I knew you could help. I hesitated to call you at a time like this, but I didn't know who else to call," he said.

"Never hesitate to call, Rick. That's what the board is for. Plus, I don't mind diversions these days," she responded honestly.

"I'll keep that in mind."

"I could put you in touch with our nephew, Tommy, too, if you would like. Maybe you could get together sometime while you are there."

"Yes, that would be nice," he said.

At his response, she gave Ricardo Tommy's contact information, then said goodbye. Ricardo went back to staring out the window. *Chicago.* He had been to the center there once, briefly, when he first took over as the L.A. director and had been on a tour of all the centers around the country, Europe, Canada, and Mexico. It was a short stay, and it had been way too long since he had been there. He had to admit that he didn't know the center the way he would like to or the city and what it had to offer. Maybe Tommy Romano could show him around. He liked Tommy, and he had liked the feel of Chicago during his brief stop.

Thinking about Tommy Romano made him think about Tommy's daughter, Alison. He had briefly spoken with her at

Jillian's home after John's funeral but didn't really know her. She seemed, however, like a nice woman, and pretty. He had thought that even when he was a ten-year-old and she was a teenager. The first time he met her was the day he and Marty were adopted, at the celebration afterward at John and Jillian's. *Too bad all the good ones are taken,* he thought to himself, and sighed.

Ricardo knew it was his own fault that he would be turning forty this year and had never been married or had children. It wasn't because he didn't want to, but he never seemed to pick the right women to care about. It seemed that whenever he liked someone, they were already in a relationship with someone else, like the girl he had a crush on all four years of high school.

In college, he had had a serious girlfriend named Tina. She was a cute and perky girl with black hair that shone in the sun. She liked sports, especially baseball. She was a huge Dodgers fan. That was one of the reasons Ricardo had fallen for her.

When he was ten, it had been Ricardo's dream to play for the Dodgers, his favorite team then and still now. He had always been a fan, even before his adoption. But after his dad, Robert, took him to see the Dodgers in the World Series when he was eleven, he was even more hooked. He lived and breathed baseball for the next eight years.

He played Little League, and later excelled in baseball in high school. He was granted "preferred walk-on" status to a college in the Los Angeles area. He made the roster, and by the end of his freshman year, he had earned a spot in the starting rotation. All of a sudden, a future in baseball became a real possibility. It was so exciting, and it didn't hurt his social life, either. Women on campus began to notice him. One of them was Tina, who was studying to become an athletic trainer, and was sent to work with the baseball athletes as part of her coursework. They had a fun time together, talking about baseball, attending Dodger games when they could, studying together at the library, going for runs, or Tina using him as her

Kathy J. Jacobson

"guinea pig" on the latest training techniques she learned in class. They would end the day with pizza or tacos, or Rick serenading her with his guitar.

Then everything changed. An injury caused him to reevaluate his future. In his sophomore season, he broke some fingers, badly enough to have surgery on one of them. Now, that isn't usually a big deal in baseball. Injuries happen all the time. But Rick—he still went by that name at that time—was also serious about his music, especially playing the guitar. He was a business major but had a double minor in literature and music.

When he was injured and couldn't play his guitar, he suddenly realized how much it meant to him. It all began when John and Jillian invited his family to a Christmas Eve service his first Christmas with the Wilson family. He had been enchanted with the guitar players at the candlelight service, Jillian being one of them. The next time they were together, Jillian let him try her guitar. His fingers were a bit small for it at the time, but it was clear he had some natural talent, along with a pleasant singing voice. His parents, Karen and Robert, went right out and bought him a three-quarter-sized guitar and signed him up for lessons. After a while, the instructor said he needed someone better than himself to work with Rick and suggested a college professor take over. He did well enough that he decided to continue his music studies in college.

Thus, Rick decided to give up baseball after his second season ended, even though his injuries were healing nicely, and he would have earned a baseball scholarship for his last two years. Some things were just more important to him, such as being able to play the guitar throughout his lifetime. Unfortunately, when he gave up baseball, Tina gave up Rick.

He was heartbroken and didn't date the rest of his college years. He had been dismissed by someone he loved, and it wasn't the first time that had happened to him in his life.

After school, he threw himself into work. He landed a position in a huge firm and made more money than he had ever dreamed of making. He invested his money wisely and devoted his time wholeheartedly to his work. He quickly climbed the ladder in the corporation. He bought a car, and three years later, a condo with cash.

On the weekends, he often played music gigs—sometimes jazz with his electric guitar or classical or folk pieces at coffee shops with his acoustic. He met a few nice women, but it would be one or two dates, then either he, or she, would call it off. Part of the reason, he believed deep down, was his great fear of being hurt once again. He had serious trust issues and learned quickly how to sabotage any real chances at romantic love.

Ricardo was aware of his sensitivity when it came to relationships. He and his therapist had talked about it fairly often after he was adopted. He had been subjected to the loss of his biological mother when he was very young, then lived with an abusive and neglectful father. When his father had been hospitalized shortly before his death, Rick went to stay at one of his favorite teacher's homes as a temporary foster home.

When his father died, it became a permanent foster placement, and later, by the grace of God, Karen and Robert Wilson legally adopted him and became his parents. He was so very grateful to them for all they had done for him. They gave him a stable home, made certain he had any professional help he needed after his rough start to his life, and supported and nurtured him in every way one can support and nurture someone. And most importantly, they loved him unconditionally.

Ricardo smiled to himself as he thought of his parents. After his travel arrangements were made, he thought he'd call his mom and see what she was cooking for dinner. She was a fantastic gourmet cook, and she loved it when she had a chance to cook for him. She still hosted her book club every month, making impressive spreads of appetizers, but it wasn't the same as cooking for "her boy," as she often referred to him, even at his current age.

He turned himself around in his desk chair and called his assistant and office administrator in for a meeting so they would all be on the same page about his upcoming adventure. They made sure his docket was cleared after the next two weeks and made certain the center's assistant felt comfortable enough to handle his absence.

His travel arrangements were handled quickly and efficiently thanks to the stellar work of the office administrator, Loretta. Once that happened, Ricardo finally began to relax. He was going to Chicago, and for some reason, he felt excited about it. He had his itinerary. He had Tommy Romano's number. He told himself it would be more than just a work trip. He would do some sight-seeing and check this place out. Ricardo was determined that he would make the best of his time in the Windy City.

Chapter Twelve

Monica sat by the pool behind her sprawling home in the foothills. She never tired of the view from the house she and Ben had built, although she barely noticed it at the moment. She was deep in thought. She had received a phone call from her agent that morning. He had surprised her with the news of Carson Stone, Jr.'s proposal to make a modern version of *O.R.* At first, she thought he was just calling to tell her about it, but then he said that Carson, Jr. had asked for her to reprise her role as Dr. Pamela Prine. She would not have to appear in every episode but definitely the pilot and, hopefully, other times throughout the season. Just how many appearances would depend on the response of the audience to her character and the direction of the storyline as the season progressed.

She checked her watch. Ben should be coming home any minute. He had gone to the store for some sparkling grape juice to go with dinner. Brent and his wife, Hannah, and their thirteen-year-old son, Luke, would be arriving soon. Monica had a huge pan of lasagna in the oven and a salad ready for its final toss with her homemade dressing. She had become a fairly good cook over the past couple of decades, and lasagna—the recipe taught to her by their former longtime cook and maid, Juliette—had become her signature dish and her only grandchild's favorite.

Monica hadn't learned to cook until they moved into their current home. Previously, Juliette had done all the cooking for the family. Juliette retired when the family moved out of their mansion in Bel Air, so Monica decided at that point that it was time for her to learn a new skill. She had enjoyed cooking much more than she would have ever believed possible and actually found it to be relaxing. Had she known that, she may have tried it earlier in her life, although it may not have been realistic with her active acting career.

A car horn honked, bringing her out of her current haze. She walked around to the front of the craftsman style house and was greeted by Luke. He was always the first one out of the car, and for a reason she could never understand, he absolutely adored his grandma. They had a very close and special bond. They could finish each other's sentences, and he would tell her things he wouldn't even tell his parents, or at least not until he had told her first.

Luke was Brent and Hannah's only child. They had hoped to have more children but had difficulty conceiving. After a number of years of waiting and praying, their dreams of a child finally came true. When he was born, Hannah wanted his name to have special meaning and asked Brent for suggestions. He took one look at his son and instantly realized what it felt like to love unconditionally. Suddenly, a lightbulb went on in his mind.

The first scripture Brent had ever read in his life was from Hannah's worn Bible which sat on the bed stand in her hospital room. He had visited her each day after he injured her, and even though she was unconscious, he would read to her. He had read several other books to her but had been afraid to touch the Bible. He felt unworthy and that he was the last person on earth God would want reading it.

But finally he found the courage to pick up the Bible and opened it to one of the pages Hannah had bookmarked. He had read the story of the prodigal son in the book of Luke. He couldn't understand how the father could be so loving and forgiving after all that the son had done. Then he read the study Bible's footnotes and learned that his heavenly Father felt the same about him. Brent told Hannah his thoughts, and there was no doubt in either of their minds, their son's name was Luke.

Luke hugged Monica tightly. Even though she saw him often, he seemed to be getting taller each time they got together. He looked a lot like his father in some ways—lanky and athletic, brown curls and eyes. Yet, there was an almost angelic aura about him, much like his mother, Hannah.

Monica looked at her daughter-in-law and smiled. Hannah still had the same special glow she had when she was a college student. Even though it had been many years, Monica still thought often about the first time she "met" Hannah. Hannah had been unconscious in a hospital room, hooked up to IVs and monitors, her leg in a cast and her face cut and bruised from the car accident caused by Brent. He had been drinking and hit Hannah while she was out for a run. It was one of the low points of Monica and her family's lives, yet the most wonderful things had come out of the situation in the end.

Her eyes drifted to Brent. She had never been so proud of him. He was an incredible man, coach, and teacher. He had taught adapted physical education at the high school level for a number of years and had been a swimming coach. Now he was an assistant swimming coach for Team USA in the Paralympic Games. His interest in such work began with his court-ordered community service helping at a rehabilitation center with people injured in accidents.

It was sometimes difficult to remember he was the same person who spent years drinking and carousing in his teens and early twenties. Brent was a different person now. It took a lot of hard work on his part, on his parents' part, the love and support of Hannah, and Monica had finally learned to admit that a higher power also helped bring him such great success.

Hannah's family, the Thompsons, had pleaded with the judge on Brent's behalf to give him a lighter sentence, asking the judge to get him some help rather than punish him. Remarkably, the judge decided to honor the request, and Brent served his sentence in a local jail rather than a prison. Hannah had come to visit Brent in jail. Monica had never seen her son light up like he did when Hannah walked into the room. Monica sensed that something very special was developing, and she had been right.

Monica thought about that first month after Brent finished his jail sentence and the surprising conversation they had one evening so long ago. She and Brent had just gone for a swim in the pool and were sitting on the deck at their Bel Air home.

Thirty years ago

"Mom, what would you consider a good first date?" Brent had asked.

Monica had been shocked by Brent's question, and almost laughed, but was very glad she hadn't. The temptation came from the fact that Brent had been on *many* first dates over the years. Monica could barely keep up with the number of women with whom Brent had been involved. He had been handsome, charming, rich, and the son of a celebrity. Everyone wanted to be around Brent, the life of the party ever since his sixteenth birthday, the day he began to drink.

But this time, his first date was with Hannah. Monica searched her memory bank for date ideas. She had remembered a quiet little seafood shack she and Ben had happened upon between Solvang and Santa Barbara. The best thing had been that no one seemed to know or care that they were celebrities. They had eaten some of the freshest seafood she had ever had, prepared perfectly, and ate it in peace—an almost unknown concept in her life at that time. Throughout the years, the small restaurant had remained virtually unchanged. It was where the "locals" ate rather than the tourist crowd. She told Brent about it. It sounded appealing to him, too, especially the peaceful part. He didn't want the paparazzi ruining any part of his time with Hannah.

Monica suggested he use her regular chauffeur to transport them. He felt bad about having to use the service, but he had no driver's license and wouldn't for quite a while. He still had money in an account he had had for years. He hadn't been able to spend anything for the last few months in jail, so he could at least pay for dinner at the restaurant.

He also knew how much Hannah loved to read and hoped he could arrange a private tour of the Hans Christian Andersen Museum in Solvang. He knew, from experience, that if the price was right, almost anything was possible.

Brent could barely wait until Friday and his date with Hannah. She had no classes on Fridays, and he thought it would be safer to be out in public on a weekday than on the weekend.

He felt like a little boy at Christmas when Friday finally came. It was a cool day, so not as many people were out and about. Brent wore a knit hat with his curls tucked up into it, sun glasses, and an old jacket over his shirt. He knew he looked ridiculous, but Hannah understood.

They were able to tour the museum privately with a stop in the gift shop at the end. Brent wanted to buy Hannah a book as a souvenir of their day. She chose *The Ugly Duckling,* saying how much she had enjoyed it as a child. Brent had admitted he didn't know the story. Hannah told him he must have had a deprived childhood, then wished she hadn't said that. In some ways, Brent and his twin, Bart, had everything as children, but in other ways, they had an unusual and sometimes lacking home life. They were primarily raised by their live-in house helper, Juliette, along with a nanny when they were younger, as his parents were always busy filming something. Hannah promised to read the book to him on the way home. She said it might be considered a child's book, but it had an important message for all people. Brent loved it when she talked like that. Hannah had such a beautiful heart.

They had stopped at the little restaurant on the way home. It was just the way he had imagined it, and even better. He especially appreciated the interior, with its weathered boards, crabs traps, nets, and colorful buoys decorating the space. The crab was strikingly fresh and was served with coleslaw and the biggest onion rings he had ever seen. He also couldn't get over the inexpensive prices and the huge portions. There was no part of this dining experience that reminded him of the price-gouging, minuscule portions, and pretension of many of the restaurants he had frequented in the city.

On the way home, he and Hannah sat close to one another in the back seat. It was getting dark, so he reached up and clicked on a dim light in the limo's ceiling so Hannah could read her book to him. He listened with childlike eagerness and was happily surprised at the end when the ugly duckling was not a duckling at all but, in reality, a beautiful swan. *What a great story,* he thought.

Hannah closed the book gently and looked up at him. Brent was mesmerized. Hannah was the most incredible person he had ever known, and he knew *a lot* of people. He could not take his eyes off of her.

"So, what did you think?" she asked softly.

"You were right. It is an important story. I really liked it, and—" he suddenly stopped speaking.

Hannah waited, but when he didn't say anything else, she surprised him. She gently put her hand on his, then rested her head on his shoulder. When that happened, Brent knew he was a goner. He was completely in love with Hannah. He didn't move the rest of the ride home.

The chauffeur waited for Brent as he walked Hannah to her front door. They stood underneath the porch light facing one another. Finally Hannah spoke.

"What was the 'and'?" she asked him.

He cocked his head. "You said you really liked the book, and then you said, 'and,'" she explained.

He moved closer to her and took her hands in his. "I was going to say ... and I really like you," he said in almost a whisper.

She smiled at him. "I really like you, too, Brent," she replied. Then she looked down a moment, looking deep in thought, then looked up at him again. "You kissed me once ... when I was in the hospital?"

He was a bit surprised she had any recollection of that, as she had been unconscious at the time. However, when he had kissed her, that's when she had finally awakened. He nodded his head and said, "Yes."

"So, I don't really remember our first kiss very much. Maybe you could remind me what it was like?" she asked.

Brent could not get words to come out of his mouth, so he just nodded again then gently put his lips on Hannah's.

That was thirty years ago—when an "ugly duckling"—became a swan.

Chapter Thirteen

Jillian jumped when the doorbell chimed. She didn't use to do that, but now every sound, big or small, seemed magnified. She noticed clocks ticking, creaks in the house, the sprinklers going on. You name it, she heard it. She had once found her sharp hearing an asset—not anymore. Now these noises made her feel ill at ease and sometimes downright scared.

She peeked through the peephole and saw Samuel, the delivery man from the dry cleaners. He held some hangers with shirts and a sports coat in one hand. Jillian had completely forgotten about them. John used to have his dress clothes sent out and returned every week, but in the past ten years he wasn't working as often, so it was only once a month, and fewer articles of clothing.

Samuel had been dropping off and picking up clothes for about fifteen years now. Usually John watched for his arrival, and rarely did Samuel have to ring the bell.

"Morning, ma'am," Samuel said. "Does Mr. Romano have any clothes he'd like me to take this morning?"

"Come in, Samuel," Jillian said, taking the hangers from the older gentleman. His weathered face looked tired today as he hesitantly stepped over the threshold. He usually didn't enter the house.

"Samuel, I have some sad news to share with you," Jillian said, trying to hold it together.

"Mr. Romano has passed away," she said.

The man looked like he might cry, and Jillian hoped he wouldn't, or she would start. She found herself consoling him, and in some way, like it had at the funeral, that helped her feel better.

"Mr. Romano was number one," he said, shaking his head sadly. "He always treated me right, and I appreciated it."

That sounded like John, Jillian thought. She went to get her purse so she could tip Samuel and told him she would get back to him soon about picking up some clothes. She hadn't gone through the closet yet, and she was certain there would be some things she should have cleaned before they were given to family or donated to the Esperanza Center. They had a room filled with "interview clothes," so people could have something nice to wear when they went job hunting.

Jillian gave him a tip, and shook his hand. "Samuel, thank you so much for your kind words about John. You are right—he was number one."

The man shook his head again as he headed back to his van. "What a shame," he said, more than once as he walked away.

Jillian closed the door, and the tears that she had been holding back for Samuel's sake flooded her eyes. The entire incident reminded her of a song from the musical, Ghost, which she and John had seen together many years before. The song was about a woman picking up some shirts at the cleaners and the worker asking about the man to whom they belonged, not knowing of his death. The woman begins to cry, then sings a beautiful, heart-wrenching tune. John had held her hand so tightly throughout that song.

Jillian slowly climbed the staircase to put away the clothes. It felt like everything she did these days was slower than usual. There was no pep in her step, as her mom would have said. She hung up the clothes, gazing about the cavernous closet. She wasn't quite ready to deal with this yet, but she told herself she would, soon. She thought she would keep a few things, the navy shirt for certain, and a few others, perhaps.

Then Tommy should look things over—not just clothes, but some other personal items. She wanted him to have John's watch to pass down to John Anthony one day and then to one of his sons after that. Maybe she could find some other special items, too, so John Anthony and his boys could each have something of John's right away.

She closed the door to the walk-in and went downstairs. It was almost time for lunch, but she, again, wasn't hungry. Jillian tried to think about why her appetite was so poor and decided that some of it, as well as her lack of energy and problems falling asleep, was not just from grief, but from a lack of exercise.

She and John had always walked a couple of miles a day, if not more. Now she only walked occasionally, when someone else was around. She didn't care for the treadmill in the fitness room. But most of all, she realized the problem was that she didn't want to do any of these things alone. When she had been single, long ago, she did these things alone all the time. It never seemed to bother her then. But she had been spoiled over the past thirty years. She had enjoyed John's company and also felt safe when she was with him. Now, she felt vulnerable outside and sometimes even inside her home.

She wrote about her feelings that afternoon in her blog, and others started to respond. By the end of the day, she had made some plans. She was going to talk to Pastor Jim about starting a walking group with people from church, meeting there and taking walks in the neighborhood.

Then she was going to see Pete and his daughter, Grace, down at For Pete's Sake. She was going to check and see what type of exercise plan they suggested for her and just see them in general. She felt like she hadn't had enough time to talk with all of her favorite people, many whom she had known since shortly after she moved to California.

Pete was one of the first people she had met in Los Angeles. He was a personal trainer who got her into shape during her first summer in L.A., and he quickly became one of her dearest friends. They had sort of briefly dated, but Pete had been in love with his former fiancée, Kelly, now his wife of thirty years. Pete had betrayed Kelly while they were engaged, but Jillian had encouraged Pete to keep seeking Kelly's forgiveness. He did, and eventually Kelly had forgiven him, and they became engaged a second time. Pete always credited Jillian with bringing them back together, but Jillian felt it was God's doing, and told him so.

Jillian forced herself to eat a good meal that evening, then made herself hop on the exercise bike for half an hour. She could feel how out of shape she was and was not pleased at all. She could also feel, however, how much better she felt after eating well and exercising, even just in one day. It also paid off in another way, as she easily fell asleep that night.

Late the next morning, Jillian went to see Pete. She walked into the original club of the four fitness gyms he currently owned and operated. He could have expanded to even more sites, but he didn't care to lose the personal touch, and stopped at number four.

Jillian watched him as he led an "over fifty" exercise group. He was still in fantastic shape, still teaching classes every day, and still turning the heads of many females. She felt sorry for the two gentlemen in the class, hoping they didn't try to compare themselves to Pete. Very few people had his physique, which coupled with his wit, energy, charm, and genuine caring for others, put him in a class by himself.

She glanced around the facility and noticed Grace working with a woman. Grace Jillian was her namesake and goddaughter, one of Pete and Kelly's twins. Grace was kind and patient. At the moment, she was gently encouraging her client, who looked like she was ready to give up.

Gus, Grace's twin and Jillian's godson, did not work in the family business. He had always helped at the clubs as he was growing up, but the summer before college, Gus had admitted to his dad that he wanted to build things. Pete had wanted to be a builder as a young man and encouraged his son to follow his heart. Pete remembered how his own father had steered him into the banking business, which he despised, and how awful he made Pete feel when he became a personal trainer instead. He would not do the same thing to his child.

So, Gus received a degree in architecture and also studied construction. He currently worked for a large, well-respected architectural and construction firm and was doing very well for himself. He, like Grace, would soon be married.

Grace loved the family business. She was petite because she and Gus were born prematurely, but what she lacked in size, she made up for in spirit. She was slim, wiry, and much stronger than she appeared. She had her dad's dark curls, which at this moment were pulled back into a long ponytail. One might mistake her for a teenager, even though she and Gus would soon turn thirty.

Gus, whom the nurses had named Bruiser in the neonatal intensive care unit, was the physical opposite of Grace. He had his mother's honey-colored hair and bright blue eyes, and a body that was a combination of Pete's muscular build and Kelly's tall, lithe frame. He, too, often turned the heads of women, but he was completely and utterly in love with his fiancée, another architect. They had met when they and their respective companies were competing for the same downtown building project.

After the bidding process was over, they had said farewell, but the two ran into one another at a convention some months later. She bought him a drink (her firm had gotten the bid) and asked him to forgive her. They ended up talking for hours that night, and by the end of it, a special bond had developed. A year later, they decided to get married and now hoped, as soon as they were able, each would leave their respective firms and begin their own together.

Pete dismissed the class and grabbed a towel to dry his sweaty face and arms.

"I'm getting too old for this," he said the Jillian, before giving her a huge hug. He pretty much swallowed up the people he hugged, and Jillian was no exception.

"No way, Pete! You're just a baby," she said, her way of reminding him that he was thirteen years younger than she was.

"Let's get out of here," Pete said.

"Are you sure you can leave?"

"Yep. I know the owner, you know," he said with a wink. "How about some lunch?"

"That sounds wonderful, Pete."

They jumped into his car, and he drove them to their favorite restaurant, Paco's Tacos. Few taco shops had such longevity, but if one makes a quality product, they can actually survive.

As they parked and entered the taqueria, Jillian felt for a moment like she had many years ago. It was like she was beginning all over again in some ways. They ordered at the counter, then settled in at a table. As she sat down, her eyes grew moist.

"I hope it's okay that we came here, Jillian."

"It's great, Pete. I was just remembering."

He nodded.

"The first time we came here I think it was the first time I realized I was falling in love with John, although you could have held a gun to my head and I would not have admitted it."

He smiled and nodded again. "And I was a miserable, broken-hearted son-of-a-gun," he said.

"Now that might best fit my description," she said honestly.

"Jillian ..."

"It's okay, Pete. I think I need to own it. I hope you don't mind if I say things like that to you. It helps if I can be open and honest with someone," she said.

"If it helps you, I'm fine with it," he said sincerely.

"Now that I've gotten that out of the way, I feel better already. So, how are you?" she said, smiling.

They talked for an hour over their unique tacos—the special of the day—made with dragon fruit salsa. Pacos was continually coming up with new concoctions.

Pete and Kelly were considering handing the business over the Grace in a few years. Pete would still help out occasionally, but Kelly had always wanted to travel the country and the world, and the biggest problem with owning a business was how it tied people down.

He felt he owed her that and admitted he felt ready for a change and wanted to see some places, too, that he had only read or heard about.

"It's almost time for a changing of the guard. And Grace. Well, I don't have to tell you about Grace. She's fully capable of running the business. She's also engaged to someone who could be helpful, too. In fact, he's kind of like a male version of Kelly—a business-minded guy—although I don't think he's ever seen the inside of a gym. That part will be the most challenging." Pete looked wistful, then continued. "They say opposites attract. I guess it's true because Grace plans to marry him," Pete said, shaking his head.

Jillian knew that Pete was very protective of his daughter, and of course, as with many fathers, wondered if anyone in the world was good enough for his daughter to marry. But he also seemed to have some legitimate concerns.

They talked a while longer, then Pete looked at his watch. "Jillian, I'd better get back to the club. I have a client coming in shortly," he said.

"Pete, speaking of the club, I want to sign up for one of your classes and perhaps a training session or two with Grace," she said. "I am getting out of shape, and I need to be around more people," she admitted. She knew that no number of classes or people could ever fill the hole in her heart, but she knew it would help and was finally able to admit her need for more social interaction.

"Great. We'll get you signed up when we get back. Jillian, this was wonderful. I miss talking to you," he said.

"Yes, we have to do this again every once in a while for old times' sake," she said.

"And for Pete's sake," he said, winking at her.

Jillian smiled at her great friend and vowed she would make this a regular event.

In her blog that evening, Jillian shared the events of her day. Many others talked about how they joined groups, clubs, or began new exercise routines to help deal with grief. One person had begun a club at her church, going out with other widowed or single members after the late service. She said Sunday afternoon had been one of her least favorite times of the week, going home alone after worship. Now, it was one of the best afternoons of the week for her and for the others in the group.

The group had grown tremendously, so there was always someone going out with someone to lunch or an event of some sort. Sometimes there were so many participants that they broke up into groups according to their interests or food preferences. It was a huge success, all because one person was willing to admit her loneliness and invite others out who might be feeling the same way. Jillian felt inspired and planned to talk to Pastor Jim to finalize her own ideas the next day.

As Jillian readied for bed, her heart felt hopeful. It had been a good day. She hadn't eaten too much for dinner after her hearty taco lunch, but ate a small, healthy dinner, then made herself ride the exercise bike again. In two days she would join the exercise class she had watched in the morning at Pete's. She would also begin working with Grace as her trainer the next week. Jillian was excited to do that and get a chance to talk with the sweet young woman.

Jillian said her nightly prayers for all her loved ones. She included, as she often did in her prayers, that she would be a helper to someone. She thought perhaps some of her plans, especially the one for the walking group at church, might do just that. She smiled, and thanked God for all her blessings, then fell asleep.

Chapter Fourteen

Drew applied the finish to the unique mahogany shelf he had been working on for the past few weeks. It was one of his best projects to date. He was proud of the craftsmanship and also enjoyed the fact that it was made with wood harvested in Peru by one of Marty's friends. The man had recently started a small fair trade logging business, and Drew was trying to support the new entrepreneur by buying his wood.

As Drew wiped his hands on a rag, he looked around his impressive workshop. Never in his wildest dreams would he have thought he would become a woodworker. It had begun as a hobby. He had whined to his wife, Greta, that he needed something to do while she was busy teaching at the college, making pottery, sculpting, or painting. She suggested he help her out by making some simple bookshelves to display her work.

The problem was he had no equipment, nor had he ever worked with wood or power tools other than a drill before. Greta told him to buy the essentials and give it a serious try. He could always sell the tools if it turned out he didn't enjoy it. So, after investing thousands of dollars in equipment he didn't really know how to use, he hadn't been sure where to begin. To say that he was a bit intimidated would be have been an understatement, but he had been determined to try. He really had wanted to make those shelves for Greta.

He watched videos online at the beginning. Then he happened to mention his new hobby and project to Greta's stepdad. He told Drew he had done quite a bit of woodworking in his younger years and would be happy to show Drew how to use his new "toys." It turned out her stepdad knew a lot and was a natural teacher. Drew wasn't certain who had more fun, and by the end the first shelving project, her stepdad decided to buy some new equipment of his own.

Now, years later, Drew considered himself a craftsman—an artist in his own right. He had a natural eye and aptitude for the work. His many years of accounting made him a stickler for detail and precision, and it paid off in his creations. But unlike accounting, working with wood made him feel relaxed. While he had enjoyed his profession, his new endeavor felt like a true gift from above.

Because of that, he decided he would share his gifts with others. Since the early years of operation of John and Jillian's Esperanza Center, he taught a class in basic accounting and household budgeting. The budgeting class was still one of the most in-demand courses the center offered. He still taught once in a while but had encouraged a number of younger accountants to share their gifts, and many had obliged.

But his other class, and his favorite to teach, was basic woodworking. Ten years ago a massive workshop had been added to the center at Drew's suggestion, along with a donation to cover the cost of the equipment.

There was always a waiting list to get in to the class. He was amazed at the young men and women and their work, many whom had never touched a tool of any sort before. Some found the same relaxation Drew often felt, or perhaps a better word might be escape, when in the shop. But, perhaps best of all, was the sense of accomplishment and pride when they made a step stool, small wall shelf, or storage container to take home with them at the end of the course.

Teaching the woodworking class was a highlight of his week, which to him was even more mind-blowing than him becoming an artisan. Drew had come a long way since his first venture into serving others at a free Christmas dinner many years before. He had done that because he was trying to impress Jillian and others at church. Now, he served because he loved it and the people.

Greta came into the workshop, wiping her hands on a rag, as she had just finished sculpting her figurines. Rags were washed almost daily at their home, a consequence of their respective art projects. Greta walked up to Drew and put her arms around his neck, pulling him close. Both of them had been more affectionate than usual toward one another ever since John Romano's death. It was a bit of a reality check, and they vowed to not take one moment they spent together for granted.

They felt terrible about John. John and Jillian had been their attendants and witnesses at their wedding, and longtime friends. Jillian had been the person who had advised Drew to ask Greta out for a cup of coffee. At that point in time, he couldn't stand Greta, and the feeling had been mutual. Jillian had sensed that perhaps Drew's disdain was in reality an unwanted attraction to Greta, and her instincts had been spot on. Drew and Greta had been together ever since they sipped those first cups of fair trade coffee together.

They both loved Jillian dearly but didn't quite know what to say to her, or how best to help. That's when Greta decided that she would express her feelings with her fingers, as she had so many times throughout her life as an art educator and artist. Together, Greta and Drew were making something special for Jillian. They would take the gift to her sometime soon. Only a few finishing touches remained.

Kathy J. Jacobson

Drew kissed Greta sweetly. He never tired of that, not even after their almost thirty years together. Greta remained the most interesting woman Drew had ever met. She was intelligent, kind, spirited, talented, and creative. Her bright green eyes were piercing and hinted at a touch of underlying sassiness.

"Don't start that now, Drew. Cleo will be here soon," she mentioned, while her husband gently kissed her neck. "Drew Alexander," she said, with authority in her voice. He knew that when she called him that, she meant business, and he reluctantly pulled back.

"Okay, okay. Raincheck," he said. "It will be great to see Cleo," he said and smiled.

Cleo Claire Alexander had been their greatest gift from God. After an unplanned pregnancy which ended in a miscarriage, Greta had blamed herself for the loss of the child. She hadn't felt ready to become a mother and thought her misgivings were to blame for the loss. With help from people like Jillian, along with professional counseling and a support group, Greta had begun to understand that wasn't the case, although a twinge of guilt had stayed with her for years.

About six months after they lost the baby, they were thrilled to find out they were pregnant again. The pregnancy appeared normal and healthy all the way through, and Cleo Claire, named for her great-grandmothers, was perfect in every way. Another six months later, they began to try for another child. That pregnancy quickly ended in miscarriage, as did the next.

After testing, the doctor told them it was absolutely amazing that Greta had ever carried a baby to full term. That was when Greta finally stopped feeling guilty about their first miscarriage. She thought she had forgiven herself, but she felt so differently after the test results, that she knew that she had still been hanging on to some guilt and blame. Once she heard the doctor's report, she truly felt like it wasn't her fault, and realized, too, what a miracle their daughter was.

After her last miscarriage, Greta returned to a support group, this time as its leader. She helped many others travel through their own journeys of loss and grief over the years. It was her way of giving back, and she knew that she always felt better when she did that.

Drew and Greta often remarked that what they might lack in quantity, was more than made up for in quality. Their daughter was precious. Cleo was an artist and teacher like her mother, although her personal favorite media were oil painting and sketching. She had recently returned from Paris, where she had studied with a painter. She planned to teach some of her advanced students the new techniques she had just acquired.

Cleo had decided to teach in a different way than her mother. After college, she opened her own studio, Paint and Pencil. She offered classes for every age and ability and also sold her own paintings and sketches in a small attached gallery. She was beginning to build a solid reputation, especially after a recent top showing at a prestigious juried art show.

With Greta's auburn hair, Drew's beautiful blue eyes, thick wavy locks, and height, Cleo had a striking look about her. It was further accentuated by a confident and reassuring presence. She made the people who came to study with her feel like they could do anything. Thus, she was making a name for herself as an instructor as well as an artist. There was a waiting list for many of her classes.

But perhaps one of the most charming things about Cleo was her singing voice. It was smooth and velvety, and she had an incredible range. She had been in choir in high school and college, but her passion was singing jazz, including the old classics from the swing/big band era of the 1930s and '40s. Her favorite singer was Ella Fitzgerald.

Cleo had briefly considered majoring in music, but her passion for art won the day. She still sang on occasion, sometimes in her gallery with a guest keyboardist or guitarist when she was having an art exhibit. John and Jillian's friend, Ricardo, accompanied her once or twice. He was very talented. Otherwise, she performed with an area band when they needed a substitute for their regular singer. Cleo's singing brought her great joy—almost as much as it did to those who heard it.

Drew and Greta were so very proud of their daughter, and admittedly, they had spoiled her tremendously over the years. The good thing was that Cleo seemed to realize she was spoiled, and she appreciated and respected her parents wholeheartedly.

Greta turned her attention to the shelf and smiled at Drew. "It's beautiful, Drew," she said. "I know Jillian will love it."

"I hope so," he said.

Greta nodded, and they walked to the kitchen arm-in-arm to get ready for dinner with their daughter.

Jillian kept working on thank you notes between her blogging and workouts at Pete's the next week. She was already beginning to feel stronger and more energetic. Her appetite was improving along with her mood, although she still had to remind herself to eat on occasion, something which was foreign to her. It was getting less frequent, however, which was a step in the right direction.

Jillian also made herself walk around the property each day, even if only to look at the flowers and foliage or pull a weed. Fresh air always made her feel better. There was also a day warm enough to swim, at least by her standards, and she knew more were right around the corner. John used to jump into the pool for a swim in winter without thinking a thing of it. She had never been that brave and got chilled more quickly than he ever had.

Jillian thought of the first time she heard the splash of John diving into the pool, in January, early the morning after she moved into the cottage in the backyard. She loved these little memories, but she was afraid she was beginning to lose them. So, she began doing something she hadn't done in years—she began writing in a journal.

Jillian decided she would journal about her favorite memories of John at least once a day. It might be as simple as a funny expression John had used or a quirk of his that she remembered, like wearing his reading glasses far down on his nose. It might be about the way he liked to eat certain foods like aglio olio, spaghetti with garlic and olive oil, eaten with a fork only. She wanted to remember everything, and never forget.

Of course, along with the recording of these memories, there were some tears, but they felt almost cleansing. She thought she might share her new activity with Carol and decided she would pick up a journal for her friend the next time she was at a store.

And most of all, she was looking forward to the first ever "walk and talk"—that's how she billed it—at church early Sunday evening. She didn't know if anyone would show up, but even if only one other person came, she would consider it a success. In would mean there would be someone to walk with and talk with— a win-win in her book.

Late Sunday afternoon, Jillian arrived half an hour before the intended walk was scheduled to begin. No one else was at the church when she opened the door via a keypad, but it was still early. But she was getting nervous when with ten minutes left to the intended start time, no one had arrived. Finally, a car slowly pulled into the parking lot, and a woman got out. At least someone came. It was a beginning.

The woman, Maybelle, said she wanted to use the restroom before they began, and Jillian decided that was a wise choice and did the same. When they came out, they were surprised to see three others had arrived. They greeted them in the narthex, then discussed a walking route outside when Janet, Pastor Jim's wife, drove in, very happy to see that they hadn't left yet.

"I have always wanted to try walking, so here I am!" she exclaimed.

The six of them finalized a plan. The two people who considered themselves faster walkers would start first, followed by those who wanted a more leisurely pace. They decided on a point where they would stop and change spots if needed, or just to take a moment's break.

After a stop at the drinking fountain, they were ready to go. They would begin with a two-mile route tonight. Jillian could tell that might be a challenge for a couple of folks who had put themselves in the final spot for walking. She offered that if they couldn't make the entire route, she would come back for them with her car. That seemed to calm their fears.

Well, Jillian never needed to retrieve anyone with her car. As what usually occurs when one walks and talks with others, the walkers lost track of time and didn't even think about what they were doing. Even the two slowest participants, a gentleman named Joe and a woman, Ann, made it easily back to the church only a few minutes behind the second group of two. They reported they never stopped talking and laughing the entire time they walked. Joe quipped that his voice needed to get in better shape if he was going to do this on a regular basis.

They all sat outside at a picnic table behind the church after the walk, deciding they should do this again the next weekend, rather than later in the month as originally planned. One walker mentioned she wouldn't be able to come the next week, but Joe mentioned that he knew of two people who had hoped to join them on this night but had had prior commitments. They decided that whoever made it, made it. They would put the change of plans out on social media, and Joe said he would call his friends. They also talked about a longer route for the next time, or possibly two different routes, one for people who wanted to do only two miles or less, and others who wanted to do more.

When Jillian drove home that evening she felt excited. The evening had been fun. She had enjoyed getting to know more about a couple of people she had only known by sight. They talked about their families, their jobs, and how they ended up at Grace Lutheran Church. Janet mentioned, too, that she had never known as much about these people, and she was the pastor's wife! She thought maybe Jim should try coming once in a while, too, although he was usually pretty tired on Sunday afternoons.

Jillian had particularly enjoyed the latest update on Pastor Jim and Janet's twin sons, Matt and Max, who were now in their mid-thirties. She and John had watched the active young boys grow into wonderful, active young men.

Matt was the program director at a bible camp in Northern California and a newlywed. His wife was a nurse at the camp. They had met during his first summer on the job when he brought a child into the nurse's station to be treated for a wound.

Max was still a member of Grace and a favorite substitute Sunday School teacher. During the week, and some weekends, unfortunately, he worked as a mason—brick, block, and stone. He was a meticulous worker and enjoyed the physicality of the work.

When Max wasn't working hard, he was playing hard. He particularly loved to surf, and after visiting his brother in the North, had become a snowboarder in the winter. Matt had joined him in that activity, and they enjoyed trying to outdo one another with their tricks. Janet confessed that she, and now Matt's new wife, tried not to think too hard about that business.

The evening had been a huge success. Jillian realized once more how good it was to be with other people. As much as she sometimes felt like hiding away, she knew she felt better when she got out and did things with others. That made her even more excited for the

Kathy J. Jacobson

future, when Marty and Michael would come to Los Angeles to live. It wouldn't be long now. She knew it was going to be a very good thing for her and hoped that it would be even better for her beautiful daughter and sweet son-in-law.

She wondered how things were going in Peru. It would be a tough goodbye, she was certain. They had been there such a long time, and their work had been tireless and life-changing. Jillian said a prayer for them as she walked through the door from the garage to the kitchen. Once inside, she grabbed a glass of water and her computer, then slid into the breakfast nook. She opened up her laptop and wrote about her surprisingly pleasant day.

Chapter Fifteen

Jillian was working on a note to Luz the next morning when the doorbell rang. She jumped, but not as much as she had the last time, so that was progress. She checked to see who it was and had to laugh at the coincidence. It was Luz!

Luz had recently returned to her Santa Monica home from her house in the southern hemisphere, as Lima's cool, gray and misty winter season approached. It was an ideal situation for someone who abhorred cooler weather as much as Luz did, even if it never really got cold in her native land. Jillian often wondered what Luz would think of a Midwestern winter.

The two women embraced, then Luz extended a box of her favorite gourmet Peruvian chocolates. "You need chocolate. I know these things," Luz said seriously.

Jillian nodded and hugged her again, and showed her into the house. The two ended up in the kitchen, as it was too windy for sitting outside. Instead, they sat at the breakfast nook, and Jillian slipped the lid off the box of chocolates.

"It's not too early for these, is it?" Jillian asked, gazing at the beautifully crafted pieces.

"It's never too early for fine chocolates," Luz said, smiling, then turned more serious. "I thought it was about the right time to see you. I remember when you came to my house—a few weeks after Carson died. You said that it was the time when everyone else went back to their regular lives, but not so for the special ones left behind. I will never forget how you were there for me, Jillian. I wanted to do the same for you," Luz said, her eyes misting.

Now Jillian's eyes began to sting. She remembered how utterly devastated Luz had been when Carson died. Never had there been a more unlikely couple. Carson Stone was a serious stickler of a director, with his loafers and buttoned-down collared shirts, his pale skin and ordinary looks. Luz was a Peruvian model and star actress, with her bronze skin and rare beauty. But theirs had been an amazing love story that lasted "until death do us part," which also produced two wonderful and talented children to boot.

Their daughter, Sol, which means "sun" in Spanish, was aptly named. She was a bright, cheerful, and creative young woman who lived in Los Angeles and was an apprentice of Jillian's friend, the famous fashion designer, Marianna.

Carson, Jr. was a director like his father and was the one trying desperately to recruit John Anthony Romano for a reboot of *O.R.* Carson, Jr. wore loafers and shirts like his father, but stood about five inches taller than Carson, Sr. had. He was muscular, with darker skin and hair. He had his father's pale blue eyes, however, which made for a stunning combination. Carson, who always felt inadequate in the looks department, was so happy his son had not inherited his height or slight build and often commented on it. Jillian, and also Luz, tried to encourage Carson to appreciate himself more, but it had been a lost cause.

Jillian made some coffee, then they each carefully selected a piece of "pure heaven on earth," as Luz referred to her favorite home country delicacies. Jillian told Luz about the "walk and talk" activity at church and invited her to join them sometime. Luz was not much for that type of exercise and still had trouble with the paparazzi, but said she would consider it.

"That sounds like a wise plan, Jillian, as are your workouts at the fitness club, especially with that sweet girl, Grace, working with you."

"She is precious, isn't she? I know I'm a bit prejudiced, as she is a namesake, but she has always had such a special spirit about her. Grace is so kind and gentle is some ways, but is a very strong woman in so many others. She has incredible energy and loves to stay active. As for her work as a trainer, she has an uncanny way of encouraging others when they aren't sure about themselves. It's a real gift."

"She sounds a lot like her namesake," Luz said with a smile.

Jillian smiled at that, then filled in Luz about Marty and Michael's new jobs and how hard it would be for them to leave Peru.

"I will miss seeing them in Lima," Luz said, "but now I'll get to see them here—and now with you, also!" Jillian was quite excited about that scenario as well.

Thinking about their respective children made Jillian want to ask Luz about Carson, Jr. and the show, but she wasn't really at liberty to do so. She didn't even know if Luz knew anything about it. She was so anxious to hear from John Anthony, one way or the other, if he would accept the role. Jillian knew he had to give an answer by the end of the day, as they needed to start shooting the pilot and begin promoting the show. It was already behind the other shows in the fall lineup, in production and promotion.

Jillian and Luz talked the morning away, then made a plan to go out to dinner together the next evening.

"It's not fun to eat alone," Luz said, "especially eating out."

Jillian nodded. She hadn't really thought about that yet. It hadn't quite sunk in how every single aspect of life would be different from now on. She was just grateful for the wonderful friends, family, and church family she had, who were making things tolerable at this point. So, as she closed the door after hugging Luz goodbye, she said another prayer of thanks.

John Anthony picked up his cell phone, praying he was making the right decision. He and Kirsten had spent the past five days discussing the pros and the cons of this opportunity. In the end, they both decided he should say yes, even though some doubts lingered.

The boys had been supportive, but he could tell it would be hard for them, especially Tommy John. The worst part of the entire deal was that John Anthony would miss almost all of his son's final football season in high school. He would probably have one break in the fall and get to see a game or two, but that was it. His son had been strong and said he understood. He probably did, but that didn't help John Anthony any. His own dad had been at every one of his games over the years, and now he was going to miss more of his son's games than he would see.

John Anthony let out a sigh and then relayed his answer to an elated Carson Stone, Jr. John Anthony would report to the set in three weeks. At least he had some time to get things organized at home before he left and, most of all, spend as much time as he possibly could with his sons and wife. After checking with Jillian, the family planned to spend a few weeks together in California in between music camp for Anthony, football specialty camp for Tommy John, and the start of his school team practices.

The time together would ease the pain a bit, for all of them. Kirsten was already working on adjusting her regular appointments to make it work. Kirsten was the best thing that ever happened to John Anthony, and he thanked God every day for her. He sighed once more, praying he was doing the right thing, especially for his wonderful family.

His parents, Tommy and Maria, were very excited for him. And then they surprised him with the news that they were moving to California, too, and his sister was buying the house in Libertyville.

He was happy for Alison and selfishly happy for himself, too, that the house he grew up in was still in the family. He was also thrilled that his mom and dad would be living near him. It sounded like things were working out well, and he hoped that he could say the same thing regarding his own family, as time progressed.

Jillian had been ecstatic at his news. She told him the guest suite in the house would be ready and waiting for him. She would have offered him the guest cottage, but she had already contracted with a company to do some much-needed remodeling. It had been over thirty years since the cottage had any major upgrades, and it was time to get it done.

John Anthony was more than happy to use the guest suite, which was almost like a small apartment. He still felt a bit guilty for just moving in, but Jillian had assured him it was her pleasure to have him in the house. He could imagine that it was awfully quiet and lonely for her, so he was beginning to truly believe her. He also knew he was going to miss his wife and children terribly, so it would be nice to have someone around the few hours of the day he would have free.

The filming schedule looked grueling, but the perks, including his salary for the show, were insane by Broadway standards. It was one of the reasons he and Kirsten felt he should do the show. They had two sons who would be in college before they knew it.

It did seem like things were falling into place, and that helped ease his mind about the venture. His script for the pilot would arrive the next day, and he couldn't wait to read it. He felt so honored to be doing this project, and to represent his great-uncle in such a way. That, perhaps, was the best part of this entire deal. He looked up and winked, "This one's for you, Uncle John."

Chapter Sixteen

Ricardo looked out the window of his hotel room in downtown Chicago. He looked down at the river below, then up to the many buildings. He loved the architecture, and he couldn't wait to explore. He took out his phone to call Tommy Romano. Jillian had told him a few weeks ago that Tommy was retiring, so maybe he would have more free time now. He hoped they could have dinner together tonight or spend the next afternoon looking around, as it was a Sunday. His work meetings would begin early on Monday, and he expected many long work days ahead of him.

Tommy answered the phone on the second ring.

"Hello, Tommy. Ricardo Wilson calling. I've met you several times at John and Jillian's home."

"Yes, Ricardo. I know you. How are you doing?"

"I am well, sir. I am actually in Chicago. I hope you don't mind me calling you at the last minute, but I wondered if you might be free for dinner this evening, or perhaps get together tomorrow? I'd like to get to know the city a little before I begin work on Monday. I'll be here for the next few weeks working at the Esperanza Center."

"Oh, that sounds nice, but unfortunately, I just sent a moving truck on its way to Los Angeles, and my wife and I will be right behind it. Our move happened a bit faster than any of us planned. Our daughter, Alison, is buying our family home, so things just zipped along, and we are on our way west now. Listen ... maybe Alison could help you out ... I'll put her on the phone. She's right here," Tommy remarked.

Ricardo was going to tell him it was okay, but Tommy cut him off too soon. He wished he could hang up, but of course, he couldn't do that. Would Alison even remember who he was? He only spoke to her briefly the day of John's funeral, and before that, he saw her a couple of times over the years, usually from afar. She probably hadn't given him a thought. And why would Tommy think that Alison would be interested in showing him around? He was sure she had a life and family of her own.

"Hi, Ricardo," a cheerful voice said.

He grimaced with discomfort as he answered her. "Hello, Alison. I don't know if you remember me ..."

"Of course I know who you are! We last spoke at Jillian's. What's up?"

"I'm in Chicago for a few weeks and had thought your dad could meet me for dinner or something tonight or tomorrow, but it doesn't sound like that can happen."

"I'd be happy to have dinner with you!"

"You would?" Ricardo felt confused. He couldn't imagine why an attractive, married woman like Alison would want to meet him for dinner.

"How about this evening? What type of food are you interested in?" Alison asked.

"I love all foods—every kind. What do you suggest?"

"Well, of course, one of our claims to fame is deep dish pizza, but the possibilities are endless."

Ricardo had considered pizza. He never tired of it. "I am a huge fan of pizza. What's the best place?"

Alison told him her favorite pizza establishment. "I'll meet you there at eight, if that's not too late? I'll make a reservation. I know the owner, so I think we can get in. Can I call you at this number if it doesn't work?"

Ricardo could barely speak. Alison was meeting him for pizza. He took down the address and sat down on the bed.

"This is very kind of you," he said. "Are you certain I'm not intruding on your family time?"

"No, it's not a problem," she answered. "I'll see you at eight."

"Thank you. I look forward to it," he said.

He sat a bit dazed afterward. He was happy to have someone to have dinner with, but he had planned on it being Tommy, not someone else's wife. Of course, he had dinner with married women on other occasions for business, so he told himself that this was no different.

He turned on the television and tuned in a Cubs game. He still adored baseball, even if he didn't play it anymore. He had often thought about joining a recreational team in L.A., but his work always seemed to get in the way. He wondered if he could even hit a ball anymore.

He enjoyed watching the local team defeat their opponent. Then, even though he had already taken a shower that morning, he took another one. He took out an iron and pressed a shirt and pants. He wasn't sure how formal to go—it was pizza after all—so he decided on business casual attire. It felt like it was business to him, which wasn't exactly what he had hoped for, but he was sure that Alison could tell him some good spots to check out in the city the next day, and that would be good.

Alison was waiting for Ricardo when he arrived. She stood up and shook his hand, then he helped her back down into her seat, as his father, Robert, had taught him to do. She was not accustomed to such manners. Her soon-to-be ex-husband certainly never held a chair out for her, or helped her back into one.

Ricardo felt nervous at first, but Alison ordered them some Goose Island beers, and he started to relax after a few sips. He didn't really think about it until the pizza came, but they hadn't stopped talking from the moment he sat down. They talked about his work and why he was in Chicago. They talked about Jillian. They talked about her parents' move. They talked about her daughter, Zoe, who would soon be a high school graduate. Alison told him about buying the family house, which she was very excited about. They talked about everyone except her husband.

When they were almost through with the pizza, he couldn't help but glance at her left hand. There were no rings on it anymore. He was quite sure there had been the last time he saw her, but he couldn't be certain. All he knew was that there were none right now, nor were there any on her right hand. He also knew that it was really none of his business, so he looked away quickly.

After gobbling down the pizza and a huge Mediterranean salad they had split, they ordered cappuccinos and sat back. "Oh, my goodness, I ate way too much," Alison remarked. "I was really hungry after helping my parents box up the tail end of their belongings. Now a cleaning service will come in and do a thorough cleaning of the house. I thought about painting a room, but I'm not sure about that yet. In general, the place is in immaculate condition, and I don't want to make too many changes, or it won't feel like home. And I need home ..." she remarked softly, her voice trailing off. She then changed the subject.

"Now, you said you wanted to see some sights tomorrow?" Alison asked.

"Yes, any suggestions you have would be great. If you are as good at that as you are in choosing pizza and beer, I'll be in for a treat."

She told him some of her suggestions, at least for a start. "Then you should do the Art Institute when you have more time, and don't forget the Field. It's a premier museum."

Ricardo entered the suggestions on his phone as she spoke, not wanting to forget them.

They lingered over their hot beverages. Alison was beginning to look tired to Ricardo.

"You've had a long day, Alison, and I've imposed on you long enough," Ricardo said.

Alison was surprised by his kindness and concern for her well-being. She just wasn't used to that type of treatment.

"You have not been an imposition, Ricardo. You have been everything but. But, I am getting tired. I have my car. I could drop you off at your hotel on my way home," she offered.

"Are you certain? That would be very nice of you," he said sincerely.

Ricardo insisted on paying the bill. His portion of the meal would be covered by his expense account anyway, and it was the least he could do. He was very grateful not to be alone on his first evening in the city. His arguments were valid, so she decided to accept it. She knew that things may be more financially tight in the near future, once the divorce was final. She wouldn't know the details of her financial status until the final day in court, which was only weeks away.

Alison drove Ricardo to the hotel. She stopped in front of the huge building. He put his hand on the door handle and was just going to say good night when Alison spoke.

"Would you like a tour guide tomorrow?" she asked suddenly.

"Do you know one?" he asked innocently.

"I was thinking of me, if that's okay?"

"That would be more than okay. I would like that."

"I'll meet you right here tomorrow at 10:00 a.m. How does that sound?"

"Wonderful. That is very kind of you. I'll be waiting. Thank you so much, Alison, for a great evening—for everything," he said. Then he exited the car and waved goodbye to her. He stood watching the car disappear into the traffic and wondered what just happened. He wasn't really sure. All he knew was that he had just had one of the nicest evenings of his life.

Alison felt a million different emotions on her way back to her house. What a day! She had helped her parents pack up the last items for the moving van, dropped them at the airport, had dinner with Ricardo, and was now on her way home to a house she would be moving out of shortly.

Alison's house had sold quickly, and for more than she had asked. It was a seller's market at the moment, which made the purchase of her parent's house even sweeter. They refused to take more than the fair market value listed on their last property tax form, even though they all knew they could have sold it for much more. But Tommy and Maria had no mortgage on the home, and the condo in California was sold to them by a friend at a good price. Plus, both their sale and their new purchase were done sans realtors. They had also made out well on the sale of the business. All those facts made it a bit easier for Alison to accept their generosity.

Earlier in the day, Alison had thought this evening would be a tough one, with her parents gone and Zoe out on a date. Instead, a pleasant surprise had occurred when her father handed her his phone with Ricardo on the other end.

It was hard to believe that the cute little boy she first met when she was a teenager was now this handsome, sweet man. She wondered how he had ever remained single. He seemed, well, perfect in every way. That kind of thinking made her feel scared, however. She had once thought that same thing about Cameron, although, she couldn't remember him ever being what she would call "sweet."

And if she was really honest with herself, she had known Cameron was not perfect very early on but ignored it. She shook her head and put the thoughts out of her mind as she pulled into her driveway.

Alison smiled when she saw lights on in the kitchen. Through a crack in the drapes, she could see Zoe sitting on the couch in the living room, the glow from her laptop lighting her face. She would miss coming home to this girl in the fall when she was away at college in Madison. At least it wasn't too far away, and it would give her a good excuse to visit her alma mater once in a while. And now, she felt Zoe would be more likely to come home to their house in Libertyville once in a while when she had a break. The thought warmed Alison's heart.

One of Alison's major concerns, she had realized that evening, was her future employment. She suddenly felt like it was time to make a break with everything from her past, including her workplace. She was in the mood for new beginnings, or perhaps, as her great-aunt and great-uncle would have said, she wanted her life to be a new creation. So, as she was certain Jillian would do, she said a prayer about it, then entered the house to greet her beautiful daughter.

There were so many sight-seeing options in the Windy City, it made Alison's mind spin. Finally, she decided the best way to begin a tour of Chicago was "the Loop" area. She warned Ricardo in a text to go casual and wear comfortable shoes, as they would be walking for miles—and she meant it.

One of her all-time favorite spots was Millennium Park. It was named that because the plan for its opening was to have been at the beginning of the new millennium in the year 2000. Unfortunately, it took four years longer than planned to create this twenty-four acre space, but it was well worth the wait.

Ricardo had heard about "the bean," the nickname for the stainless steel structure named Cloud Gate. It was just as fun and unique as he had heard it was. After the obligatory photo in front of it, they walked the area around it. There were many other great pieces of art and architecture throughout the park—more pieces and exhibits were added annually—but they would have to wait for another visit. Today was just a "taste of Chicago for the beginner," as Alison coined it. Otherwise, the park itself could have been an all-day event, or more.

They walked around Navy Pier and rode the Ferris wheel. Ricardo had to admit it frightened him a bit, but Alison was having so much fun that he couldn't help but smile from time to time. He just hoped she didn't notice his white knuckles.

As their tour neared its end, Alison introduced him to Fannie May chocolates, which Ricardo decided he would buy for his mother before he went back to California. His mom truly appreciated fine chocolate. Maybe he'd get a box for Jillian, too. He wasn't certain why so many women he knew seemed to be so crazy for chocolate, but after tasting the candy that day, he decided he could become a dedicated fan himself.

While they sat with cups of coffee and a plate of hand-selected chocolates, the subject of Wrigley Field and the Cubs baseball team arose. That caused Ricardo to talk about his love of the Dodgers and his dream once upon a time to play major league ball. He told her about his brief college playing career, his injury, and his tough decision to give it up.

"Wow—that must have been a really hard thing to do," she remarked.

"It didn't seem that hard at the moment, but later on, I second-guessed myself, especially after I lost the possibility of a scholarship, and—" Ricardo stopped mid-sentence. Alison didn't need to hear about the end of his only real relationship, so he changed the subject. "So, what piece is your favorite?" he asked.

"I guess if I had to choose only one, it would be the Pixie, but I love them all—milk, dark, filled, plain, with nuts, no nuts," she said smiling, but then she changed the subject back to baseball.

"Well, since you like baseball, you really should see a Cubs game if you get a chance. Wrigley Field is a classic. That alone is worth the price of admission," she said.

"Maybe I will. It all depends on work, I guess, and how long I end up being here. Tomorrow I'll see what I have to work with and hopefully start the ball rolling on some applicants for the directorship." He told her more about the woman who was leaving for serious health reasons.

"That is so sad. If she needs any suggestions for doctors, let me know. I know quite a few."

"Thanks. If the subject comes up, I'll be in touch."

Alison didn't mean to seem like she was anxious to get going, but she looked at her watch. They had walked close to twelve miles, she reported.

"Awesome," Ricardo responded.

"I'll be sore tomorrow," Alison said. "I usually walk about two miles every day, but rarely log double digits."

"Thanks for the tour, Alison. I feel like I have some idea of where things are and what I would like to check out in the future. It was really kind of you to do this with your work and your upcoming move, too."

"It was my pleasure. It's fun to see one's home area through someone else's eyes once in a while. I forget how blessed I am at times," she said smiling.

"It's a great city. Thanks, again," he said.

Alison realized at that moment she didn't really want to go, but she knew she should. "They say all good things come to an end. I really should go home and make supper. I know Zoe could scrounge something up, but I like her to eat regular meals most days."

"I understand. I have a mother who thinks the same. She would still cook for me every day if she had the chance," he said, a huge smile crossing his face. His white teeth were gleaming against his skin, and his dimples were even more pronounced. Alison had to look away. This man was truly adorable—in so many ways.

They stood up and Ricardo cleared their plates and trash, then they walked toward the hotel. Alison was parked in a parking garage a block away from it, and Ricardo saw her to the entrance.

"Thank you again, Alison. I really appreciated today and last night."

"It was fun, Ricardo. I hope you enjoy the rest of your stay. Call me if you have any problems or questions," she offered.

"I will," he said.

It was one of those awkward moments for both of them. Do you shake hands? Do you hug? They decided on a sort of hybrid hand-shake that morphed into a slight hug.

"Have a good evening," Ricardo said.

"You, too," she said and entered the parking structure. She took the stairs once inside, and when she got to the first landing, she looked out the window. She could see Ricardo's back as he walked toward the hotel. She was glad he didn't have much further to go, and she couldn't wait to get to her car. She was physically exhausted but realized she also felt the best she had in a very long time in every other way. She felt very thankful for that as she opened her car with the key fob.

Kathy J. Jacobson

Chapter Seventeen

Jillian was very grateful for Luz since it seemed like everyone else was off on an adventure or in transition mode. Their dinner at a restaurant was a much-needed outing, although there had been one member of the paparazzi who just couldn't help himself and had to snap a photo of them sharing a meal. Luckily, the owner of the establishment guided him out the door immediately afterward, and they ate the rest of their ceviche and aji de gallina in peace. They had dined at Luz's favorite Peruvian restaurant. Luz might not miss the winter weather in Lima, but she did miss the food.

When Jillian returned home from dinner, she realized that she should begin planning her own needed transitions. She was going to tackle the closet—finally. It would not be fun, but it had to be started, at least.

Jillian had hosted Tommy and Maria the night they arrived in California from Chicago. She had offered to help with the move-in the next day, but they said they had it under control. They had ordered all new living room and bedroom furniture through their favorite local furniture store, but instead of having it shipped to Libertyville, it went to Los Angeles. It had been delivered the day after they arrived as planned.

They had one large hutch and its contents that came from Illinois two days later, along with artwork and personal items that were special to them, and most of their clothes. They had done a good job of filtering through their closets, which had been one of the things that got Jillian on track to do the same.

Tommy had gladly, and emotionally, accepted John's watch. Together they selected some items for John Anthony and the boys including John's Northwestern jersey and other items from his college football years as well as some ties, tie tacks, and cuff links. Once that was done, Jillian felt she could begin her piles of "keep," "throw," and "give away."

She also needed to make some decisions about the guest cottage. The contractor was waiting for her final say on paint, tile, carpet, light fixtures, and the patio. The man had been very patient with her, knowing of her recent loss, but he also had a business to run, and a schedule to try to reasonably maintain. She made herself sit down, look at her options, and made some selections. She chose them based on her own personal preferences, as if she herself were living in the cottage.

Jillian also attributed some of her new energy to her increased exercise and better eating habits. The church "walk and talks" were becoming a hit at the church with more people joining all the time. Jillian also signed up for another group exercise class once a week and for more workouts with Grace at the club. Those were some of her favorite times. However, she felt that something was a bit off with the young woman these last few sessions. Grace was usually one of the most upbeat people Jillian knew, and they usually talked the hour away. But lately, Grace had seemed quiet and distracted, and even a bit melancholy. Jillian decided that if she was like that at her appointment the next day, she would ask her if everything was alright.

Jillian continued to blog almost every day and was beginning an outline for a second book, this one on issues of loss and grief. So many people on her blog and her author page mentioned that she hoped she would write it, and that inspired her even more. She also felt that after John Anthony and Carson Stone, Jr. got *O.R.* off the ground, she would approach Carson with her own project request.

Yes, life was continuing on. There had been moments in the first few weeks after John died, when she wasn't sure if she would ever be able to really enjoy life, get excited about something, or be motivated to complete a project again. But thanks to God and the special people God had placed in her life, she was thankfully doing just that.

The next morning during her workout with Grace, when Jillian asked how the wedding plans were coming, Grace looked like she might cry.

"We started our pre-marriage work with our priest a few weeks ago," she said quietly, then stopped.

"That's good ... isn't it?" Jillian finally asked, noticing the color drain from Grace's face.

"I thought it would be," she said quietly.

"Is there a problem?"

"I don't know if it's really a problem, it's just ... the priest asked us what we like to do together. We talked about how we go out to dinner, to movies and shows, things like that. Then she asked us if there was anything we wish we did together, that we don't do already. I mentioned how much I like to do things outside and other active things both inside and outside, but we don't seem to do that. When my priest asked Christopher if he might try some of these things in the future, he said he didn't see that happening, but whenever I wanted to do them with other people, that was fine with him.

"I don't want to do everything by myself, or without him. But I really miss biking, swimming, going to the beach—especially surfing. My best friend who I have surfed with since high school recently moved many hours away. I didn't surf at all last season because of Christopher, and now my friend is out of the picture, too. I guess I was hoping Chris would do some of these things after we were married, but it doesn't sound like he's willing to even try. It's just so ... disappointing," she said.

Jillian sat and thought a moment. She didn't feel that she should be the one to pose the question but wondered if Grace was truly happy with her decision to marry this person. Instead, she thought that maybe Grace would feel better if she had someone to surf with, and she had just been reminded of someone who loved to surf—Max.

"So, Grace, do you believe that Christopher is truly okay with you surfing with other people?"

"That's what he said. I guess I won't really know until I try it," she said.

"I know a young man from church who loves to surf. I'm sure he wouldn't mind going out with you. He works a lot, but when he's free, he's usually at the beach. Would you mind if I gave him your number?"

"I guess that would be okay," she said. "I don't think I can stand the thought of never hitting the waves again," she said sadly.

"Okay, I will give Max your number," Jillian said.

Grace just nodded, then their time was up.

Jillian wondered if she had done the right thing after giving Max Grace's phone number. She did remember that Pete had mentioned that Grace's intended seemed like someone who had never seen the inside of a gym, and Pete had reservations about him. Jillian wondered how they even got together in the first place, but love is a strange beast sometimes. She sat down and prayed that she had not made a mistake, and that Grace would have some active fun, and Christopher would truly be okay with it, as he said he would.

Max arrived before Grace at Zuma Beach. Standing at the back of his SUV, he combed the wax on his board. He whistled as he worked. He was so happy to be at the beach. He'd been working way too much lately, and this was the first really good day he'd seen for surfing so far this spring. He couldn't wait to get into the water.

As he finished, a small car arrived with a board on top. When it stopped, a petite young woman in a wetsuit popped out. She unfastened the board like she'd done it a thousand times, then headed toward him. Her steps were springy, and her long, dark ponytail bounced behind her. Jillian hadn't mentioned how cute her "namesake" and godchild was, but she had mentioned Grace's boyfriend didn't like outdoor activities, and that her previous surfing partner had just moved away. He gathered, from the mention of Grace's boyfriend, that Jillian wasn't trying to set him up, as did so many other women at church, including his own mother.

But this didn't stop Max from staring. There was something about this woman—a vivaciousness, a freshness, a unique aura about her he couldn't quite put his finger on. Max could tell by the way she moved that she was in great shape, and he remembered Jillian mentioning that she was doing personal training sessions with Grace. As his eyes took in the athletic form approaching him, it was very believable.

"Hi, you must be Max," Grace said, extending her hand to shake.

"I am, and you must be Grace," he said, and in the back of his mind, the title of the hymn "Amazing Grace" came to mind. "First time out this year?" Max asked.

"First time out in two years," she said, a hint of sadness in her voice, but then she smiled. "I'm ready to make up for wasted time," she said, and ran with her board toward the water.

Max watched her sprint for the ocean, then followed suit.

They surfed for hours. Max was not used to surfing with too many people who could keep up with him. In fact, there was a moment when he wasn't sure he could keep up with Grace. He was happy when she finally said they should call it a day.

They went back to the cars, and Grace pulled out a small cooler with water, juice, and high-energy snacks. Max had to admit, this woman knew what she was doing.

Max pulled out a beach blanket, and they sat on it practically inhaling the nuts, energy bars, fruit, and juice. He was impressed by Grace. She had fallen quickly on her first run, but that only seemed to make her mad and more determined. After that, she was on fire-carving out and cutting back turns like a pro, giving him a real run for his money on the waves. It was the most fun he'd had surfing in a long time, and Max enjoyed the challenge of surfing with a truly talented athlete.

It was quiet for a moment as they ate, but then they talked about their work. Max told Grace about some of the projects he had done, which was an impressive list. His favorites were outside—patios and fire pits. He told her to check out Jillian's fire pit the next time she went there, as that was one of his creations. He had also worked on a cool interior stone kitchen and a floor to ceiling stone fireplace. He spoke with enthusiasm about the sense of accomplishment he often felt when a project was complete.

Then Grace told him about the fitness clubs. Max had heard of the For Pete's Sake clubs but had never been to one. He told Grace that he got quite a physical workout on the job, so while he did some running and lifting on his own, he rarely felt like going somewhere to work out at the end of a long, active day. When he did have time off, however, he surfed, went bike riding, or snowboarded in the winter in Northern California, where his twin brother lived.

Grace lit up when he said that. "You're a twin?"

"Yes, I am. We are considered identical, but my brother always says he got all the looks," Max said grinning.

His smile made Grace feel self-conscious for some reason, and she looked away. His eyes were kind and bright, his face tanned and framed by brown hair streaked with blond from the sun.

"I don't know if Jillian told you or not, Max, but I'm a twin. I have a twin brother, too, but we're not identical," she said in a smart tone and looked up at him again.

Max liked this funny, feisty, yet gentle in other ways, woman. "Well, that's probably good," he said kiddingly. That made Grace smile, and then she started to laugh. It was the first time in a few weeks that she had felt like laughing.

They talked about their respective families. Grace knew that Max was from Jillian's church, but she didn't realize he was the pastor's son. She had once been introduced to his parents at Jillian's, and of course, she had attended the renewal of vows ceremony—and just a week later, John's funeral. Now she wondered if Max had been at that service as well. There had been so many people there, it had been mind-boggling. She didn't feel like talking about sad things like the death of her godfather, so she didn't ask.

They lost track of time and talked for almost two hours. Then they watched the surf, quietly enjoying its sound and beauty for a few minutes.

Finally Grace spoke. "I hate to ruin a good time, but I've got to do some paperwork for the clubs tonight and have to be in really early tomorrow. Thanks so much for meeting me here today, Max."

"It was great, Grace. I should be thanking you," he said sincerely.

They packed up and headed back to their vehicles. Grace easily put her board on top of her car. She had mentioned that she would like an SUV like Max had, but she was so short that it would be too hard to put her board on a taller vehicle, even the smaller models.

They said goodbye and climbed into their vehicles. Max waited for her to pull out before he did. It was what his dad always did with his mom, making sure she got off safely if they were driving separate cars. Max watched her car disappear as it turned onto the highway. He didn't know anything about her boyfriend, but he was one lucky guy. *She's one amazing Grace,* he thought to himself, then started his engine.

Chapter Eighteen

Jillian was in heaven. Not only were Tommy and Maria settled in, but John Anthony had arrived, and they were joining his parents for dinner at their condo. Maria had been cooking up a storm in the huge kitchen. It had been the selling point for Jillian's friend Nancy when she and Buck first bought the condo many years before, and it was the clincher for Maria as well.

Maria made several of John Anthony's favorites, which had also been huge sellers in her recently sold Italian deli shops. It was time to celebrate the sale of their business, their successful move, and their son in L.A., indefinitely. Tommy and Maria were thrilled that John Anthony would be in California. It had been an unexpected bonus of their move. Their close proximity was certainly a good thing for their son, too, who was now three thousand miles away from his wife and children.

They lingered over the soft, moist tiramisu and strong coffee after the meal. Jillian was expecting she would not sleep a wink that night, but it was worth it. They talked about John Anthony's show. The table read was Monday morning and filming began two days later. He sounded excited and a bit nervous. The show was being thrown together at a furious pace.

If anyone could do it, the young "rocket" of a director, Carson Stone, Jr., only twenty-eight, could pull it off.

John Anthony mentioned that they hadn't even cast one of the main characters yet. They thought they had someone to play the hospital administrator, a character who was supposed to be a decade or so younger than Monica Morgan, and often at odds with her in the series. Apparently, Monica's character, Dr. Pamela Prine, had accused this woman of having an affair with her husband, Dr. Nick Caruso, the character John Romano had portrayed in the original series.

The actor they wanted thought she could get out of a commitment, but a studio sued her and her agent, and she had to honor her former contract, which overlapped the filming of the pilot and a good number of episodes. So, now they were in a bind. It wasn't that simple to find someone who was just right for the part—middle-aged, beautiful, intelligent, and available to begin work in the coming week.

All of a sudden, a lightbulb went on in Jillian's mind. She excused herself from the table and called Carson Stone, Jr. The call went to voicemail.

"Carson, this is Jillian Johnson Romano. Please call me back when you get this message. I think I may have the solution to your hospital administrator character problem."

The phone buzzed the second she hung up.

"Hello, Jillian. I was swimming laps, trying to work out some stress. I thought we had this all ready to go, and now Missy Blackburn can't get out of her contract. You think you know someone?" Carson asked breathlessly.

"Actually, I think you know her, too, Carson—very well, in fact. How about your mother?"

"My mother? My mother! Jillian, you are a genius. I'll call you after I talk to my mom!" Carson said and hung up the phone.

Jillian smiled as she sat back down at the table.

"You look pleased with yourself," Tommy remarked.

"I'll let you know if I am or not in a bit," she said with a smile.

The talk then turned to Alison. She would be moving into the house soon, right after her divorce was finalized in court and Zoe graduated from high school. John Anthony would be filming, and his family had work and exams, so they would not be able to see Zoe walk across the stage. But Jillian and Tommy and Maria were flying to Chicago for the occasion. Maria mentioned she hadn't heard much from Alison in a few days. She was certain she was extremely busy and preoccupied with the upcoming big events, both the bad and the good.

"What a roller coaster of emotions for Alison," Jillian remarked. She decided she would call Alison the next day to see how she was doing.

"Truly," said Tommy, looking sad. "Keep praying for her."

Alison tossed and turned in bed. She hadn't been sleeping well lately. So much was going on. But deep down, she knew that was not the only, or biggest, reason. It was Ricardo.

The week after their dinner and city tour she couldn't stop thinking about him. In her mind she saw his dimpled smile. In her ears she heard his laughter and kind voice. Then on the Friday after their dinner, a colleague at work had announced he had two tickets to a Cubs game he was not going to be able to use that Sunday afternoon. Alison found herself calling Ricardo and asking him if he was interested in going with her. He had been thrilled with the prospect and readily accepted. The day had been picture perfect for baseball, but that was the least of the greatness of that day. The Cubs won, and Alison recognized that Ricardo was also winning her heart.

It was an exciting feeling. She hadn't felt that way in many years. It was also terrifying.

So, now she couldn't sleep. It didn't help that Ricardo had texted her that day the cutest photograph of himself with a little five-year-old boy named Antonio who had attached himself to Ricardo during a tour of an Esperanza Center project site. The little boy was the foster child of a client and had taken an immediate shine to Ricardo. Alison understood how the little boy felt. She felt the same way. She had looked at the photo over and over again throughout the day.

The worst part was that he would soon head back to Los Angeles, and if she kept letting herself think about him, she would be hurt once again. More hurt was the last thing she needed in her life. She needed to put this young man—he seemed young to her, as she was almost six years his senior—out of her mind, for her sake, and for his, she told herself.

The plan to forget all about Ricardo was easier said than done, though. He was so fun to be with and so nice to her. Alison wasn't used to "nice" anymore, which made her feel bad and mad. Why had she put up with Cameron for so long? She told herself it was for Zoe's sake, but she wasn't sure she had truly done her daughter any favors by staying in a bad relationship. What kind of example had she set for her daughter, to put up with disrespectful behavior?

She grabbed a tablet of ibuprofen from the drawer of her nightstand and downed it with water from the always present glass on her nightstand. Finally, after another twenty minutes of what seemed like torture, she drifted off to sleep.

Ricardo tossed and turned. His workday had begun at 6:00 a.m. and ended at 9:00 p.m., and still, he couldn't sleep. His mind bounced back and forth between the hiring process at the Esperanza Center and Alison.

The assistant to the former director was definitely an *assistant*. He was not even close to having the right qualities for the top leadership role. At least Ricardo discovered this quickly and easily, but that was the only positive in the situation. There just weren't many qualified candidates for the position or candidates willing to work for the lower pay of a non-profit organization. Ricardo knew it would have been much harder for him to do had he not made so much money his first six years out of college.

Ricardo thought he had secured a person to step in as an interim director, but two days after the person had made a verbal agreement, he called to say he had gotten another offer that was too good to pass up. Now Ricardo was back to square one.

He was trying to find ways to make the position more attractive. Even something as simple as a free "L" train or bus pass might be helpful as well as an expense account for lunches. The center couldn't really afford big things, he knew, but little things like that might be the difference between finding a candidate, or not. He was going to call Jillian the next day to discuss some of his ideas.

Then there was Alison. She was the biggest surprise of this Chicago experience. She was pretty, fun to be around, and he had never felt so comfortable around anyone before. Maybe it was because they had somewhat known each other for years, but their past experiences were few and far between, and their age difference had been much more pronounced in their younger years.

And he also knew that in a short time, he would be leaving. Alison would be moving further from the city, and she was in the process of a divorce. She probably had no interest in dating anyone at a time like this. It just seemed like the deck was stacked against him, but yet, he still wanted to play his cards. He just didn't know how it could work out, and the thought made him feel miserable.

His head was beginning to pound. He got up and found his shaving kit. He had put some aspirin in it, he was certain. He popped two tablets into his mouth, swallowed them dry, and plopped back down into the bed with a heavy sigh.

Two calls came through on Jillian's phone at the same time. One was coming in from Carson Stone, Jr., another from Luz. She wasn't sure which one to answer, and which one to ignore temporarily. She opted for Carson, since she was the one who had called him first.

"Jillian, your idea about my mother is fantastic. I'm just not sure she will do it. She's going to call her agent, then call me in the morning. I won't sleep a wink tonight. Maybe if she heard it from you, she'd say yes for sure."

"Carson, I don't think I should pressure her, but I will speak with her. She probably just needs to talk it out with someone," she said. Jillian knew that Luz and Carson, Sr. had many long talks together before she signed contracts, and she was sure Luz missed that. Jillian got that, as she often wished she could ask John what he thought about something, but it wasn't possible.

"Okay, that's fair. I just hope her answer is yes. She would be fantastic. I'm a bit embarrassed that I didn't think of it myself," he said sincerely.

"Don't be too hard on yourself. Your mom just came back to the States, and sometimes our closest friends and relatives slip our minds when it comes to things like that."

"I guess you're right. Okay, then. I'll keep my fingers crossed, and wait for her answer."

"And I'll keep my hands folded, and do the same," Jillian responded.

Luz was excited, and scared, by the proposal. "Carson said it was your suggestion," she said into the phone.

"Yes. John Anthony told us at dinner about the collapse of the deal with Missy. He said it would be hard to fill, as they needed a middle-aged woman who could pull off playing a beautiful and intelligent hospital administrator. You instantly came to my mind."

Jillian still remembered how stunned she had been to find out John was a leading man opposite Luz many years before. Luz took people's breaths away with her striking beauty, her talent, her sharp wit and intelligence. She was the "whole package," and the combination was rarely equaled in Hollywood. That was why Luz was still in demand, although she was quite choosy these days with her work projects.

"Do you really think I would be good in this part?"

"I think you would be perfect. But of course, it is up to you. I do have to say, I'm a bit partial to this project, as it was John's show for so many years." She told Luz the premise of the proposed character and the conflicts with Monica's character.

"It sounds like it could be fun. I have only a few small commitments coming up—nothing that can't be worked around. And I do feel in some way that I should do this show—for John." Luz's voice sounded like it was starting to break.

"Your real-life affection for him will surely make your part easier and most convincing, I would imagine."

"You are right, Jillian. I will call m'hijo back after I speak to my agent. I would imagine my son would have a better night if I tell him sooner, rather than later. Thank you, Jillian, for thinking of me. I am excited at the prospect," Luz said sincerely.

"I am too," Jillian answered, equally sincere.

Carson called Jillian back shortly afterward and thanked her profusely.

"If there's ever anything I can do for you, Jillian, please let me know," the excited young director blurted into the phone.

"Actually, Carson, there is, but I won't ask you until you are done shooting this pilot. I'll be in touch in a couple of weeks with my idea," she said.

"I will try my best to be of assistance to you, Jillian, as you have been to me," he said. The way he spoke—he sounded just like his late father, and it made Jillian's eyes mist. Carson, Sr., then John—too many good people gone way too soon.

"Thank you. Have a good night, Carson."

"It will be a good night now, thanks to you."

Jillian thought about that and wasn't sure there wasn't a little bit of extra help from heaven involved in this latest development. She was sure that Carson, Sr. and John would both heartily approve.

Max was on a rooftop building a chimney, but his mind was riding the waves, and he wasn't riding them alone. Ever since the surfing outing with Grace, he had thought of little else. He tried to shake the thoughts and forced himself to focus on the work before him.

Two of his friends were going surfing the next afternoon, and he hoped to join them if he got his current project done on time. They were two of the better surfers he knew and genuinely a nice couple. The thought made him step up his pace a bit, but not enough to compromise his attention to detail. He was known for his meticulous work and didn't want that to change. In the meantime, thoughts of curves and cutbacks and a dark ponytail dripping with saltwater and whipping in the wind kept their steady invasion. He sighed deeply and plugged away at the bricks and mortar.

Kathy J. Jacobson

"A penny for your thoughts," Pete said to his daydreaming daughter.

"It would cost you more than a penny for these, Dad," Grace answered matter-of-factly.

"Everything all right, honey?"

"I'm not sure," she answered honestly.

"Anything I can do to help?" he asked, as he folded the clean white towels Grace had intended to fold, and put them on the shelf.

"I'm not sure about that either, Dad."

Pete waited for her to go on, a trick he had learned from Jillian long ago. She was one of the best listeners he knew.

"We've been doing our pre-marriage work with Pastor Vicki," she said. "She asked us what we like to do together, and the only things we could list were eating out and going to shows. I like those things, but I like a lot of other things more," saying that last word softly. "I went surfing the other day with a friend of Jillian's. Christopher told me to go ahead and do my outdoor adventures with others, but he made it clear he would not be joining me. Then when I told him I had gone surfing with Max, he seemed upset. I feel like I am doomed if I do, and doomed if I don't."

"Do you think you could live like this—forever?" Pete asked.

"I guess so."

"That doesn't sound very convincing, Grace. Also, being able to, and wanting to, are two different things," he said.

"But Dad, we already have everything planned, and you put all that money down on ..."

"Grace Jillian," Pete said in a more serious tone. "Your mom and I care first and foremost about you and your happiness. We don't give a hoot about deposits or anything else that money has bought. We only want you to live a happy life and be loved and appreciated the way you deserve, and if that means changing or postponing your current plans, so be it. If you aren't ready to get married right now, or ever, to Christopher, or anyone else, please do not do it."

"But I'm almost thirty ..."

"Grace. Really? You have no idea how young that is. This is your future you are talking about. Age doesn't matter, but love does. I was wildly in love with your mother when I married her. I couldn't imagine living my life without her. If you don't feel that way about Christopher ..."

"I don't believe I do anymore," Grace whispered.

"Then I think you have your answer, Grace. But it's up to you. We will support your choice either way. But please, honey, be happy. Be with someone who appreciates you for the special person you are. If you can't be yourself—the person you enjoy being—around Christopher, perhaps he isn't the right one, or he isn't yet. Life isn't a race, Grace."

"Thanks, Dad," she said.

"Your ten o'clock is here, Grace," the woman at the check-in desk called to her.

"I've got to go, Dad," she said softly, then gave him a peck on the cheek.

Pete watched Grace as she greeted her client in her usual friendly and perky manner. He didn't like what he had just heard. And he didn't appreciate people who didn't appreciate his daughter or treat her right. And he was *really* glad that Christopher wasn't anywhere near him right now.

Chapter Nineteen

Marty and Michael were flying out of Lima early the next morning. They sat at their usual table at their favorite restaurant in the La Molina District. Whenever they were in the city, it was their first stop.

They sipped a smooth Peruvian wine. The wine industry in Peru had greatly progressed since the early days of their arrival twenty-nine years ago. Where had the time gone?

"To think I didn't really want to come here," Marty said. "Now, it's so hard to leave," she said, her throat tightening.

Michael put his hand on hers. "Luz said we can come back and stay at her home anytime, Marty, whether she is here or not," he said, trying to reassure his wife.

A few months after they had arrived in Peru for the final leg of their medical training, Michael proposed to Marty at Machu Picchu, with a beautiful ring made of silver mined in Cuzco. It was the best he could afford at that point in time. Years later, he bought her a diamond anniversary ring, but her silver ring was still her favorite.

They were married in Los Angeles at Grace Lutheran on their first holiday break home, with just their two sets of parents, along with Tommy and Maria, John Anthony, and Alison present. It was perfect. It was the only time Marty got to meet Michael's mom and dad, who had dedicated their lives to mission work on the reservations in South Dakota. It was one of the biggest drawbacks of mission work, as Michael and Marty knew quite well themselves. One doesn't see family very often.

But now, they were going to live near family—the closest either had lived to another family member since they were undergraduates in college. They were definitely ready for it and also excited for some new professional challenges. Even though they loved their work and the people in Peru, they believed their lives would be enhanced by their new positions, and they would be doing something important for others in a new way. And with John's unexpected passing, it almost seemed like their move was all part of a bigger plan.

They held hands between servings of their favorite alpaca appetizer, followed by entrees of *lomo saltado and arroz con pato*. The host and manager for the evening, one of the daughters of the former manager, came and sat with them for a while to talk, just as her father had always done before he retired. After she got up to greet another table, she had the waiter bring them several desserts on the house as a parting gift to them. They would sorely miss this special place, but they knew they would come back—someday.

The weather was perfect for surfing. Max had completed his work project and was meeting Jamie and Moxie at the beach just before one. He was loading up his SUV when he found himself texting Grace on an impulse. "Surf's up at Zuma," the text read. He didn't know why he was texting her and was pretty certain she was at work, but something made him do it anyway. He still couldn't seem to get her off of his mind, no matter how hard he tried.

Jamie and Moxie had been Max's friends for almost ten years. They were a unique pair. They were supposedly engaged, but they had been in that same status for as long as he knew them, and still no wedding plans had been made. They were fun people to be with, though. They were great surfers and friendly, kind people. They both worked at the same surf shop and seemed content to live a simple lifestyle.

Max loved surfing, but he didn't think it could be the only thing in his life, like it was for his friends. He had grown up with parents who tried to introduce their sons to all kinds of activities and interests, and then let them choose the ones they wanted to pursue, most of the time.

Max laughed to himself as he thought about the piano lessons he had painfully endured as a seven-year-old. He just could not sit down long enough to practice. It was like pure torture to be glued to a hard wooden bench in the living room while the sun was shining outside. There were times when he was older that he wished he had continued his lessons for a longer period of time. At least he did learn how to read music—the basics, anyway, and also to how to appreciate different types of music. But his body needed more activity than the piano could provide. He thrived on fresh air and action. That's why he loved his work as a mason so much. His work was often outside, and even if he was inside, he was almost always moving.

Max was riding a huge wave when he noticed Grace's car drive up on the beach. He immediately lost his concentration, then his balance, and down he went like a beginner. Max only hoped Grace hadn't noticed. She was pretty far away, so he thought she probably hadn't seen him fall.

He grabbed his board and got out of the water, heading toward her car.

"Grace," he said as he met her. He was at a loss for other words.

"Nice run," she said, with an impish smile. For some reason, she had felt comfortable enough to kid around with Max right from the moment she had met him.

"You saw that, huh?" He could feel his cheeks and ears turning red. "I can do better," he said.

"Prove it," she said and started for the water.

They paddled out together, then rode a great wave all the way in, both of them staying up the distance.

"Better," she said, as they stood in the shallows. Just then Jamie and Moxie waded over, and Max introduced them to Grace. She liked their easygoing personalities from the start, as well as their playful relationship with each other. And after watching them surf, Grace was impressed. She could tell they were accomplished surfers.

"Moxie used to be a fierce competitor. That's how she got her nickname. I don't even know what her real first name is," Max informed her later. "She was injured in a car accident, and that ended what could have been a professional career. You'll always see her wearing a wet suit, no matter how warm the water is. She has quite a collection of scars—at least that's what Jamie told me," he said.

Grace felt bad for Moxie. It was hard to see a dream come to an end due to an accident. She suddenly thought about her father's words to her earlier that day about her future. She thought perhaps she was ending some of her very own dreams, not by accident, but on purpose—and realized that wasn't a very intelligent thing to do.

Grace was quiet as she surfed the rest of the afternoon. It felt great to be outside. She had convinced her colleague to take her afternoon shift and promised to switch with her when she needed time off. Grace had thought she might go in for a few hours this evening to do some work but now felt there was a more important matter which needed attention. So after another two hours on the waves, Grace knew it was time to pack it up and do what she needed to do.

"Want to join us for some crab, Grace?" Max asked as she put her board on her car.

"Perhaps another time, Max. I, unfortunately, have plans for this evening." She paused a moment. "Thanks for the text," she said and smiled.

Her smile was so sweet. She was so sweet. Max again, could not take his eyes off her as she hopped into the car and drove off.

"I like her," Jamie said as he walked up beside Max.

"Me, too," was all that Max could say.

That evening, Grace made the boldest move of her life. She ended her engagement to Christopher. He hadn't made it easy. In fact, he was very rude. He seemed more angry than he seemed hurt. He had a way of making her feel like everything was her fault, and he tried to intimidate her into changing her mind.

At that moment, she realized how often he tried to make her feel less about herself than she ought. She thought about the great marriages she had grown up around—her parents' and John and Jillian's. They loved each other and respected each other. She never heard any of them talk to each other like Christopher had just spoken to her. It seemed that the only time he was truly kind and loving was when things were the way *he* wanted them. She should have noticed this before, but what she had thought was love had blinded her.

Tears filled Grace's eyes on the way home. She would have to tell her mom and dad the next morning. They would lose money on the banquet facility. She would have to tell her brother, Gus. She would have to call her priest. She was not looking forward to any of this, but a feeling was growing in her heart that she was doing what was best. And for once, she started to believe she deserved more. So while she felt a loss, she also felt like she was gaining in other areas, like her life and her self-worth.

The day of Alison's divorce had finally arrived. The past few weeks had been very busy with work, getting ready for Zoe's graduation, and preparing for her family coming in early Friday morning before the commencement that evening. They were having a small party at the house on Saturday. A number of Zoe's closest classmates and their parents would join them.

Alison was also getting ready for the big move, which in this case meant packing up only things she didn't want the movers to touch. Cameron was paying for a professional moving service to pack, deliver, and unpack at the house Monday morning as part of the agreement the judge had just ordered.

She was grateful she had taken the next two days off. She was an emotional wreck. She was relieved that the day in court was finally over, but she had never felt so empty inside. Cameron had been at his worst in court, especially after the judge gave him the news about his alimony, support to Zoe for college, and more. The judge had not been impressed with Cameron's unfaithful behavior, and it showed in his decision.

So, even though the settlement was more than Alison expected, and she and Zoe would be better off financially than she had previously believed, Alison had never felt so small in her life. She felt embarrassed, foolish, and for some reason, undesirable.

She was relieved that Zoe was at a friend's house all evening. Exams were over and the seniors had no school the next day. Only graduation rehearsal on Friday morning remained for the members of the graduating class. Thus, Zoe and a few friends were celebrating with a pizza party at her best friend's home.

Alison was grateful to be alone. She was not good company—at all. She had once thought she would feel like celebrating at the end of this day, but she felt nothing of the sort. She felt angry, hurt, and like she would begin to cry at any moment, as she sat with a glass of wine on a wicker rocker in the three-season room.

She was startled when her phone vibrated on the glass table next to her. She hadn't remembered to put the ringer back on after court. It was Ricardo. Alison almost hadn't answered it, and later wished she hadn't.

"Alison," he said. "How are you doing?" Ricardo asked.

She didn't know if he knew this was the day in court or not. They hadn't really talked for more than a few minutes since the Cubs game, and she didn't remember if she had mentioned a timeline. Life had been too crazy for both of them.

"Okay," she lied. "How about you?"

"Good. In fact, more than good," he said excitedly. "I filled the interim director—"

Alison cut him off. "That's great, Ricardo, but could I call you back another time? It's been a long day, and I've got company coming, a graduation, and a move on my plate."

"Oh, I'm sorry, Alison. I should have known that this was a busy time for you, but—"

She cut him off again. "Yes, it is. Another time, okay?"

"Sure. Good night, Alison. Congratulations to Zoe," he said, disappointment in his voice.

If Alison thought she felt bad before Ricardo's call, now she felt horrible. She had just treated Ricardo terribly, the one bright spot in her life outside of her beautiful daughter. Alison almost called him back but then thought the last thing he needed was for her to unleash her baggage on him. Ricardo deserved better. *Better than someone like me,* she told herself. As these thoughts flooded her soul, she let herself go, and a waterfall of tears rushed down her cheeks.

Chapter Twenty

Alison felt excited Friday morning. The flight from L.A. was on time, and the thought of being with her loved ones in only minutes brightened her spirits. Zoe was at graduation practice. She would join them at a restaurant for a late lunch/early dinner before reporting back to the school at 6:45 to put on her cap and gown and line up with her fellow graduates.

Alison had reflected the day before that part of the reason she had felt so bad recently were all the "endings" occurring at once. Her marriage, her daughter's high school days and soon Zoe's time at home, and leaving the house they had lived in for all of Zoe's life. It was a tough combination for anyone.

Zoe was handling it all admirably and was truly excited about it in some ways. Alison knew that she was sad to be leaving her friends, though. It helped some that her boyfriend was going to be working at a music camp in Michigan all summer and would not be around. Zoe was already prepared to be missing him, not only this summer, but when they both went to colleges many hours apart in the fall. Another good friend of hers was going to be working full-time and would have little free time.

While these things made it a bit easier, leaving the only house she had ever lived in, even if the last few years hadn't been the

Kathy J. Jacobson

happiest for her family, was still challenging for the young woman. Zoe was a trooper, though, and worked hard to move on. She had recently applied for a job at a nursing home in Libertyville and had an interview on Tuesday for a CNA position. She had received her certification during the school year and had worked one shift a week the past semester in a facility in their current location.

Alison was confident that if Zoe wanted the job in Libertyville, she could easily have it. Zoe was a conscientious worker, very kind-hearted, and smart. She was graduating third in her class of three hundred students and had won a number of local scholarships for those going into the medical profession.

When her parents' and Jillian's smiling faces came walking through the gateway at the airport, Alison didn't know whom to hug first, so they all ended up in a group hug. Alison had tears in her eyes, and her mom gave her hand a firm, extra squeeze as they walked to the car. Maria could tell how much her daughter was hurting, and it hurt her heart.

The combination of sharing time with family and watching with pride as her daughter graduated with top honors, was beginning to work its magic on Alison. Her heart felt like it was recharging, slowly, but steadily.

That night, after everyone went to bed, Alison went down to the kitchen. She was going to pour herself a glass of milk, when she heard someone enter the room. It was Jillian.

"Sorry if I startled you, Alison. I'm still on California time, I guess," she said, pulling up a chair next to her great-niece.

Alison got Jillian a glass and handed her the glass bottle of milk. Plastic bottles had been a thing of the past for the last ten years in Illinois and many other states.

"You've have quite a week," Jillian said softly.

"You can say that again," Alison said, with a slight sigh.

Jillian waited for her to continue. "They say things come in three," Alison said and relayed the three big changes occurring in her life.

"That's a lot to deal with, for even the best and strongest of people," Jillian said.

Alison just nodded. Then her eyes misted.

"And then, to make things worse ..." She couldn't finish her sentence. Her throat tightened, and her eyes filled with tears. Jillian waited again.

"I was really mean to someone who has been nothing other than wonderful to me since I met him," she said.

Jillian cocked her head in a questioning manner.

"You know that Ricardo Wilson has been working out here for the past month or so. I had dinner with him and gave him a city tour when he first arrived. He had called my dad, but Dad and Mom were moving that day. I volunteered instead, and now I wish I'd never met him." Her eyes filled with tears.

"Why do you say that?" Jillian asked.

"Because ... I like him ... and he's going to leave, and ..."

"Didn't Ricardo tell you?" Jillian asked.

"Tell me what?"

"About the interim director position?"

"He called me the other night to say he had filled it. It was just hours after my court hearing, and I was a mess. I couldn't stand the thought of hearing how he'd be leaving."

"Alison, he took the interim position himself. He said his assistant in L.A. was doing a great job in his stead, and that he really liked Chicago, the center, and its programs. And while he didn't say it—he only told me about the things you had done together—I think he really likes you, too. I've known Ricardo for a long time, and I've never heard him so happy or excited."

Alison's head snapped back in shock. Ricardo had been calling to tell her he was staying, at least for a while, and she had blown him off like he meant absolutely nothing to her. Alison's eyes burned with tears as she relayed the phone conversation to Jillian.

Jillian put her hand on Alison's. "I'm sure that was an awful day for you. I'm also sure that if you told Ricardo why you acted the way you acted, he would understand. He's a pretty special man," Jillian said.

"Yes, he is," Alison said softly and sadly. "But Jillian, I'm afraid."

"I totally understand that," Jillian said, meaning it. She told Alison the story of how she quit her job cleaning John's home when she realized she really cared for him. She was so afraid of being hurt again. She had almost missed the last thirty wonderful years of her life with him because of fear. "Fear is a four-letter word, Alison, in more ways than one," Jillian remarked.

"I don't know, Jillian. I was really awful to him."

"Well, at least consider it. Don't throw away the possibility."

Alison nodded her head in agreement.

Saturday morning the family went out for breakfast so they wouldn't mess up the house, then went home to make sure everything was ready for the party. Alison had wisely chosen to have it catered by her and Zoe's favorite Mexican restaurant. She didn't know who was more thrilled—Zoe and her friends, who loved the food, or Alison, who didn't have to cook for a small crowd or clean up afterward.

Zoe's friends and their parents began to arrive at noon, greeted by Zoe and her grandparents, Tommy and Maria. Alison and Jillian were helping the caterers set up on the deck. It was a picture-perfect day. Even though they had plenty of room, they were happy they didn't have to move the party inside. Only dessert would be served in the house. A large cake adorned the dining room table, ready to be cut and served with ice cream.

Alison had rented white patio chairs and tables from the caterers, too. The backyard looked perfect, and the guests comfortably sat and visited as they munched on crispy tortilla chips and the restaurant's famous homemade salsa. After all the invited guests had arrived, Tommy and Maria joined everyone else in the backyard.

Zoe was just about to go back herself when the doorbell rang again. She answered it and smiled at the handsome man holding a bouquet of flowers.

"These are for you, Zoe. Congratulations," Ricardo said, as he put the beautiful yellow roses interspersed among spring flowers into her hands. He hadn't known what else to get on such short notice. He had received a call from Alison less than two hours earlier inviting him to her home for the celebration. She mentioned that Tommy, Maria, and Jillian would be there, too, and he was very anxious to see them again.

"Hi, Ricardo," said Zoe, then she gave him a hug, which took him by surprise. He was happy she remembered him and even more thrilled at this friendly reception.

Early that morning, Alison had knocked on Zoe's bedroom door. Alison had sat on her daughter's bed and asked her if it was okay if she invited a friend of hers to the party.

"Ricardo?" Zoe had asked, surprising her mom.

"Ah ... yes," Alison had stammered.

"I like him. He makes you smile. Of course, Mom," she said. Alison had kissed her daughter on the forehead and called Ricardo a bit later.

Ricardo and Zoe walked to the backyard. The air was filled with laughter and friendly chatter.

"Ricardo!" Maria, Tommy, and Jillian shouted in unison. Alison had wanted Ricardo to be a surprise to them, and she had succeeded. They hugged one another, then Ricardo noticed Alison. She smiled at him, and he smiled back. The smiles were not lost on

Tommy and Maria, who looked at each other with a mix of surprise and happiness. Jillian just smiled her own huge, knowing smile.

After Alison introduced Ricardo to the rest of the guests, she stepped to the side with him for a moment. She looked down as guilt and shame made a momentary appearance.

"Ricardo, I am so sorry about the other night. I had court that day. It was not a good day," she said, her voice breaking.

"It's okay, Alison. I understand," he said kindly. Then with excitement in his voice he said, "I just wanted to let you know that I filled the interim director position—*with me!*" He smiled brilliantly. His dark eyes were sparkling, and Alison felt like they were piercing hers. They nearly knocked her off her feet.

"I can't lie. Jillian told me last night, and I'm glad," Alison admitted, looking straight into his eyes.

He moved a step closer to her, which made her heart beat faster. "I'm glad that you're glad," he said softly. Just then Zoe came bounding over with the flowers from Ricardo, which were now in her mom's favorite vase.

Alison smiled at Ricardo, then looked to her daughter. "We'd better find a good spot for these. That was kind of you, Ricardo" Alison remarked. "Please excuse us," she said, giving him another smile, then walked away with Zoe. Ricardo's eyes followed them both.

Alison and Zoe decided to put the vase near the cake in the dining room. The colors coincidentally matched the yellow roses and blue trim on the cake's frosting, Zoe's school's colors. The yellow roses brought to Alison's mind the flowers her uncle John always gave Jillian, and she felt like it was some sign as the two walked back to their guests.

The party was more enjoyable than Alison would have ever dreamed. Perhaps it was the great food. Perhaps it was being with her loving family and friends. Perhaps it was because she had faced her pain, let herself feel it, and was beginning to heal. Perhaps it was the kindness and smile of someone special. Or maybe it was the combination of all of those things. All Alison knew was, she now felt something refreshingly new in her life—hope. The future seemed promising and full of possibility, for the first time in a very long time.

The weekend whizzed by. Sunday morning the family attended Mass together at Zoe and Alison's church, then enjoyed a Sunday brunch. Before she knew it, Alison was taking her parents and Aunt Jillian to the airport.

Alison and her mom had had a wonderful talk after the party the evening before. Maria had been so happy to learn about Ricardo being a part of Alison's life, even if Alison was unsure exactly what part that was at this point. All Maria knew was that her daughter seemed to light up with joy whenever she was near the man, and that made Maria extremely happy. Alison's life had been too dark and too unhappy for way too long.

It was Monday, and Alison and Zoe were on their way to Libertyville, their vehicle packed to the brim with special treasures. The movers were on their way to the new house as well. Alison had never seen such efficiency. Some workers wrapped quickly, but carefully, while others boxed, and others did the heavy lifting. It was an impressive operation.

Alison felt truly excited as they drove the well-known route to her childhood home. She was looking forward to sleeping in the familiar house on the familiar, quiet street. This move was feeling wiser by the minute.

Most of all, Alison was looking forward to seeing the look on her daughter's face when she received her graduation gift. It was currently parked in the garage. It wasn't a brand new vehicle, but it was only a few years old and had low miles. It had a great gas mileage rating, was compact and easy to park in a city, and would be an excellent car to take to Madison in the fall. Tommy had helped her obtain it through his friend in Libertyville, the dealer he always used for their family cars. She had given the man the code to the garage and had received a text the day before that it was ready and waiting for its new owner, the keys in a packet on top of the hood. Alison couldn't wait to watch the garage door go up when they arrived.

The car was a huge hit. Zoe had hugged her mom, then cried tears of joy. She couldn't believe she had her own car. She hadn't really needed one at their old house, as there was a bus stop a block away and the "L" just beyond that. But in her new locale, a car would be a godsend. She and Alison drove it around town for a while, finding the nursing home where Zoe would have her interview the next day. It made them both feel better to know that she actually knew where she was going.

They drove past Pasto, the original deli her parents' had owned. It looked like its popularity was still intact, although it had only been a couple of months since the new owner took over, so the proof would be in its status down the road. Alison prayed it would have many more successful years, mostly for her parents' sake.

The deli had been her mother's brainchild, and Maria had created its menu, with family recipes handed down over generations. In addition to cooking and baking, she had run the business end as well in the first year, until it almost ran her into the ground in exhaustion. That's when Tommy decided to leave his employer of many years and had taken over as the business manager for Maria. When he did that, the place had been taken to a new level, as was Tommy and Maria's relationship.

They drove around the block, then came back, having decided they would take home carryout dinners for their supper. Tony, the new owner, was behind the counter and had been extremely excited to see them. He looked around to see if Tommy and Maria were with them and was disappointed when they were not. Alison told him her parents would be back in a few weeks when she and Zoe were all settled into the house.

Tommy, Maria, and Jillian had decided they needed to come back for a longer stay. Tommy and Jillian planned to bury some of John's ashes at John's parents' gravesite. They had considered doing it over the past weekend, but there wasn't much time, and they didn't want to take any time or focus away from Zoe's special milestone. Jillian also hoped to spend a day or two in Wisconsin, her home state, when they returned. They would have a housewarming party for Alison, too. Maria was already busy making plans. Everyone was excited about the prospects, and it couldn't come soon enough.

John Anthony stretched out on a chaise lounge on the pool deck, soaking in the sunshine. It was his first real day off in almost three weeks, and he was beat. He was also excited—for many reasons. The filming of the pilot had gone very well. He had done little television work in the past, so there was a learning curve, but Carson was an impressive director, the cast was stellar, and Carson's screenplay was top-notch. John Anthony wondered how someone so young could be so competent. He guessed he inherited some of his gifts from his parents.

Luz was absolute perfection in her role, as was Monica Morgan. The two made quite the pair of adversaries in the show. They were so convincing that John Anthony almost wondered if they truly hated each other in real life, until he witnessed them talking and laughing as they ate lunch together. It was then he realized the immensity of their talents.

Most of all, John Anthony was excited because in only weeks his family would arrive. The only drawback to his new show was that he missed Kirsten, Tommy John, and Anthony like he had never missed anyone, or anything, before in his life. It helped some that the workdays had been really long during the shooting of the pilot. And when he had time off, Jillian had been a wonderful host. She was accustomed to dealing with an actor's life and was a great comfort and resource in his few wakeful hours at home each day.

It had not been fun when Jillian was gone to Zoe's graduation. She was going to leave again soon for a week, along with his mom and dad, and he wasn't looking forward to that at all. But when she came back, his family would be right on her heels. Jillian was already planning a party at the Malibu beach house to celebrate, and the boys had been sending texts and links with hints for all the places they wanted to go and things they wanted to do. One of the things the boys wanted to do was learn to surf, and Jillian told them she had at least two friends who might be able to help out with that request.

When Jillian had been away, John Anthony gained insight into why Jillian was so pleased to have him there. It was hard coming home to an empty house. It was especially hard knowing that John was gone—for good. It was difficult at times for John Anthony to deal with that fact, so he could only imagine Jillian's pain. He wished there was something he could do to ease it, but he guessed that his being at the house temporarily, when the wounds were so fresh, was the best he could do.

He put his head back on the soft chaise, sighed deeply, and closed his eyes. Within minutes, he was sound asleep.

Alison opened several drawers in the kitchen until she finally found the dish towels. They were not in the same drawer in which her mom had kept them. She would change that later, but for now, she just wanted to dry the dishes they had used for the lasagna and pesto penne with chicken they had just devoured, and sit down. She was so grateful for the wonderful, fresh, and convenient food she had purchased that afternoon. Her mother had been a genius developing this business that served high quality homemade entrees suitable for family dinners and special occasions.

Having this food tonight made her feel even more like she was home. She may not have had her mom to cook for her in person that night, but her mother's recipes prepared by a cook at the deli were the next best thing. She was certain that she and Zoe would be regular customers at Pasto.

Zoe was upstairs deciding what outfit she would wear to her interview in the morning, and then she was going to go to bed, which meant she would spend an hour or so on the computer or phone with her boyfriend or other friend, and then finally go to sleep. Zoe had chosen Alison's old room as her bedroom. She had picked it over John Anthony's former room and the guest room. Perhaps it was because they would often stay in that room when they came home for visits as she grew up.

Alison had purchased a new bedroom set for the master bedroom. She wanted nothing to do with the bed she had shared with Cameron, especially knowing that he had defiled it probably more times than she could possibly know. She needed no reminders of that part of her past. It was time for a fresh start.

Luckily, her parents had recently painted the room in a soft, neutral color that went with anything. Alison had enjoyed picking out new linens and bedding and planned to add accents to the room over the summer.

Alison wiped the dishes and put them into the cabinet then sat down at the table. She pulled out her cell phone and checked it. She saw that she had a message from several hours earlier. She had been too busy to pay much attention to her phone that day.

It said, "Thinking of you and Zoe. Hope the move went well." It was from Ricardo.

She texted back, "All is well. Good to be home." She wanted to say more, but didn't. It was getting dark, and Alison was emotionally and physically drained. What a week it had been—actually not even a full week, but quite a roller coaster ride. Gratefully, the ride felt like it was finally slowing down and arriving safely to a halt.

Alison decided to follow Zoe's lead and go to bed, except Alison would actually go to sleep. The alarm would be going off before she knew it, her day beginning forty-five minutes earlier than before, one of the few negatives of her move. At that moment, Alison regretted not taking an extra day off—or even the rest of the week, but she would already be taking the upcoming Friday afternoon off for the closing of her former home.

She also knew she wanted to visit her parents in Los Angeles sometime before the summer's end and maybe take a short trip with Zoe before she left for college. Perhaps she should ask her mom and Jillian to join them, too. She'd have to put on her thinking cap and come up with some ideas about that one. At least these were all fun and positive things on which to focus.

She crawled between her new, soft Egyptian cotton sheets on the plush bed. For once, she had spared no expense and purchased a top-quality mattress. It was worth it, as she felt like she was floating on a cloud. She said a prayer of thanks for the end to the former chapter in her life and the beginning of a new one. Then she closed her eyes and didn't open them again until her alarm went off.

Zoe was hired on the spot at the nursing home and began work the next day. She had wisely taken her social security card with her when she interviewed and got her paperwork completed for her paychecks. She was pretty much guaranteed full-time hours, with the possibility of overtime under certain circumstances. She was thrilled with the hours, the facility, and had been impressed with the director of nursing. Her former boss had been a bit on the negative side, even though she had given Zoe a glowing recommendation. Perhaps the woman didn't know how to convey her good thoughts in person to her workers.

Alison had a busy week at work. It was the beginning of summer, and with that came accidents and other issues of all sorts. One man fell off his roof doing repairs. Several others had injuries from overdoing it while getting back to their summer sports and hobbies. One had injuries from falling off a jet ski, another from doing tricks on a skateboard.

Alison was grateful for the busyness in some ways. It helped her keep her mind off of Ricardo—at least somewhat. She was trying her best not to seem overeager, yet found herself texting him late Friday morning after Zoe informed her she was pulling a double shift and wouldn't be home until after eleven that night. Zoe had been so excited because she was going to get overtime pay for working sixteen hours straight. Alison remembered those days earlier in her nursing career. They weren't quite as exciting anymore, not even with extra pay. She was happy for her daughter, though.

Ricardo texted back and asked if she was available to take a call. She had a very short break, so she said yes. When he called, Alison found herself asking Ricardo out to dinner to help her celebrate her house closing and because Zoe had to work and she'd have to eat alone—at least those were her excuses.

Ricardo had thought the food at Zoe's party was outstanding and had complimented the caterers on his way out.

"Would you like to see where that great Mexican food at the party came from?" Alison suggested.

"You bet," he said.

Just then Alison's next patient was ready, so she had to go. She told him she would pick him up at the hotel at six.

Alison didn't understand why it was so easy to talk to Ricardo. Not only did they talk pretty much nonstop over their tamale sampler, mango salsa enchiladas, and chicken poblano at the restaurant, but for hours afterward.

After their meal, they walked around the neighborhood near the restaurant. They passed a small park and sat on a bench, talking and talking about anything and everything. Alison finally looked at her watch and saw that it was nearly ten. Ricardo knew Alison hoped to be home when Zoe got home, so he stood up and said they should start for the car. Neither one of them truly wanted to go, so they just stood there a moment.

Ricardo spoke softly as he turned to her. "This week was a week of good surprises. First, you asked me to Zoe's party. That was so nice, and it was very special to see your parents and Jillian again. Then tonight, another pleasant surprise. You're spoiling me, Alison."

Alison didn't know quite what to say. "Good," was all she could come up with. Then she started walking back toward the restaurant's parking lot, Ricardo walking quietly by her side.

They rode in silence during the fifteen-minute drive to the hotel.

She parked as close as she could to the front entrance of the hotel, but there were several taxis and other cars lined up. She pulled in behind them.

"I had a great time, Alison," Ricardo said, his hand on the door handle. He was about to get out when Alison put her hand on his left arm.

"How about one more surprise?" she found herself saying.

He turned toward her, a quizzical look on his face. When he did that, she leaned toward him, gently pulled his face toward hers, then kissed his lips. She pulled back, hardly believing what she had just done, but not feeling too sorry about it at the moment. "I've got to go, Ricardo. Good night," she said softly.

He looked at her, and spoke quietly, touching her face softly with his fingers. "That was the best surprise of all," he said, then reluctantly exited the car.

Alison had beaten herself up all the way back to Libertyville. Why had she kissed Ricardo? Why was she always so impulsive? What must he think of her now, although hadn't he said it was the best surprise of all? Question after question invaded her mind.

She had gotten home only ten minutes before Zoe. She had washed her face and thrown on her nightclothes in record time, then sat in her favorite chair with a book in her hands, like she had been reading all night. Alison suddenly felt like she was the teenager and Zoe was the mother. She didn't know what she would say if Zoe asked her what she had done all night. She guessed it would be okay to mention the dinner, but she would definitely skip the rest.

Luckily, Zoe had no interest in chit-chatting after her sixteen hours of work. She was grateful her shift the next day was from three to eleven p.m., and not the seven to three. She kissed her mom goodnight and headed for bed—this time to actually go to sleep.

Alison sat in the chair a while longer in the dim light of the single lamp. She couldn't stop thinking about the kiss. Ricardo's lips were soft and warm, and she loved the feel of his five o'clock shadow on her fingers. She couldn't remember the last time she had kissed a man, and the thought made her feel sad. It also made her feel scared for the future. She was terrified of loving someone again—

Kathy J. Jacobson

and them not loving her back. She let out a heavy sigh, then mindlessly looked at the book until she fell asleep in the chair.

A new week at the Chicago Esperanza Center was underway, but Rick's mind was elsewhere. It was back in a car in front of the hotel with Alison's sweet lips on his. He couldn't get it out of his mind, no matter how hard he tried. Even his recent change of living quarters could not release his thoughts.

He had spent Sunday afternoon moving into a furnished, short-term rental apartment. There wasn't much to move, actually, just his suitcase, a new suit, and some dress shirts he had purchased. He hadn't planned on shopping, but he hadn't brought that many clothes with him, as he didn't think he'd be staying in Chicago so long.

He had walked to the nearest grocery store the evening before, then took a taxi home with several huge reusable bags he had purchased filled with food and other essentials. Ricardo had been tired of eating out almost every night and trying to make breakfast, lunches, and a few dinners with only the small refrigerator and microwave in his hotel room. Now he could actually cook, something his mother had taught him well.

As he sat eating his fresh pan-seared fish, he wished he had some of his mother's homemade fish sauce. He also wished he had some motherly advice to go with it. He had enjoyed Alison's kiss very much. It had surprised him. It had also scared him. His past insecurities were surging more than they had in a long time, perhaps because it had been a long time since he felt the way he was feeling at this moment.

Ricardo felt like he was falling in love. How could this possibly work? He'd most likely be leaving in a month or two, and then what? He pushed away the rest of his dinner, suddenly losing his appetite. All he could see was heartache ahead—for both of them.

Chapter Twenty-One

It was a most pleasant day when Jillian and Tommy reached the cemetery in Belvidere. Tommy held Jillian's arm as they crossed the uneven grass, which was badly in need of mowing after a week of intermittent rain and hot sunshine. In his other hand, he held the small urn of ashes. Jillian held in her grasp five roses she had brought—four red and one yellow to put on the graves.

There was a slight breeze, and the scent of pine trees wafted into their nostrils. Jillian inhaled deeply. She missed this smell. It reminded her of the pines she and her father had planted—a 4-H project—on their farm. They had been only saplings bundled in newspaper when they brought them home to plant. Now they formed a grove of giant firs.

A space had been readied for the ashes near the head of Tommy's grandparents' graves, right between the two of them. Tommy had called that morning to make certain everything was ready. He didn't want any glitches.

Jillian had never been to the graves before and gazed for the first time at the ceramic photo disk John had permanently attached to his parents' headstone. It was a photo of his parents holding him and his brother, Anthony, when they were small. His mother and father were looking adoringly into one another's eyes. John had received the original photo from his relative when they were in

Italy. He had never seen it before and had never seen his father seem as happy—or loving—as he had been in that photo. John had the medallion made not long after he and Jillian were married and put it on the stone.

Remarkably, it was still intact and looked in good shape. Tommy's parents' graves were right next to his grandparents. Jillian thought about the baby Jesus figurine John had buried at his brother, Anthony's grave that same day long ago, a "peace offering" after many years of strained relations. The brothers had always fought over who got to put it in the manger of the family's nativity set each Christmas. It had been a special act of reconciliation and love on John's part toward Anthony.

A small pile of dirt sat near the headstone, and a top layer of grass was sitting next to the new space ready to be placed back like a lid.

"Should I do it, or do you want to, Jillian?" Tommy asked, his eyes suddenly red and teary.

"Go ahead, Tommy. He loved you so very much," she said, her own eyes stinging.

Tommy gently put the small vessel into the space, pushed dirt from the pile on top of it, and replaced the cut piece of topsoil and grass. "There you go, Zio," he said softly, as he patted it down with his hand.

Tommy stood up, wiping his hands on a small towel he had brought. Jillian gave him two of the red roses to put on his parents' graves. He did that as she placed the two other red ones on John's mom and dad's graves, then finally laid the yellow one on top of the new space.

"I'll love you forever, John," she whispered as her fingers left the stem of the rose.

As she stood up, a stronger breeze came up and the pines swayed. She looked up at them and saw the most brilliant male cardinal riding one of the branches, his crimson feathers shining in the sun. He called out his beautiful song, then flew away.

Jillian had once heard that cardinals were representatives of passed loved ones, and that they came to you whenever you were thinking of them, or perhaps needing them most. Some also said it was a sign that they were well. She thought there might be something to this, as she felt John's love in her heart so strongly at that moment, and was confident that he was happy and well cared for.

"I hear you, John," she said to the bird as it flew away.

Later, on the way home, she told Tommy her thoughts about the cardinal. He said he didn't doubt it. He had felt something special, too. Jillian was so grateful for Tommy. He was so much like his uncle John, and also like a brother to her. What a wonderful family she had, and she thanked God for him, and all her family, once more.

Before they knew it, the travelers were back home. It had been a wonderful visit with Alison and Zoe. Jillian found it interesting, however, that Alison hadn't mentioned Ricardo once during their stay, and when Jillian had a business lunch with Ricardo, he had not mentioned Alison. She decided that she was not going to bring up the subject with either of them.

Ricardo had been excited about the projects in Chicago and mentioned they had received a couple candidates that seemed promising for the directorship. His assistant was checking out references, and afterward, they would begin the interview process. One of the applicants, who looked strongest on paper, was not available to begin working with the center for two months, but Jillian told him if it was the right candidate, they would wait.

In the meantime, she thanked him for taking over and helping the center continue to thrive. She also gave him the latest updates on his parents, which made him very happy. Being so far away from them had been a challenge—for both parents and son.

Karen had mentioned to Jillian that perhaps their next trip

should be to Chicago—a city she had never visited. Robert had been there only once, but it had been many years ago on a short business trip. Ricardo perked up at that idea. He thought he was beginning to know the city well enough to do the basics with visitors, at least. Thinking about that made him think about Alison and her "Chicago for beginners tour." He had made himself put the thought out of his mind.

Now Jillian was back in Los Angeles getting ready for John Anthony's wife and sons to descend upon the house. It reminded her of when Tommy, Maria, John Anthony, and Alison came for visits. The cupboards and refrigerator were brimming with food, including Anthony's favorite sugared cereal for breakfast. Kirsten had tried to get him to give it up, but finally she gave up. She decided she could surrender this battle, as he otherwise ate fairly healthily.

Jillian had also decided to have the party at the beach house on July the seventh, John's birthday. One of the people responding to a recent blog post had mentioned that it was okay to honor and remember a loved one's birthday by doing something special or something the person had often enjoyed on their special day. Going to the beach house and celebrating with family was one of those things. Jillian was already planning the menu and having someone set up a volleyball net on the sand.

"Tears and cheers" was the best way to describe the reunion of John Anthony's family. Although they talked every day and often video-chatted, it just wasn't the same. Jillian remembered that well from the many years of Marty living far away and was so grateful and still a bit in the unbelieving stage that her daughter and son-in-law now resided in the same city as she did.

The days the family were together in Los Angeles were filled with fun and sunshine, and it seemed like time was fast-forwarded, which usually happens when one is having a great time. Kirsten and the boys had already been in California for ten days and still had another eleven to go. The boys were in the pool constantly—it hadn't seen that kind of action in eons. They had gone to Disneyland with their parents on John Anthony's day off and even gotten in a surfing lesson with Max one day. They had been thrilled and both wanted to do it again. Max didn't know if he would have time while they were still here, but he suggested Grace might take them out and mentioned she was a really good surfer.

They had the birthday party at the house in Malibu, complete with John's favorite grilled seafood, loaves of his favorite Italian bread, and almond cake for dessert. Jillian had learned to bake this cake, perfecting Katerina's recipe from Italy and garnering tips from Leo's family, too, over the years.

The boys adored the beach volleyball and had split into teams with Anthony, John Anthony, and Marty on one team, and Michael, Tommy John, and Kirsten on the other. Tommy, Maria, and Jillian were the cheerleaders and were called on to be line judges from time to time. It was an interesting job, as the lines were drawn in the sand, and the wind kept blowing them closed.

A great time was had by all, and Jillian could feel John with them when they all sang "Happy Birthday." It was a special day, and Jillian blogged about it afterward, thanking the person who had suggested celebrating in such a way. She thought it might very well become a new tradition.

The entire visit was going along splendidly—until Kirsten got a call from the physical therapist in her office. The PT was keeping the office open in Kirsten's absence, doing her own appointments and a few clients of Kirsten's who needed regular visits. The woman's father had just had a massive heart attack and was being kept alive by artificial means at this point. Her mother was awaiting her arrival, as the family was considering taking him off life support. The woman was a mess and needed to get on a plane—

pronto. She was one of only two siblings, and her brother was not in good health himself. She had no idea how long she would need to be gone.

Kirsten talked it over with John Anthony. While he was heartbroken, he knew that his wife was going to have to leave. They had a long discussion, trying to come up with a better solution, but there was none, or one that could be implemented quickly. Kirsten would take over the appointments that week, missing only one day—the next one—as she traveled back to the other side of the nation. The PT thanked her profusely and told her that the office assistant was ready to call the individuals who had appointments the next day that would have to be canceled.

When Jillian heard the news, she was very sad, especially for John Anthony. She knew what it felt like to be without the one you love. He had missed Kirsten fiercely the past few months and had been so happy to have her with him, finally. Jillian used to hate it when she or John had to travel for work and were apart. And, of course, now she had an even keener understanding of that longing.

Jillian had suggested John Anthony and Kirsten go out that night and offered to stay with the boys. But they both wanted to be home—with their sons. So instead, Jillian ordered in pizzas from Leo's restaurant—they did deliveries these days. They ate, then Jillian excused herself, leaving the family together around the firepit afterward. The boys were still in swimming suits and diving into the pool from time to time throughout the evening, throwing around a soft, floating football. John would have loved it.

John Anthony and Kirsten snuggled on the outdoor couch, Kirsten's head on John Anthony's strong shoulder, just watching the boys. They hated to have to end the night and were not looking forward to telling them about what was happening. Finally, they called them both out of the pool and gave them the disappointing news.

Anthony seemed to be okay with it, but Tommy John was very quiet. He was always the sensitive one. John Anthony put his arm around his eldest son's shoulders and hugged him to his side.

"It'll be alright, bud," John Anthony told his firstborn, wishing he believed his own words.

John Anthony's call was at 6:00 a.m., so he sadly kissed his beautiful wife goodbye while it was still dark. Kirsten couldn't sleep after that, so she packed her bags, then went downstairs to the kitchen. She made some coffee and sat at the counter, wishing so much that she could stay. Jillian joined her shortly and they talked together. Jillian wished she could find the words to make things better, but there really weren't any.

Kirsten had tears in her eyes as the boys bounded down the stairs for breakfast, and she wiped them away quickly. Anthony poured himself his usual huge bowl of cereal, and Jillian made omelets for Kirsten and Tommy John.

They were taking Kirsten to the airport after breakfast, then Jillian had a surprise for the boys—and for John Anthony. She had called Carson the night before, and after explaining the situation, asked if they could stop in for lunch and watch the production the next afternoon.

"Anything you want, you've got it, Jillian," he said. He was so thrilled about the way things had turned out with the casting and thought the show was going better than he would have ever dreamed.

"Watch out, Carson. I'll take you up on that. I still have a favor to ask, but it can wait until my company is gone. We'll see you tomorrow at lunch."

They deposited Kirsten at the airport. Everyone was trying their best to act bravely, but their hearts were hurting. After kissing their mother goodbye, it was a quiet ride into Hollywood for the usually talkative boys.

Kathy J. Jacobson

"This isn't the way we usually go home, is it, Aunt Jillian?" Tommy John asked. The young man noticed everything.

"No. We're taking a little detour today," she said and smiled.

They pulled up to a gate where a guard stood in a booth. "Hello, Ms. Jillian! We're expecting you," he said with a smile, and the gate lifted.

"Thank you, Ralph. It's nice to see you again," she said, smiling back at the kind man.

It was the same studio where John, Luz, Carson, and she had shot their award-winning movie, and many memories came flooding back. They traveled the "streets" and parked the car. Entering a huge building, Jillian asked the woman inside where lunch was being served today. The woman, too, was expecting them, although she did not know Jillian by sight.

"Are you Jillian?"

"I am," Jillian replied.

The woman gave them all visitor passes to hang around their necks. "Right this way," the woman said and led them down a few halls to the room where the meal service was set up.

They stepped into the room, and John Anthony spotted them immediately, almost dropping the tray of food he was in the process of carrying to a table. Hugs ensued, then the boys helped themselves to the buffet. They were in heaven. John Anthony introduced them to the cast, and the boys were almost too excited to eat—*almost*. They cleaned their plates and went back for dessert. Jillian had a great time sharing a table with Monica and Luz, who Jillian sensed were fast becoming friends.

Then lunch ended, and it was time for filming. John Anthony wasn't in the first brief scene, so he proudly sat between his sons as Monica and Luz's characters snarled at one another. Then it was his turn, and John Anthony was "on." They turned their chairs to face a set that was an operating room. John Anthony was helped into scrubs and warned the boys that it could get pretty gory, to which the response was "cool."

They enjoyed the afternoon immensely, even with the gore. The scene went well. It really was an amazing cast and crew. One thing bothered Tommy John a bit, though. One of the female "doctors" assisting his dad in the scene, obviously had a crush on his character, based on the lines they were reciting back and forth. He knew his dad and the woman were actors, and it was just a script, but it still bugged him.

Anthony, on the other hand, noticed only the blood and guts and wondered how they made everything seem so real. He announced afterward that he thought he knew what he wanted to do when he grew up—work in Hollywood in special effects.

Around seven o'clock, John Anthony was given the okay to finally go home. Jillian told the boys to go ahead and ride with their dad, and she would follow behind. It was strange watching John Anthony hop into the driver's seat of John's vehicle. He looked more like his great-uncle to her with each passing day, and she noticed how he had many of John's mannerisms, too, as did his father, Tommy. He and Tommy also had John's heart. She sure did love these special Romano men, including the young ones who were currently fighting over who got to ride shotgun.

Jillian had worried the boys would be lost without their mom during the daytime hours, but they were anything but. The combined forces of Tommy and Maria, Marty and Michael, and Jillian helped make the rest of their time in California a true success.

Tommy and Maria had taken them to Universal Studios. Afterward, Anthony reiterated his desire to work in special effects and

Kathy J. Jacobson

design. He had been truly impressed, even with some of the early expressions of the art. He spent the next morning surfing the Internet for colleges that were best in those areas, and at dinner that evening, he announced he was going to do everything he could to get into the California Institute of the Arts when he graduated from high school. John Anthony looked surprised, then pleased.

While the boys had been gone that day, Jillian had stopped by to see Grace and ask if she could fit a surfing outing with two teenage boys into her schedule. She was working the desk that day. It was supposed to be one of her days off, but a worker had called in sick. Jillian had told her that Max had suggested she contact her and passed on his compliment about her being a very good surfer. Grace had smiled and blushed a bit when Jillian had mentioned Max—even before the compliment.

Jillian noticed this but was in a hurry to get going. She was meeting Carol for lunch. It had been too long since they had had one of their talks. Luckily, they seemed to do less crying now and more talking and laughing. It had been so healing for both of them to feel and remember—not only their pain, but the love which preceded it.

Grace had a day off coming up and agreed to an outing with the boys. Grace suggested the same beach they had surfed at with Max, saying, as had Max, that it was best for beginners. They would meet by the board rentals at 7:00 a.m. and catch the first waves.

Jillian thought about Grace as she drove to meet Carol. Jillian wished she had signed up for a session with her when she had the chance. She hadn't had a workout with her for weeks now, with all of her travels to the Midwest. Something seemed different about Grace today. She seemed more positive than she had in a long time. She was more like her old self, yet, there was something else. She seemed more mature, or perhaps more self-confident. Maybe the wedding details were going better. Jillian hadn't spoken with anyone in the family for weeks, she realized. She would have to call Pete later in the day and say hello.

During lunch, Carol relayed to Jillian that she thought her husband, Jerry, might be one of the kindest and wisest people on earth. He had come up with the idea that Carol, her children, and grandchildren should go to Madison and have a "remembrance celebration" at her late husband, Len's, grave. Now, it had become an official plan. Even her daughter, Carrie, would participate, which Carol said she would truly believe when she saw it.

Carol rarely saw Carrie, although she had come to California for Mark and Lena's wedding and one other time briefly for a visit when she had been in the area for some new software technology training. Carol knew that Carrie had always struggled with her father's death. While Carrie hadn't displayed the angry, defiant problem behaviors her brother had, she had detached from her family after her loss. She had never wanted to return to her home in Madison and had become distant with her mother and brother.

Carrie had dedicated her life mainly to her work. Carol had been pleasantly surprised when Carrie announced she had gotten married over her final spring break of college. Even though she wished she would have had a wedding in Madison, she had been grateful her daughter was not completely alone in the world.

Tears filled Jillian's eyes when she heard the plan, not because she was sad, but because she thought it was one of the nicest things she'd ever heard. She asked Carol if she could anonymously blog about it. Carol gave her permission, saying it might help other people in similar situations. Jillian then told her about her own visit to the cemetery in Belvidere. It had been a good day, and she reported the story of the cardinal, too.

"That gives me goosebumps, Jillian," Carol said, her eyes moist.

"It gave me them, too. And it also gave me a little extra reassurance," she said.

Carol put her hand on Jillian's and nodded.

Kathy J. Jacobson

"Pete, how are you?" Jillian asked on the phone. They had been playing phone tag for hours and had finally connected.

"Hey, Jillian. Okay—busy. One of our attendants is sick today. Grace has been holding down the fort for her since seven. I'm on my way to "number one" so I can relieve her. She shouldn't have to do that on her day off," he said. "Number one" was Pete's nickname for his first fitness center, built with a wedding gift from his in-laws.

"I saw her earlier today, matter of fact. I wrangled her into taking John Anthony's sons surfing before they head back east."

"Great, that will make her happy. She loves to surf."

"Speaking of happy, Grace seemed more positive—more relaxed. Her wedding plans must be moving along well," Jillian said.

"We haven't talked in a long time, have we?" Pete said. "I'm sorry, I should have told you this a few weeks ago, but Grace's plans have changed. She and Christopher are no longer engaged."

"Oh, my. She didn't mention it, but we only had a few minutes to talk. She was working, and I was rushing off to have lunch with a friend. Is she okay?"

"I think she is more than okay. She was the one who called it off. I can't say that I was too upset about it. It didn't seem like a natural match to me, and maybe I shouldn't say this, but I sometimes felt like she was 'settling,'" Pete said.

"Well, if that was the case, she most likely made the right call."

"Only time will tell, I guess," Pete responded. "I'm just pulling in at the club now, Jillian. How about lunch at Paco's next Monday at noon? We can catch up."

"It's a date," she said.

"Sure—*now* you want to date me," he said kiddingly.

"I love you, Pete," she said sincerely.

"Right back at ya, Jillian," he said.

Jillian smiled as she put down her phone. Pete and his entire family—true blessings from God.

Chapter Twenty-Two

Ricardo threw his arms around his parents as they exited from the long hallway at O'Hare into the baggage area. It had only been a couple of months, but it had seemed like a lifetime in some ways.

He had given his assistant some extra duties this week so he could have some time off with his parents. They were only visiting for a week, and he wanted to make the most of their time. Of course, the main thing his folks wanted to see was the Esperanza Center and its satellite projects. Ricardo had spoken so excitedly and proudly about them, and they were equally proud of their son for choosing to work for such an organization.

Robert and Karen themselves had shared their talents with the original center. Karen taught people how to read or improve their reading and later began a book club there, which was still going. Robert had been instrumental in the legalities of getting the original non-profit off the ground. Ricardo had always been so proud of them, and their example had led him to his eventual work with the organization.

Ricardo loved his current work. It didn't even feel like work most days. However, he did admit he was often grateful for his years making a ridiculous amount of money at a huge for-profit firm.

It had allowed him to do this work now, for less pay, and still have assets like his condo, some investments, and a reliable vehicle. He was amazed sometimes at how things worked out in life.

As he had waited for his parents to arrive, he thought about how their family had come to be. It all began when his mother decided to go back to college after many years and became a reading teacher. Ricardo had been a student in his mother's classroom, and he had gravitated toward her kind, motherly ways from the very beginning. When his father was sick and dying, and no family member could be found to take him in, a social worker asked him if he knew any adults with whom he might stay. He had told her, "My teacher." His teacher became his foster mother, and eventually, his mother. Now, his mother, Karen, and his dad, Robert, were here to visit him—in Chicago.

Their first afternoon in the city, they took a walk around Ricardo's new neighborhood, then stopped at the grocery store. Karen was going to cook for "her boy," for the first time in months. Ricardo was very excited.

While they ate fish with Karen's fish sauce she had brought from California at Ricardo's request, they made plans for the week. They would begin with the Esperanza Center the next day, then hit some of the "basics" over the rest of the week, when Ricardo's work schedule allowed. On Friday and Saturday, Ricardo would be off and show them some of his favorite sights and take in a "Broadway in Chicago" show. On Sunday afternoon, he would take them back to the airport to catch their flight home.

They made a list of Ricardo's favorite restaurants and a couple of others he wanted to try. At one point a while back, he had thought about asking Alison out to one of them, but he hadn't heard from her since "the kiss." He, too, had not called or texted her since that night, even though he could not stop thinking about her. He had picked up the phone several times, but each time, he chickened out. Then his parents had announced their plans, and the right time hadn't presented itself—or at least that is what he told himself.

Midway through the week, Karen pronounced Chicago one of her favorite cities. She loved the architecture, but most of all, she loved the food. Karen loved to cook and was considered an excellent cook. She also loved to eat good food and appreciated the variety of offerings. She also commented on the heartier portions at smaller prices in the midwestern city. Karen also enjoyed the lake and its cool breezes, although she mentioned it must cause a lot of bad hair days.

Thursday night's restaurant choice was the Mexican one that had catered Zoe's party and where he and Alison had gone "that night." Ricardo had almost suggested another place, but he knew his mom would love this spot, so it stayed on the agenda.

Zoe had a day off on Thursday. As a newer CNA, she worked many weekend shifts. Actually, she was working much more than she had ever dreamed she would. She was getting many overtime hours, and while it was tiring, all of her friends were gone for the summer and she liked the idea of having a lot of spending money for her first year in college. Her tuition, housing in the dorm, meal plan, and books would be covered by her parents—most of it by her father. That meant that whatever she made during the summer was hers to spend on clothes and recreation during the year. That pleased her greatly.

Zoe was getting excited about school, remembering how much she had enjoyed the campus tour. A friend from her high school, who would be a junior at UW-Madison in the fall, had contacted her to get together when she arrived. It was nice to know someone else in town, even though one of the things she liked about the large university was the chance to be anonymous for a while.

Even though her friends had been kind and didn't bring it up to her, she knew everyone was talking about her parents' divorce and the reason for it. She had always tried to pretend that things were fine at home, when she knew they were not. Her father had rarely been home, especially in the past few years, and when he was, he was distant—like he was just playing a part. It turned out he was.

She had known he wasn't a good husband to her mom, but she had never dreamed that he had been cheating on her so often and, most recently, with a young woman he was now planning to marry. He was going to be a father again, too. Zoe suddenly felt sorry for the baby and hoped he would be a better father to him or her, but she wasn't sure he was capable of doing that.

Her dad had rarely been interested in her while she was growing up. She remembered him coming to a dance recital once when she was little. He came to school once when she received a science award in sixth grade, but he hadn't even come to her senior awards night and looked less than thrilled at her high school graduation. That night after the ceremony, he had given her an embarrassingly huge spray of red roses, posed for a photo with her and the flowers, pressed a few hundred dollar bills in her hand, and then he was off.

She wasn't sure how someone as nice as her mom ended up with someone like him. She felt her mom deserved someone better than that. Her mom was always so thoughtful and kind.

"So, what do you want to do on your day off?" her mother had asked her the evening before.

"Sleep," was her first answer.

"Good plan," Alison said. "How about dinner? May I take you out to dinner somewhere? Your choice," she added.

"How about our favorite?" Zoe asked excitedly.

Alison's face froze. All she could think of lately was that last dinner out with Ricardo—and what happened in the car.

"I could meet you there," Zoe said. "I have a car now," she said smiling.

Alison didn't like the idea of Zoe driving all the way in to the restaurant, so she suggested meeting at a certain spot, and she would drive from there.

"It's a date!" Zoe said happily.

Karen and Robert loved the Mexican restaurant. The only problem, his mother proclaimed, was not being able to try all the items on the menu.

Rick had gotten off early, and they went to the restaurant with the intent of beating the work crowd. Even on weeknights, the restaurant was popular and often bustling. It was a good idea, as the place was filling up as they ate their desserts of chocolate enchiladas, ice cream with mango bits and guava juice, and another ice cream dessert topped with pistachios and fried cinnamon wheat sticks. Karen was taking notes on the foods she had that evening, planning to offer some of them at a future book club meeting at her home.

After paying the bill, the family exited the restaurant just as Alison and Zoe were about to enter it.

"Ricardo!" Zoe exclaimed, and hugged him.

Ricardo was in shock, not from the hug, but from seeing Alison again. He pulled himself together somewhat and stammered through the introductions. They talked for a few minutes, Ricardo reminding Karen that Alison and Zoe were Jillian's family. Karen remembered meeting Alison at Ricardo's adoption, but Alison had only been a teen then. The attractive teenager had grown into a beautiful, mature woman with an eighteen-year-old daughter of her own. She and Robert had not gone to Jillian's house after John's funeral—Robert had been feeling under the weather—or they may have met once more.

Alison reminded her daughter that they had a reservation, and they excused themselves. Alison could hardly stand to look at Ricardo, yet her eyes kept gravitating to his. Whenever they connected, she averted her eyes as quickly as she could. She could feel heat moving up her neck and hoped she wasn't as flushed as she felt.

Ricardo had seemed equally ill at ease, yet his eyes kept moving to Alison as well. He thought about her day and night. His parents' visit had helped relieve some of that, but even company couldn't completely stop the thoughts of how much he wanted to kiss Alison again.

That night, Ricardo could not sleep. He got up and paced on the small balcony of his apartment, then sat down on a patio chair and put his head in his hands. In a bit, he heard faint footsteps, then the sliding screen door opening behind him.

"I'm sorry," he said, turning and seeing the outline of his mom. "I hope I didn't wake you."

"It wasn't you. I ate too much food tonight, and I always have trouble sleeping when I do that," Karen admitted, sitting down on a chair next to her son. "But it was worth it. How about you?"

Ricardo didn't want to tell her what was really on his heart, so he talked about his other pressing concerns. "There's a lot going on at work. Monday morning we're meeting with two candidates for the directorship."

"That's good—isn't it?"

"I guess ... yes," he said.

"That doesn't sound very convincing, son." She was quiet a moment. "Have you considered taking the job yourself?"

Ricardo almost fell off his chair and was glad it was fairly dark on the porch so his mom couldn't see the surprise on his face. He had, indeed, thought about it.

"It's pretty far away from home ... and you guys," he said.

"Ricardo, we know how to get on an airplane, you know," she said. "We really have enjoyed it here. Your father even wondered how much one of these little short-term lease apartments cost. He said he could see spending more time in this place. And of course, if you were here, we'd be back for certain."

Again, Ricardo felt shocked. His parents had lived in California their entire lives, and while they had traveled a lot, he had never heard of them wanting to spend any major amount of time anywhere else. He also knew how much his mom missed him even when they lived in the same city, let alone two thousand miles apart.

"I think it may be too late for that, Mom," he said.

"That's too bad. The center is wonderful, Ricardo, and doing such special things in the community." She paused once more. "And there are such nice people in Chicago, too," she said in an unusual tone. Ricardo wished he could see her face so he could read it better.

"Yes, there are," he said quietly.

There was silence for a minute, then his mom began to speak again. "Did I ever tell you that before you came along, there was a time I thought your father's and my marriage might be in jeopardy?"

Ricardo had never heard such a thing before and expressed great surprise.

"Well, it wasn't good. Your dad and I had grown apart after our many years of failed attempts to have a family. He worked all the time. I was home alone—a lot. I was not happy. I did not know how to get his attention or fix our situation. Then Jillian came to my book club and we became friends. She told me about her parents and some of the tactics her mother used with her father when he worked too much. I tried them—and they worked. That was the beginning of a new chapter in our lives."

She paused, "Ricardo—relationships are a lot of work. They are not always perfect. They are risky. There are peaks and valleys, times of great joy, and sometimes times of hurt—because we are people—human beings. But all in all, having someone special to love in one's life is worth every bit of it."

Ricardo was quiet. He had never heard his mother talk this way before. He didn't really know what to say, so he said nothing.

"I think my stomach has finally settled. Goodnight, Ricardo," she said, putting her hand on his shoulder. He put his hand on hers. He sure won the lottery when it came to his parents.

"Good night, Mom. I love you," he said.

"I love you, too," she said and kissed the top of his head like she used to when he was little.

Chapter Twenty-Three

John Anthony was sitting by the pool, staring at it and thinking about how much his sons had enjoyed swimming in it. He had been pretty miserable since his family went back to New York, but he was trying hard not to show it for Jillian's sake. Fortunately, he loved the show, his co-stars, and everything else about the situation. He had discovered he enjoyed acting in front of a camera—a lot. If only his family were with him, he would be in paradise.

Jillian sat down next to him. "It's so quiet, isn't it?"

He nodded. He was afraid if he spoke, he might become quite emotional.

"It's okay to miss them, John Anthony. It means we have people we love," she said.

Again, he nodded, then sighed. Then, as if his thoughts had brought it on, his cell phone rang. It was Kirsten and he happily answered it. Jillian excused herself and went back into the house.

"Hi, sweetheart! How are you?" John Anthony said, grinning a classic Romano smile. His smile faded seconds later as Kirsten relayed a call she had just received from Tommy John's football coach.

He said that Tommy John was not participating wholehearted-ly in practice and had wondered if there was a problem. She had asked their son, but he said that nothing was wrong, but she could tell that there was.

John Anthony didn't know who to talk to first—the coach or his son. Maybe he should hear the coach's side of it first, and said he would call him as soon as they hung up.

"How are you, Kirsten?"

"I'm okay, but I miss you so much," she said. "I'm so sorry, again, about having to leave in the middle of our visit. It was the right thing to do, but I absolutely hated it."

"I hated it, too, but you did the right thing. You always do. That's one of the reasons I love you so much," John Anthony said sincerely.

"I love you, too. Now, maybe you should call the coach. Perhaps it's just all a misunderstanding."

"I will, the second I hang up. Kirsten ..." He couldn't finish his sentence.

"I know, Jay." Kirsten sometimes called him that. It was how one pronounced his initials, J.A., "Jay." She was the only person in the world who called him that.

"Talk to you later," he said. He was beginning to loathe the word goodbye.

He immediately called the football coach. Tommy John had been on the varsity team since his sophomore year and took over as the starting quarterback after just a few games that season. He loved his coach—and football. John Anthony thought perhaps something had happened with a teammate, or maybe a girl problem. Tommy John didn't mention anything, but one never knows with teenagers.

The young man the coach described on the phone did not sound like anyone John Anthony knew—especially not his eldest son. While Tommy John might have some struggles academically, he was usually the model student in every other way. He was bright, hard-working, kind, and respectful. The coach told John Anthony that if things didn't change soon, he would have to start another quarterback. He couldn't have a person who didn't seem to care, was arguing with teammates, and was not paying attention to the coaches, as the team's leader.

John Anthony's day off was three days away. He wondered if he should try to go home for twenty-four hours. He had told the coach he would check in again after the next day's practice to see if things were improving.

John Anthony went into the house. He needed someone to talk to, and his Aunt Jillian was one of the best listeners he had ever known outside of his wife. He could sure understand how his great-uncle ended up falling in love with someone like her. He thought that they were two really lucky and spoiled men.

John Anthony didn't have to call the coach the next evening, the coach called him. He told him that Tommy John had almost gotten into a physical fight with another player on the field. The coach was genuinely concerned about the boy. He had told Tommy John not to come to practice the next day. He wanted him to have a long weekend to think over his behavior.

John Anthony knew the coach loved his son. He was doing everything he could to help him succeed and was also trying hard not to officially suspend Tommy John from the team. John Anthony appreciated that, and told the coach he would talk with his son this weekend, hopefully in person.

He ended the call, called his wife, and then called Carson Stone, Jr. He explained that he had a family situation and asked if there was any way he could leave early on Saturday. Carson looked over the production schedule, which was all on his tablet. He played around with it for a few minutes.

"I can do better than that. Take Saturday off, Romano," he said.

John Anthony could barely believe his ears. He booked a flight home for late the next night.

John Anthony sat at his kitchen table with Tommy John late Saturday morning. Kirsten was in the next room, waiting until the right moment for both of them to talk to their son together.

"What is going on, son?" John Anthony finally asked, as Tommy John was not talking.

"Nothing," was his first answer.

"I'm sorry. It's not 'nothing' when your mother and I get calls from your coach saying you are not working hard, are not listening, and are arguing—almost fighting—with teammates. It's not 'nothing' when you have to sit out a practice."

Tommy John's eyes reddened and grew watery.

"What is it, Tommy John? You can tell me. There isn't anything we can't handle. We love you no matter what," John Anthony told his obviously hurting son.

"You're getting a divorce, aren't you?" Tommy John finally said, his voice quivering.

"What?!"

"You and Mom—you're getting a divorce, aren't you?"

"Son, I don't know what gave you that idea, but we are not getting a divorce—not now—not ever."

"That's what my friend's parents said, too, just before his dad moved out, and they got a divorce."

At this point, John Anthony called the waiting Kirsten into the room. He wasn't sure how to proceed. John Anthony and Kirsten sat next to each other at the table. John Anthony filled her in on what he had just heard and asked his son if he had relayed it adequately, to which he just nodded.

"What would ever give you that idea?" Kirsten asked.

Tommy John went on to list his main concerns—his father moving to the other side of the country, then his mother leaving in the middle of their California visit. And then he added that Aunt Alison just got a divorce, and he never thought she would, either.

The two adults at the table had to remember that they were not seventeen and how these things might appear to someone who was.

"Why can't we all just live together?" Tommy John asked.

John Anthony was never so sorry he had taken his current role. He tried to calmly explain that it was a huge opportunity for his career, and for the sake of their family in the long run. He also had taken the role to honor his late uncle John and explained more about that.

Tommy John was a very sensitive and thoughtful young man, and he really did get those things—especially honoring Uncle John, to whom he had looked up to himself.

"I get that, but why can't we all be together and do that?"

"Mostly, because your mom has worked hard to open her own office ..." John Anthony started to say.

"I could do that anywhere," Kirsten cut in.

"Really?" John Anthony looked at her, a bit of surprise in his voice.

John Anthony continued, "And one of the other biggest reasons was football. We thought you would want to finish out your high school years on your team. It's meant so much to you in the past ..."

"It did ... it does," Tommy John admitted. "But, I'd rather be with you," he said.

John Anthony's heart was breaking for his son, but it was also full of love. He didn't quite know what to say next. He thought for a moment, then proceeded.

"Tommy John. I love you so very much. I love your mother so very much. I love Anthony so very much. We will figure this out, okay? It might take a while, but we will figure it out. And again, we are not getting a divorce—ever. Your mom and you and your brother are

Kathy J. Jacobson

the best things in my life, and don't forget that."

It was like a mask had been taken off of his son's face. He now appeared to be the real Tommy John again.

"May I be excused?" Tommy John asked.

"You may, but you are not leaving the house," John Anthony said.

"I know—I'm grounded, aren't I? That's okay. I have to write an apology to coach, and to Jason, and maybe the entire team ..."

"Start with your coach," John Anthony said. His son had a way of being way too hard on himself.

John Anthony wondered if he would have any voice left by Monday morning, after all the talking he, Kirsten, and the boys did over a twenty-four hour period. They finally came up with a possible plan.

Since it was almost time for school to begin, it seemed silly to make a big move right then. They also didn't know if, or when, the show might be renewed. They decided the boys and Kirsten should stay in New York for at least the first semester. Tommy John could finish his high school career with his football team.

If they knew the show was renewed by then, they would evaluate the idea of a move after the first semester. If they didn't have that information yet, they would wait until the spring to make a decision and move during the next summer, if needed. In the meantime, Kirsten would put some feelers out about selling her practice. People did it all the time. Sometimes they were serious and went through with it, other times not. John Anthony had been surprised by her willingness to give up her practice, but she said she had missed him so much that it definitely came in second to being with him.

Most of all, John Anthony was amazed at how much the boys seemed to enjoy the idea of moving to the opposite end of the country. It made some sense, he guessed. Anthony was still gushing on about how he was going to go to college in California and wanted to work in Hollywood, and both boys were constantly reminiscing about swimming in the pool and surfing in the ocean.

Tommy John and Anthony had also mentioned that their grandparents now lived there and Aunt Jillian, too, and they would love living near them. The boys had had a blast going to Universal Studios with Tommy and Maria, and Jillian treated them like her own grandchildren. John Anthony had never considered that that would mean so much to them, as they had lived far away from family their entire lives, but he was glad it did.

"So, was it a good weekend off?" Carson Stone, Jr. asked John Anthony at the crack of dawn Monday morning.

"It was more than good. Thank you so much, Carson," John Anthony said sincerely. "If there's ever anything I can do for you, let me know."

"As Jillian would say, you might regret saying that one day," Carson responded.

"I mean it."

"We'll see," Carson said with a sly smile.

While John Anthony had been gone, Jillian had called him, as she had promised she would. She was ready to ask her "favor" of him. She explained it to him in detail and was waiting for his answer.

Carson told her he would consider it and get back to her. First, they had to get this show "on the road," as he put it. The pilot would air in six weeks. He thought it was very special, but Hollywood could be fickle. What one person thought was fantastic, could be labeled a flop, and vice-versa.

Jillian said she was willing to wait. Carson's next steps were to get through the airing of the pilot, then, if it went reasonably well, he would say yes to Jillian, and then help encourage the other person she hoped would be a part of the plan—John Anthony. When the time was right, Carson would try his best for Jillian.

Carson, Jr. had gotten to know John Anthony and Jillian better over the past couple of months. He had known them for years—especially Jillian. But now as an adult, he realized these people were not only extremely talented people, but true quality people. His mom and dad had often alluded to that, but he had been way too young and immature before to really get it. Now he got it. His mother had told him once that the Romanos were like familia. He now knew what she meant.

Chapter Twenty-Four

Early on Sunday afternoon, Alison picked up her phone, then put it back down, picked up her phone, then laid it down once more. Since Thursday evening, all she could think about was Ricardo. What were the chances of them running into one another at the restaurant? It almost felt like she was being forced to deal with the situation, once and for all. She needed to talk to him. She needed to explain—why.

It was Sunday afternoon, and Ricardo had just said goodbye to his parents at the airport. Now he was sitting at a gas station a mile away from O'Hare. He had filled his tank, but didn't know which way he was turning when he left the lot. He held his phone in his hand with Alison's number pulled up. He needed to talk to her. He needed to tell her—why.

Ricardo finally pressed the number as Alison simultaneously hit his. They both went to voicemail. They were disappointed until each noticed the call from the other, and dialed again. Ricardo was a bit faster than Alison was this time, and the call went through.

"Alison, can we talk?"

"I was just calling you to ask the same thing. Yes, I think we should," she said.

Zoe had just left the house and was working until eleven that night. It was the perfect time to connect.

"I could come to you," he mentioned. Ricardo had rented a car when his parents had arrived and had it for another two weeks. "You commute every day. You don't need to on Sunday, too."

Why did he have to be so nice? "That's very considerate of you, Ricardo," she said and agreed to meet him at a park on the edge of Libertyville, as it was a beautiful afternoon.

He arrived half an hour later. Alison watched him as he stepped out of the rental. Why did he have to be so attractive?

They walked for a bit, then spied a bench and sat down. They both began to speak at the same time, saying the exact same thing, "I'm scared."

"You first," Ricardo said softly.

Alison told him everything. She relayed how she had fallen for Cameron, then about his philandering ways from the very beginning. He had had a number of affairs, but his latest was different. He was having a child with this woman and planned to marry her. When she finished, she told him, "That's why I'm scared." She thought for sure this information would make Ricardo want to head for the hills. "Your turn," she said, wondering what Ricardo must think of her.

Well, once Ricardo had finished talking, she felt like crawling in a hole. She knew that he was adopted, and that his home life prior to that had not been good, but she hadn't realized the level of abuse and neglect he had endured for many years. He also told her that his family had a history of violence and alcohol abuse, and sometimes he wondered if deep down, one reason he shied away from relationships was because he was afraid he would somehow pass these awful things down to yet another generation. Then he mentioned the other main reason for his fears—Tina. Alison was the only person, other than his parents, with whom he discussed his history with Tina.

When he finished he said, "That's why I'm scared."

"How did you end up being such a nice person with all of that?" Alison asked, almost like she was thinking out loud.

"I believe I was saved—just in the nick of time—by two people God put in my life, who showed me what real love is." And then he added, "And they were also wise enough to get me into therapy shortly after I walked through their door. I am eternally grateful for all of that," he said.

"I am too," Alison said softly. "They helped make the man ..." She couldn't say what she wanted to say—the man with whom she was falling in love.

Ricardo turned to her, took her hands, then looked into her eyes. "I think we could both use another surprise," he said, in almost a whisper.

Alison nodded, then their lips met.

The interviews for the director of the Esperanza Center had been a disappointment to almost everyone—except Ricardo. The interview team—leaders of the various programs and projects—met with him afterward, wondering what they were going to do. Then Ricardo surprised them all.

"I believe there is one more candidate to consider," he said after each had given their wary assessments.

They all looked at each other. They hadn't heard of any other applicants, and the two they had interviewed so far had not met their expectations.

"Did you receive another application?" one of them asked.

"Not exactly. This person just decided yesterday to put his hat into the ring, so to speak," he said.

"Do you think this person is better than the other applicants?"

"I'll leave that answer up to you," he responded, then told them he was interested in the position.

First, there was a look of shock on their faces. Then, the cheers began. Ricardo had endeared himself to everyone at the center over the past few months. No one had been looking forward to him leaving. People were shaking his hand and saying the nicest things about him. Bertha, the head of the after-school homework and summer school tutoring programs, came over and hugged him fiercely. "I've been praying to God to send us the right person! God sent you!" she exclaimed.

Ricardo thought Bertha was on to something and was so excited about what appeared to be God's plans—for both his professional and personal lives.

Karen and Robert had been thrilled when they heard their son's news. Of course, they would miss him, but as Karen spoke into the phone, Robert was already surfing the Internet for rentals in Chicago. Karen and Robert had done very well for themselves over the years financially, and had had only one child to raise from the age of ten to adulthood. They had the time and the resources to visit him often and were certain that would make the transition easier for their son—and for them.

Ricardo had been concerned about Jillian's reaction to this news. She would now need a new home office director, but she had told him she was very happy for him. "And Alison," she had tacked on at the end of that sentence. *How did she always know these things?*

Alison tried to hide her excitement at Ricardo's news but couldn't quite conceal her surprise, and then her joy, over the phone. She invited Ricardo out to the house for dinner that evening to celebrate. Zoe was going to be home, too. Knowing her daughter, and the way she had hugged Ricardo at the restaurant, she was quite certain this news would make her happy, too.

Ricardo told her he was cooking, so get ready for some enchiladas that were just as good, if not better, than their favorite restaurant's. When Alison expressed her surprise that he cooked, he made certain to credit his mother for his expertise in the kitchen. Alison was thrilled.

Jillian was back to her workouts with Grace once a week, even though she had gotten back into good shape. She enjoyed spending time with her goddaughter and had been pleased that Grace seemed to be doing better. However, it still felt to Jillian like something was hanging over the young woman's head, and her spirit.

To begin a conversation, Jillian asked if Grace had done any surfing lately. When she asked this, Grace's face had instantly turned a dark pink, and she seemed flustered.

"Did I bring up a bad subject?" Jillian asked.

Grace didn't answer that question, but instead answered Jillian's first. "The surfing lesson with the boys at Sunset Point was my last time out," she said. "I really need to get back out there. I'm just not sure when I'll get the chance, or who to surf …" She didn't finish her sentence.

"You went with Max once, didn't you?"

Grace's face went from pink to scarlet.

"Ah, yes. Well, twice, actually. Once with him, and the next time was with him and his friends."

"It didn't go well?" Jillian asked.

"It was fine ... it was great ... he was great ..." She stopped speaking and looked like she was searching for words. "He is a great surfer," she finally said.

Jillian waited. She could tell there was more, but Grace just couldn't get it out.

"You didn't care for him personally?" Jillian asked finally, a bit surprised to think that Grace would not have liked Max. Everyone she knew adored him and wanted to be his friend.

"I like him ... a lot," she added, softly.

Jillian was surprised that she hadn't picked up on this more quickly. Grace liked Max but didn't necessarily want to like him. Jillian herself had once known that feeling—when she was falling in love with John.

"You read books, don't you, Grace?"

Jillian's namesake nodded affirmatively. "I'll drop a copy of *Noted!* off for you this afternoon. I'm working on the screenplay for it now. I'd love some feedback from a younger reader like you—maybe get your thoughts on which parts would be best for the screen, or best left out," Jillian said.

Grace had been way too young for the book when it first came out, and Jillian thought there may be some situations and insights in it that might be helpful to Grace now that she was a grown woman who, Jillian believed, was fighting her feelings.

Jillian did indeed drop the book off to Grace later that day. Grace wasn't going to read it right away, but she started it, and then found herself not being able to put it down. She read the "author's note," and realized that the story was based on Jillian and John's own story. That made her want to read it even more. Luckily, the next day was one of her days off.

By the following afternoon, she had finished the book. She had cried when Jillian had planned to leave the house, and John, and again when she thought it was too late to reconsider. She understood why Jillian had wanted to run away, though. She had wanted to do the same ever since she called off the wedding. It's not that she was really sad about it. In fact, she felt relieved.

But she didn't trust herself in matters of the heart. She had thought Christopher was so special and then felt he was nothing of the sort. Then she met Max ... and he was too good to be true. There had to be a catch.

She closed the book, then mindlessly flipped through the pages once more. She hadn't noticed the first time, but Jillian had signed the book to her and written a message:

"Grace—don't be afraid to follow your heart."

Chapter Twenty-Five

It was November—almost time for Thanksgiving and the holiday season. Everyone had warned Jillian how difficult those "firsts" would be—the first birthday, the first holidays, the first anniversary, etc., without one's loved one. Frankly, Jillian had gotten through John's birthday about as well as she thought humanly possible, so perhaps the holidays would be okay, too.

She was looking forward to spending Thanksgiving with Marty and Michael at the home of Drew, Greta, and Cleo. It was also Drew and Greta's thirtieth anniversary, so they would be celebrating. They had invited John and Jillian almost a year before to join them on this occasion, as they had been the best man and matron of honor at the wedding ceremony. Jillian was bound and determined not to disappoint them. She was certain there would be difficult moments, but she was happy to be with close friends and family on this particular occasion—the first major holiday without John.

Jillian knew deep down, too, that she wasn't as worried about all those "firsts," as much as she was about all the seconds, thirds, fourths, and so on. Life without her best friend and lover was a reality, and it was a harsh reality, and one that could realistically go on for a good deal of time. Some days she thought she was getting more used to it. Others—not so much.

The "not so much" days were what Jillian called her "wallowing days." She just needed to "have it all out," it seemed, from time to time. But once she did that, she often felt better and was strengthened to go on. Once she let that pain out, it was like she was purging her body and soul of it. So, she let herself have those days. The good news was that they seemed to be fewer and farther between. She was grateful for that, and also that they often seemed to be followed by stretches of wonderful creativity and achievement.

It was after one of those days months before that she had called Carson Stone, Jr. and told him she was ready to cash in on a favor he had promised. Jillian told Carson how she had been approached just prior to John's death about adapting her book, *Noted!*, the story of how she and John ended up together, into a screenplay. There was a company waiting to hear from her.

Of course, after John's recent death, they had been after Jillian even more, saying the story would be of even more interest now that John had died. Even though they were trying to be sensitive to her pain, she knew they hoped to capitalize on the situation.

Jillian, however, had needed some time to even begin thinking about writing the screenplay. She needed to distance herself somewhat from that event so she could write more clearly. On the other hand, she didn't want to lose the passion for the story, and she knew that more people could be reached if it came out in a timely fashion.

So, on that day a few months ago, she felt she was ready to begin the project but only if Carson Stone, Jr. would direct it. She also asked that hopefully he would cast and encourage John Anthony to play his great-uncle, John, in the movie. Watching John Anthony over the past few months had given Jillian the idea. He was so much like John. He would be perfect, just as he had been in the return of *O.R.*

O.R. was a bigger success than anyone would have ever believed, with perhaps the exception of Carson Stone, Jr. who had envisioned it, created the remake, and brought it to life. Carson had recently called Jillian to say that they had already been "picked up" for a second season, which was almost unheard of in Hollywood. Therefore, Carson told Jillian he was "in" on the *Noted!* movie project, and he would talk to John Anthony right away. If he said yes, they could begin production possibly as soon as their winter filming break assuming they could cast it quickly enough and Jillian was ready to go with the screenplay.

Otherwise, it would have to wait until the entire filming season of *O.R.* was over. Luckily, Jillian had just finished the first draft of the screenplay. She would begin editing immediately and hoped Carson would look it over, too. The rest of the casting would be up to him.

The renewal of *O.R.* was an answer to John Anthony's family's prayers. Kirsten was going to sell her practice to the other therapist in her office, and another therapist was on board to come in and take her patients. She had scoped out the employment situation in Los Angeles, and the possibilities were endless. First, she said, she just wanted to enjoy being with her family for a while.

The boys were excited, too, and seemed happy to move mid-year, especially Tommy John. Outside of football, high school was sometimes a painful situation for him. He had discovered that fall that he was only two courses shy of what he needed for graduation at his current high school. He met with a wonderful new guidance counselor who mentioned that if he wanted to, he could take an online course for one of the requirements and do the other one remotely. If he completed those things, he could graduate in the spring with his classmates in New York.

Tommy John was ecstatic over that news. He was also thrilled that a California university had shown interest in him as a quarterback for their football team. After the rocky start in preseason practices, he did a 180 and had a stellar season and was the team captain. Now, his mission was to find out what type of support the college offered for students with academic issues like his.

The Romano families, therefore, were all feeling very grateful at Thanksgiving and were ready to celebrate at Alison's. They went out of their way to refer to the house as "Alison's" now, as she was its owner. John Anthony, Tommy, and Maria would be flying in late Wednesday night. Kirsten and the boys would be coming in from the East Coast early Thanksgiving morning. Zoe was home from college in Madison. It would truly be a day for giving thanks.

Alison was nervous as she put the turkey in the oven. She had gone over her mom's notes thoroughly. Even though her mom was in the house, she was trying to give her a bit of a break. Maria had been the one making Thanksgiving dinner for longer than Alison had been living. It seemed like she deserved to be cooked for, for once.

Alison was making all the family favorites as well as a few new items she had found online and another recipe from a friend at work. She was anxious to see how everything turned out. But dinner wasn't the only thing she was anxious about.

She had invited Ricardo and his parents, who were visiting from then until Christmas, to the dinner. She hoped her parents and brother and his family didn't mind and trusted it would be a good surprise. Her family had been supportive of their dating for the past almost six months, so she was quite sure they would be okay with it. Zoe had been excited—more than Alison would have expected.

Alison had timed her dinner just right. There was just a bit of time before everything would come out of the oven or refrigerator and be served. Everything was ready—except her. Luckily, all she needed to do was to slip on her new dress, the one that Zoe had insisted she buy for Thanksgiving dinner. Alison really did like the dress and thought Ricardo would too. She smiled at that thought.

Tommy answered the door when the doorbell rang. Alison had decided she had better tell him what was going on before she went up to change, so she had informed her father about their guests. Now Tommy greeted the Wilsons. "This is wonderful! Come in, Wilson family," Tommy said cheerfully as he opened the door. He guided them into the house, took their coats, and then introduced, or reintroduced them, to the rest of the family.

Maria and Kirsten were in the kitchen with Zoe opening bottles of wine and sparkling juice. Zoe ran to meet Ricardo and hugged him, as was her ritual. He always seemed pleased at that, and they smiled hugely at one another. The scene warmed Maria's heart.

The next stop was the family room, where John Anthony, Tommy John, and Anthony were engrossed in the pro football game that was airing. John Anthony muted the sound, and he and his sons stood up to greet the guests. This was turning into quite a party.

The boys moved over, and the Wilsons sat down on the plush sectional couch. While John Anthony and Ricardo's family talked and watched football, Tommy had gone to the kitchen to carve the turkey, then carried the huge bird to the table. Some traditions were worth keeping, Alison had thought, and she had wanted her father to do the honors.

The table was filled with delectable food. Alison used her grandmother's china and silver, two of the things Maria insisted be left at Alison's for just such occasions. Candles were lit. Small carved pumpkins hosting bright fall flowers in their carved out centers adorned the table, along with arrangements of Indian corn and gourds. It was perfect.

Zoe had gathered all the guests to the table. Alison was the last person to emerge from the kitchen. She could feel Ricardo's approving gaze as she moved toward the seat next to him. He couldn't take his eyes off her as he pulled the chair out for her.

Tommy or Maria usually said the blessing, but her mom suggested that Alison do it this year. It was her home. She was hesitant at first, but she knew her mom was right. She said she would give it a try. They all held hands around the table. Alison gripped Ricardo's extra tight for support.

"Lord, I am thankful today. I am thankful for this food. I am thankful for each person at this table, especially for their love." When she said that, Ricardo squeezed her hand, and she almost lost her train of thought. Then she continued. "I am thankful everyone arrived safely from both near and far, and I am so thankful we can be together today in this house—this home. We are truly blessed, and we give you thanks and praise. Amen!" There were resounding "amens" around the table.

The dinner tasted even better than it looked, and that was saying something.

"Remember to save room for dessert," Zoe advised as they were passing bowls and platters around for seconds. There were four kinds of pie cut and waiting on the kitchen table. Zoe took "orders," and she and Kirsten said they would bring the plates to everyone. Maria retrieved the large silver coffee pot and began pouring cups for the adults and Tommy John, who insisted he was old enough. His parents didn't argue with him this time.

"I'm not sure I can eat any pie right now," Alison said when Zoe asked what kind she wanted. Zoe's eyes flashed, and she looked at Ricardo. Alison didn't notice, thankfully.

Kathy J. Jacobson

"Mom—it's un-American not to have pie on Thanksgiving! How about a little slice?"

"Okay," she relented. "I'll take pumpkin, but just a sliver."

"Great, pumpkin it is," said a relieved Zoe.

Kirsten and Zoe served everyone pie beginning with the boys, who were bottomless pits. On the side of each plate of pie, Zoe had placed tiny fall-colored organza bags tied with ribbon. Inside were fall candies. Alison decided that this was why her daughter was so adamant about her having a piece of pie. It really was a cute idea. Zoe seemed pleased with the compliments she was receiving and remarked that she got the idea from the Internet.

Alison was the final person to be served. The boys were thinking about seconds on pie and asked what kinds were left. Alison could only shake her head. She was so full, she could barely eat the one small piece on her plate. She did admit, it did taste wonderful. And she would have to at least open the little goody bag Zoe had taken the time to make. Zoe seemed so proud of them, and they were adorable, Alison thought.

Alison slowly untied the bag. Inside were a few pieces of candy corn and a couple of what she assumed were chocolates wrapped in foil in various sizes. One had her name on it. *Personalized candies. What will they think of next?* "My name's on this one, so I'd better eat it," she said while unwrapping it. But the inside was not what she expected. It was a tiny rectangular wooden box with a small hinge on one end. Her name was on the box as well. "What is this?" She opened the box, and she felt her head begin to swim for a moment as her eyes took in a solitaire diamond ring.

Ricardo grabbed her around her shoulders, concerned for a moment. "Are you okay?"

She looked at him and nodded. Then he pulled his chair out and dropped to one knee. "I've never been as thankful for anything, or anyone, as I am for you, Alison. I love you so much. Would you marry me?"

"Yes," she whispered, as tears trickled down her face. Ricardo hugged her, then kissed her gently.

There was applause all around the table followed by more hugs and kisses. Anthony, who had been instructed by his cousin Zoe to have his camera ready during dessert, captured most of the event, cued silently by Zoe when Alison was opening her goody bag.

"Welcome to the family, son," Tommy said to Ricardo and hugged him.

Zoe was the last one to hug her mom. "I don't know what we would have done if you wouldn't have had a piece of pie, Mom! You really had me worried," Zoe said, a huge smile on her face.

"You were in on this from the start?" Alison asked, looking her daughter in the eye.

"From the moment Ricardo asked me if he could ask you to marry him," Zoe responded.

Alison looked at Ricardo. She didn't believe she had ever loved anyone in her life as much as she loved this man at this moment.

Jillian so enjoyed Thanksgiving at Drew and Greta's, even the tofu turkey. She did admit, though, that she was grateful they had prepared a small turkey breast as well. Jillian had been in charge of the pies—one vegan pumpkin, a regular pumpkin and an apple.

Greta and Cleo shared some exciting news during the meal. Cleo's business was booming, so much so that an interested investor had offered to help it expand even more and had secured the building next to the one she was currently renting for the expansion. At first, Cleo had been reluctant. She didn't feel she could handle much more by herself. That's where Greta came in.

Greta had just informed the college that the upcoming semester would be her last. They were disappointed to lose their long-time professor and chair of the art department, but they were happy for her opportunities working with her daughter. Greta would teach pottery classes, create pottery and sculptures, and show and sell them in the gallery. It was a dream come true for her.

"What are you going to do with yourself, Drew?" Jillian asked.

"I haven't figured that out yet. I will continue to work with wood, but I don't want that to become like work to me. So, I have been thinking about going back to work—maybe part-time. However, just doing accounting like I have for so many years sounds boring to me now. I think I need a new challenge."

A lightbulb went on in Jillian's head. They had been functioning at the Esperanza Center with an interim director, and still hadn't found the right person to take over Ricardo's position in Los Angeles. The assistant decided she didn't know enough yet to take over, and Jillian agreed.

Drew most likely wouldn't want to work for many more years, but they would be good and valuable years for the organization, she had no doubt. He would be a good mentor to the assistant, and perhaps the foundation could provide education for her in the meantime. It may be worth the money spent in the long run. She was creative and smart but didn't have the formal education the position required yet.

"Drew, I'll call you tomorrow. I have an interesting proposition for you," Jillian said.

Just then Greta came to the table with a beautifully decorated box and began to speak.

"We were going to give this to you a while back, but it just didn't happen. Maybe this is a better time anyway. We made it for you. I did the sculpture, Drew, the wood. We hope you like it, Jillian."

Jillian lifted the top of the box, then carefully unwrapped the two pieces. The wooden piece had been fashioned to look like a love seat—like the one in the library at her home—and had been worked out of mahogany. Drew's craftsmanship was amazing, and he mentioned that the wood came from Marty's acquaintance in

Peru. Not only was it beautiful, but the piece could be a small wall shelf, or could sit on a table.

The next piece made Jillian nervous to open, but Greta told her it was stronger than she imagined. Marty helped her unwrap it, helping to ease her fears. The protective paper dropping away, Jillian lifted up the intricate sculpture. She just stared for a few moments—then tears began to flow.

"We thought you'd like it," Greta said softly, putting her hand on Jillian's shoulder.

The sculpture was of Jillian and John, sitting down and reading a book together. John was holding the book, his reading glasses down low on his nose. Jillian's head was on his shoulder, as she snuggled against him, her legs curled up to her side. It was as if Greta had taken a photo of them while they were sitting in the library.

"May I?" Drew asked, indicating he wanted to seat "John and Jillian" on the love seat shelf. It worked together perfectly. They had made certain of that before putting it in the box.

"It can sit on a table, or it can hang on a wall, Jillian. Whichever you prefer," he went on.

Jillian still could not speak. What an incredible gift! She nodded her head, and Marty handed her a tissue and gave her a hug, her own eyes filled with tears.

"I'm sorry," Jillian said finally. "It's beautiful—it's perfect—and I love you guys."

"We love you, too," Drew and Greta said in unison. There were hugs and a few more tears all around, but happy ones.

Jillian held the box containing her treasures all the way home while Marty drove and Michael fell into a food coma. What a precious gift! What precious people there were in her life. What a wonderful day, and it wasn't over yet!

Alison and Ricardo, along with their families, video chatted with Jillian, Marty, and Michael that evening to give them the exciting news of the engagement. For the second time that day, there was a downpour from Jillian's eyes. When she recovered, she congratulated the newly engaged couple, as well as their parents. Karen and Robert were beside themselves with joy. Karen had shouted out that she was going to have a daughter! Jillian knew how much that meant to her. Zoe seemed sincerely happy, too, which made Jillian's heart happy.

The Saturday after Thanksgiving, Marty and Michael had gone back to their condo and Jillian could just feel the emptiness of the house. The quiet was deafening, too. She couldn't wait for John Anthony to return, although that would not be until late the next evening. Today, the members of the Romano family were all busy doing fun things in Illinois.

John Anthony, as a former athlete, had a ticket source for the home football game at Northwestern, so he and his sons, his father, and Ricardo and his father, were off to the game. Ricardo had been thrilled, as was Robert. Robert reminded Ricardo about the Northwestern football jersey and youth-sized football John and Jillian had given to him the first Christmas he was at the Wilson home. Ricardo had insisted on wearing the jersey to the Christmas Eve service that night, the first real church service he could remember attending. That was the night he had fallen in love with the guitar, too. Ricardo smiled with excitement, as he remembered he now had his guitar in Illinois, too, as his parents just brought it with them.

When Ricardo got to the football game that day, the first thing he did was go to the college shop and buy a jersey. He proudly wore it over his heavy sweatshirt in honor of John and John Anthony, his soon-to-be brother-in-law.

Alison, Zoe, Maria, Kirsten, and Karen opted for art over football this time, taking in a new exhibit at the Art Institute and recording the game to watch later at home. It was a clear but chilly day, and they were not complaining about not sitting in the bleachers this time. They enjoyed lunch out at a new restaurant, sincerely grateful they were not sipping hot chocolate and eating hot dogs in the stands trying to stay warm.

Jillian wouldn't have minded either of those outings. Instead, she rambled about the house, which seemed larger to her all the time. She had found a spot for her special gift in the library. The wood matched the woodwork in the room perfectly, and she suspected that was purposeful. While trying out different spots for her piece of art, she had opened up one of the cabinets in the room, and the hinge squeaked loudly.

Since she had nothing better to do, she decided she would hunt for some household oil to fix the noise. She looked in the kitchen to no avail, then the garage. Then she thought she should try the cabinets in the laundry room.

Jillian dug through a few of them, but had no luck. She knelt on the floor as she pulled out the contents of the final, lower cabinet. She had forgotten what was stored in that one. There were the ceramic dishes with the name "LUCY" on them. Behind them were a few of the orange-haired cat's favorite toys. This cabinet hadn't been opened in fifteen years, since their beloved pet's death at the ripe old age of nineteen.

Jillian held the dishes in her hands. She remembered all the times she served Lucy her food in this room. In her mind, Jillian could see Lucy sleeping on the low windowsills in the sun. There were tears in Jillian's eyes, but she was also smiling at the memories. Suddenly, Jillian stood up, put the dishes down, and did something she never thought she would ever do.

The sign at the Rescue Center said they were not able to accept any more animals at that time. They were completely full—and then some. Jillian had thought perhaps she would get a cat just like Lucy—or maybe a calico cat like she and Marty had once had. She ended up with neither.

"What kind of cat is this?" Jillian asked, looking at the solid brown cat with huge green eyes.

"He's a Havana Brown, named supposedly because their coats resemble the color of a Cuban cigar," said the worker with a chuckle. "We've never had one of these before. He's only about two years old, but no one seems to be interested in him. I think he is just too different looking for the average person. That's too bad, because they are super friendly and affectionate, and actually like to be with people."

Jillian stooped down to look more closely at the unique cat. When she did that, he walked toward her and meowed—and that was that. She filled out the adoption papers, then hurried to a store to get a carrier and some food. She bought the kind the shelter used and the brand she and John had always bought for Lucy. Jillian thought Lucy's long life certainly should be an endorsement for the product. She also bought a litter box, litter, and a brush. She was back at the shelter within the hour and took her new friend home.

Jillian hadn't named the cat yet. He had a name at the shelter, but she didn't think it fit him at all. She poured some of Lucy's favorite food in her old bowl—she'd get the cat his own bowl once she came up with the perfect name—and suddenly it came to her. The first cat Jillian had loved in this house was an orange-haired feline named Lucy. This newcomer was brown-haired and was often called a Havana or a Cuban brown cat. She petted the purring animal as he gobbled down the tasty, moist food. "Welcome home, Desi!"

Chapter Twenty-Six

Kirsten and the boys moved into Jillian's house in January, as soon as the first semester of school was officially over. John Anthony assured Jillian it was only temporary. The items they wanted to keep from their home were packed up into a moving cube, ready for whenever they found a place to put them. Jillian secretly hoped it was a long time before that happened and mentioned that they were welcome to stay for as long as they would like.

Alison and Ricardo would be married at Grace Lutheran in February, the Saturday after Valentine's Day. They figured since most of the family lived in California now, it was the logical choice. It was also the warmer choice, which everyone appreciated.

Everyone was excited about the chance to be together again. They had had so much fun at Thanksgiving and Christmas. The Wilson family and the Romano families were a natural fit for one another. Jillian and Karen like to reflect, too, that now they were officially family, as well as friends, and Karen happily bragged about that at book club.

Carol and Jerry were hosting Carrie and her husband for a few weeks. Carol would have never believed it possible, but when they had done the "remembrance" for her late husband, Len, in Madison, something special had happened.

Jerry had waited at the hotel, about two miles from the cemetery, while the family gathered for the ceremony. He did not want to intrude on this special and important time, even though he was the person who had thought of it.

The family members who had known and loved Len shared some of their favorite memories, then spoke honestly about their lives without him—both early on and in the present day. Those who had never met him said how much they wished they could have known him and how much they loved the family Len had helped create, who were now a part of their lives.

The plan after the cemetery was to go out to dinner at one of Carol and Len's favorite supper clubs, which was still remarkably in existence. When they got to their cars, Carrie asked Carol if Jerry would like to join them. Carol's eyes had filled with tears as she called her husband to ask him. Jerry readily agreed. That evening Carrie had talked more to her family than she had in many, many years, and she had a real conversation with Jerry for the first time. It was like someone flipped a switch, and she was a different person.

And now, Carrie was visiting her family members in California and was ready to make some new and happy memories with all of them.

Desi had settled into the household without a hitch. He really did like people, even the louder, faster-moving boys. He particularly liked to sit on Tommy John's lap when he was on his computer. Jillian thought it was the combination of the boy's sensitive nature and the warmth of the laptop, which was so attractive to the kitty.

O.R. was on its winter hiatus, but John Anthony was hard at work filming *Noted!* Jillian felt a bit guilty that he was spending his break this way, but he had been incredibly honored to play the role. He had thought his series role honored his uncle John, but this one was in another league altogether. He also reminded Jillian that his family was around, and he felt like he was on vacation all the time now that they were living under the same roof.

Jillian was so happy for him—and for everyone. Still, there were times when she felt a bit sad, especially those times when everyone seemed to have a partner, except her. Carol and Jerry, Karen and Robert, Marty and Michael, Tommy and Maria, Pete and Kelly, Monica and Ben, Alison and Ricardo, Darius (a.k.a."The Mayor") and Keisha, and even Buck and Nancy—at their advanced age—were still hanging on together.

Grace and Max were dating. Moxie and Jamie had requested Grace come surfing with them and Max at dawn on New Year's Day. When she and Max arrived separately, Moxie was dressed in a new dry suit, holding a small bouquet of flowers with Jamie at her side. A wedding officiant stood on the beach with them, two surfboards leaning up against each other, making an arch behind him.

Grace and Max had been the witnesses to their marriage, then they all celebrated by riding the waves and later going out for a crab dinner. At the end of the day, Grace and Max discussed the possibility that they had been set up by the couple, and both confessed, they were not sorry about that.

Pete told Jillian he thought they were getting serious, which made him happy. He loved Max, and he was quite sure his daughter did, too. He was grateful that Jillian had introduced the two.

At Jillian's weekly church "walk and talks," Joe and Ann had announced that they were officially a couple, too. Of Jillian's family and closest friends, only Luz remained single, but during the current filming break, she was back at her home in Lima.

Jillian wasn't the least bit interested in a romantic relationship. She couldn't imagine that she could ever love anyone like she had loved John. But she did admit at times it would be nice to have a companion of sorts—a special friend to do things with once in a while. Her friends and family members were wonderful to be with, but she sometimes felt like she was taking away from their own family/partner time. Even though they said they did not mind, she did not want to monopolize or intrude. So finding a companion would be nice. She just had no idea how that would ever happen.

Jillian felt a lot like she had when she first moved to California and knew no one. She had had to create a new life back then. She guessed she would have to create a new one again now. She loved her family and was eternally grateful to God for them, but she knew she could not rely solely on them for her happiness. She said a prayer to God to help her find the answers.

The wedding weekend had come and gone, and Alison and Ricardo were back home in Libertyville. They both commuted into the city each day, but not for long for Alison. A private practice doctor in town had just hired her as her nurse practitioner, and she would work ten hour days Monday through Thursday. Alison was thrilled with the new opportunity.

Ricardo was in heaven at the Esperanza Center. The new programs were up and running, and the building project was completed. Even his assistant was improving in the leadership area. The man was bright enough to watch Ricardo closely. He considered Ricardo his mentor and was learning how to become a true leader, and a compassionate one.

Zoe was midway through her second semester of college and loving it. She also adored her car and came home from time to time. As Alison had hoped, her daughter felt comfortable coming back to the house in Libertyville—a place where much love had been shared over the years and a place where love now continued on.

And the latest development—the little boy who had attached himself to Ricardo early in his tenure was in need of a new foster placement. Ricardo and Alison were in the process of filling out paperwork. They hoped the boy could come to live with them on a permanent basis if all worked out well.

Chapter Twenty-Seven

Jillian awakened on March the twenty-seventh to the sound of a splash. It was only 6:00 a.m. Could someone really be swimming so early? Then she heard a second splash and the sound of laughter and happy voices. She sat up in bed. The first thing that came into focus was the sculpture of her and John reading a book together, sitting on its unique love seat shelf, straight ahead of her and attached to the refinished wall where a television had once been anchored. Below the artwork was the love seat itself. She smiled as she looked at them, then climbed out of her bed and peeked through the cottage window blinds toward the pool.

Tommy John and Anthony were racing each other. Shortly, Anthony would be off to school, and Tommy John would have breakfast, then "sit in" with his classmates three thousand miles away. The boys filled her with joy, and she could tell it would be a good day.

She turned and looked around the completely remodeled cottage. It had turned out just the way she had wanted. It had been decorated to her personal taste, although at the time she had picked out paint and trim, carpet, tile, and many other new touches, she never dreamed that she would once more occupy this space as a residence.

Jillian had convinced John Anthony and Kirsten to live in the house—just them and their family. She still ate a meal with them once or twice each week, but otherwise, the family had their privacy for the most part. Jillian used the library from time to time but made sure it was a convenient time for the family first.

Otherwise, she had everything she needed in the cobblestone cottage. In addition to the updates, she had also recently expanded the abode. A walk-in closet, along with another room, had been added to the back. It served as an all-purpose room. Desi the cat's belongings took up part of the room, and a pull-out couch, a large flat screen television, various odds and ends of her favorite furniture pieces from the house, along with a bookshelf with her very favorite books, filled in the rest. It could serve as a guest room in a pinch, although most of Jillian's friends and family members either lived in the area now, or they used the unoccupied bedrooms in the main house when visiting.

Above the new room was what Anthony had dubbed the "Castle Room" because it was a round, turret-like structure as one would find on a castle, with many large windows looking out over the entire grounds.

Jillian found it a great place to read, or just sit, think, and pray. It was also her favorite spot to write. She had just finished the first draft of *Where Broken Hearts Go (When a Loved One is Gone)*. The book dealt not only with issues surrounding the death of a loved one but also the ending of relationships by other means, which were often equally painful and devastating. Her publisher hoped to have it out before the summer's end. There would be a book launch and a book tour upon its release. It would be an interesting, busy summer ahead for Jillian between the book coming out and the premiere of the *Noted!* movie on July the seventh, John's birthday.

Jillian climbed the steps to the space and gazed out the windows, one by one. What a special place she had come to long ago. And now, all the memories—even the not so happy ones—made it even more special.

She thought about the plans for the evening—the first anniversary without John. The family was going to meet at the beach house in Malibu for dinner, then she planned to stay there overnight, by herself.

And then Jillian thought about the upcoming Saturday. She was going to meet a new friend named Stan for coffee. He was a widower who had reluctantly joined a bike ride hosted by the church a few weeks before. Jillian guessed he was a decade younger than herself, but she wasn't sure. He was the father of a member of Grace Lutheran and had been visiting his daughter that day. His wife had died only six months before, and his pain was still very raw.

His daughter had introduced them at church, and Jillian had encouraged Stan to come along on the congregation's maiden bike ride, an offshoot of the popular walk and talks. He was very hesitant. He also didn't have a bike with him and lived an hour outside the city. Jillian said she had an extra one he could use—John's. He finally said yes and met the group going out from the church parking lot at one o'clock.

Jillian and Stan seemed to keep catching up to one another on the ride and found it comical. After returning to the church, they talked over bottles of water near Stan's car, then at the picnic table behind the building. They talked for a long time, sharing a common bond—both losing the love of their life suddenly and without warning.

They both had wonderful, loving family members and friends but missed their spouses tremendously. They also mentioned they missed having a companion to do the little things with, like go out to lunch, to a movie or concert, or just a cup of coffee. They talked about how uncomfortable it could be at certain gatherings, especially those where everyone else seemed to be part of a couple. Sometimes each felt like the odd man out.

Jillian was able to give Stan an understanding ear as well as tell him some of the things that had helped her over the past year. He said he felt better after talking about it, and it made Jillian feel good to be able to make someone else feel better. She guessed that was the "helper" in her that she hoped would never disappear. And as often happens, by helping someone else, she felt better herself.

Stan suggested that maybe they could get together once in a while and do some of those little things they both missed so much. That was how the coffee shop plan came about. Jillian felt like her prayers had been answered and was happy God had brought a new and understanding friend into her life.

Jillian looked at the clock and headed back down the spiral staircase holding the rail tightly, as Desi so often seemed to be underfoot. Jillian had been invited to have breakfast with Kirsten and Tommy John in the breakfast nook that morning because it was a special day.

Tommy John had made eggs and toast for Jillian and his mom, with fresh fruit on the side. The three were just finishing up when the doorbell rang. Tommy John ran to answer the door, then came back and told Jillian it was for her.

Jillian walked to the door, Desi following closely behind. The soft, brown feline purred and rubbed against her ankles as she opened the door. There stood the same young man from the floral shop—the one who had delivered the thirty yellow roses to her exactly one year before on this day.

Today, he stood with just a single yellow rose lightly wrapped in floral paper. There was a folded note attached to the paper. She thanked the young man, gave him a tip on his tablet, and closed the door. She opened the note with a shaky hand and stared at it. It was written in John's handwriting, which took her aback for a moment.

Kathy J. Jacobson

My dearest Jillian,

If you are reading this note, it means I am no longer with you on earth. I just wanted to send you this rose as a remembrance of our special day— the day we two became one—and as a reminder of our singular love, which will never end. I know how I would feel if I were in your shoes, but please, Jillian, enjoy each and every moment of your life. That would make me most happy. In the meantime, sweetheart, remember that I am in good hands. So, until we meet again, my beloved Jillian, I'll love you forever. John

Jillian's eyes were brimming with tears, but her heart was absolutely overflowing with the unique and extraordinary love that belonged to only John and her. She knew few others were blessed with a love like theirs, and she also knew John was right—it would never truly end.

She carefully removed the rose from the paper and inhaled its sweet scent. She looked up and smiled. "Until we meet again, John, I'll love you forever."

The End

Questions for Discussion

1. After a wonderful renewal of vows ceremony and celebration with family, Jillian suffers the significant and sudden loss of John, her beloved husband of thirty years. Shortly afterward, Alison is served divorce papers by her husband of twenty years, affirming her suspicions of an affair, and announcing he is having a child with the woman. Have you, or someone you know, ever been dealt a similar "blow?"

2. Which do you find more difficult—sudden losses or those which are more drawn out over time?

3. When a death occurs, people express their condolences in various ways (e.g., food gifts, calls, flowers, notes, and just being present). Which do you find most helpful when you are grieving a loss? Which do you find the least helpful? What way(s) do you tend to express your sympathies to others?

4. Carol had a way of taking charge and taking care of business when John died, which Jillian appreciated. Do you know someone like Carol? While Carol's strength in times of crisis is good in some ways, it is not without pitfalls. Discuss some of them.

5. Marty and Tommy both wanted or needed to share a eulogy at John's funeral. Have you ever given or written a eulogy? What do you think are the benefits of doing so? What are other ways that one might share memories of a loved one?

6. More than once, Jillian mentions that she can't imagine going through a loss like hers without the benefits of her family and faith. What helps you most at a time of significant loss?

Kathy J. Jacobson

7. On the evening of John's death, Jillian drove to a place that was very special to them both, where many memories were shared. If you lost someone special, where might you go, or what might you do?

8. Jillian experiences what she perceives to be "the presence of God." Have you ever had a similar experience?

9. There are many losses in life other than physical death. John Anthony suffered a football injury that changed the course of this life. Alison's marriage ended. Ricardo suffered years of neglect and abuse, and later the loss of his first love in college, both which contributed to his fear of committed relationships. What are some losses you have experienced? How did they affect your future life? In the case of these characters, things eventually turn out very well, despite their losses. Has this ever happened to you?

10. Alison immediately felt better after telling Jillian about the divorce. Sometimes sharing painful news with a trusted person can be very helpful. Have you ever experienced this?

11. Life can be very joyful one moment and very sad the next. Discuss a time in your own experience when this was the case.

12. Tommy and Maria consider changing their plans to move west when Alison announces her divorce. Eventually, they make their big move. Do you think they made the right decision? Why or why not?

13. Tommy and Maria, as well as Drew and Greta, feel a renewed and heightened appreciation for one another after John's death. It was a real "wake-up call" to them. Has this ever happened to you?

14. John Anthony makes a very difficult decision to take a role that has a sentimental element to it and could greatly benefit his career and his family's future financial security, yet is not without risks in other ways. Have you ever had to make such a decision? How did it turn out? Do you believe John Anthony made the right call?

15. While adjusting to the "new normal," Jillian notices little things—the house creaking, clocks ticking, the sound of sprinklers turning on, and slipping into the "too cool sheets" on her bed. She also experiences times when she turns to discuss something or share some news, only to remember that John is not there to talk to. Have you, or someone you know, had similar experiences?

16. Jillian takes steps that help her deal with her loss (i.e., blogging, writing a new book, developing the screenplay of her personal love story, going to book club, having regular talks with Carol, initiating a "walk and talk" group at church, and being open to the idea of a companion). She also allows herself to have her down days (her "wallowing days" as she refers to them). What has helped you most in times of loss and grief?

17. Monica Morgan did not realize the scope of her affection for John until he was gone. Have you ever discovered that about someone you've lost?

18. Carol and her children have carried their unresolved grief for many years, each in their own way. Greta had held on to the pain and guilt of her first miscarriage until after the birth of her child, two subsequent miscarriages, and tests which revealed a physical cause for the loss of her babies. Have you ever held on to pain or guilt in such a way? What were the ramifications?

19. When Jillian sees a cardinal at the cemetery, she believes it is a sign. What do you think? Has anything similar happened to you?

Kathy J. Jacobson

20. When John Anthony moves to Los Angeles and Kirsten has to cut her visit with the family short, Tommy John fears his parents are getting a divorce. Do you think his fears were reasonable? Discuss.

21. Despite some questions in her heart, Grace almost marries a man because she is "almost thirty." What might have been lost had she gone through with the marriage?

22. Many different people make a move in this book, including Jillian, who ends up in the same residence she lived in when she first came to California many years before. Do you think the people involved made wise moves? Why or why not?

About the Author

Kathy J. Jacobson lives with her husband in the beautiful "Driftless Area" of Southwestern Wisconsin. They are parents of three grown children. Kathy is an avid traveler, having visited all fifty states and six continents. She is a huge fan of all genres of music, the theater, and the Wisconsin Badgers. *Footnotes* is the fifth book of the *Noted!* "faithful fiction" series. You might also enjoy her recently published devotions in *The Word in Season* (*July, August, September, 2018, Augsburg Fortress.*)

Photo by Michael Mowbray

Check out the entire NOTED! series.

" Kathy J. Jacobson has truly outdone herself with Footnotes. Through the characters we have come to know and love, Jacobson taps into her background to help us explore the different stages people go through while grieving. Jacobson then shows us how powerful the love of family, friends, and faith are when dealing with life's losses. Truly inspirational! **"**

Joyce McPhail, RN
Hospice Director